Love
&
Lyrics

De-ann Black

Text copyright © 2024 by De-ann Black
Cover Design & Illustration © 2024 by De-ann Black

All rights reserved.
No part of this book may be used or reproduced in any manner whatsoever without the written consent of the author.

This is a work of fiction. Names, characters, places, and incidents are either products of the author's imagination or are used fictitiously. Any resemblance to actual persons, living or dead, businesses, companies, events, or locales is entirely coincidental.

Paperback edition published 2024

Love & Lyrics

ISBN: 9798874405755

Love & Lyrics is the third book in the Snow Bells Haven series.

1. Snow Bells Christmas
2. Snow Bells Wedding
3. Love & Lyrics

Also by De-ann Black (Romance, Action/Thrillers & Children's books). See her Amazon Author page or website for further details about her books, screenplays, illustrations and artwork. www.De-annBlack.com

Action/Thrillers:
Knight in Miami.
Agency Agenda.
Love Him Forever.
Someone Worse.
Electric Shadows.
The Strife of Riley.
Shadows of Murder.

Romance:
Love & Lyrics
Christmas Weddings
Fairytale Christmas on the Island
The Cure for Love at Christmas
Vintage Dress Shop on the Island
Scottish Island Fairytale Castle
Scottish Loch Summer Romance
Scottish Island Knitting Bee
Sewing & Mending Cottage
Knitting Shop by the Sea
Colouring Book Cottage
Knitting Cottage
Oops! I'm the Paparazzi, Again
The Bitch-Proof Wedding
Embroidery Cottage
The Dressmaker's Cottage
The Sewing Shop
Heather Park
The Tea Shop by the Sea
The Bookshop by the Seaside
The Sewing Bee

The Quilting Bee
Snow Bells Wedding
Snow Bells Christmas
Summer Sewing Bee
The Chocolatier's Cottage
Christmas Cake Chateau
The Beemaster's Cottage
The Sewing Bee By The Sea
The Flower Hunter's Cottage
The Christmas Knitting Bee
The Sewing Bee & Afternoon Tea
Shed In The City
The Bakery By The Seaside
The Christmas Chocolatier
The Christmas Tea Shop & Bakery
The Bitch-Proof Suit

Colouring books:
Summer Nature. Flower Nature. Summer Garden. Spring Garden. Autumn Garden. Sea Dream. Festive Christmas. Christmas Garden. Flower Bee. Wild Garden. Flower Hunter. Stargazer Space. Christmas Theme. Faerie Garden Spring. Scottish Garden Seasons. Bee Garden.

Embroidery books:
Floral Garden Embroidery Patterns
Floral Spring Embroidery Patterns
Christmas & Winter Embroidery Patterns
Floral Nature Embroidery Designs
Scottish Garden Embroidery Designs

Contents

Chapter One	1
Chapter Two	19
Chapter Three	38
Chapter Four	56
Chapter Five	76
Chapter Six	94
Chapter Seven	113
Chapter Eight	132
Chapter Nine	150
Chapter Ten	167
Chapter Eleven	184
Chapter Twelve	201
Chapter Thirteen	219
Chapter Fourteen	236
Chapter Fifteen	255
Chapter Sixteen	267
Chapter Seventeen	285
About De-ann Black	313

CHAPTER ONE

She's lightning in a bottle
When she's near I feel the spark
But I sense trouble brewing
Will she break my heart?

The small town of Snow Bells Haven blinked awake against the early morning sunlight as Brad drove down the main street. He sang along to the demo he'd made, drumming his fingers on the wheel, wondering if his new song would make the cut for his latest album. He needed a hit song, preferably a few, and that's why he'd decided to open a second music recording studio, away from his main studio in the city. Snow Bells Haven was the perfect location. Not too far from New York, yet set in beautiful countryside with a nearby cove. He hoped that this was the type of quaint location where he could relax, find inspiration and focus on his song writing.

Pulling the car over, he parked outside his new premises, a former hardware store he'd had refurbished as a recording studio that was a match for his city studio. Cutting edge equipment, two main rooms for recording, a master control room, and everything soundproofed and kitted out to a professional standard. No expense spared. Brad, a successful recording artist, had the money to equip his new venture. His albums sold well and when he toured, his performances were sold out. Money wasn't the issue. New songs, new hits, that's what he needed. Fresh inspiration.

He grabbed his guitar from the back seat and dug out the keys to open the front door of the studio. The sun highlighted his thick, blond hair, and he wore black jeans with a dark denim shirt and boots. Expensive, but low–key. Tall, broad–shouldered but rangy, his busy lifestyle kept him lean and fit.

'Hi there!' A man, similar in age to Brad, early thirties, tall, well–dressed with a lawyer–type mien, came hurrying along the street. He walked with a gait of measured self–assurance, tilting his head to one side as he smiled, hoping he wasn't too much of an interruption to Brad's day.

Brad clicked the studio door open, but paused and glanced round at the man. His pale blue eyes squinted against the sunlight trying to figure out whether he knew this guy or not.

He guessed not as the man extended his hand along with a pleasant introduction. 'I've been meaning to welcome you to Snow Bells Haven, but our paths haven't crossed these past couple of weeks.'

Brad shook hands with the stranger for a second before the man revealed his occupation.

'I'm Mark, the town's new mayor.'

Brad thought he was kinda young to be the mayor.

'The youngest the town's ever had.' Mark seemed used to explaining without being asked. 'I took over when the previous mayor retired recently.'

'Pleased to meet you, Mark. I'm Brad, but you probably know more about me than I do about you.'

People usually did. It came with the territory of being a successful singer and songwriter.

'I have your last album. I enjoy your music.' He glanced at the studio door ajar. 'Is your studio open yet for business?'

'Opening in a few days. Just smoothing things over, getting everything right.'

Mark nodded. 'Sure.' There was a confident but excited tone in his voice. Not quite an all–out fan, but nonetheless impressed by the latest addition to the town.

'Are you a performer as well as mayor?' It was always a question that Brad liked to ask. People often had ambitions to sing or play and many an amateur had wanted Brad to help them up the ladder regardless of whether they had any real talent.

'Nooo, I'm a listener, not a singer.' Mark looked at the guitar. 'I don't play any musical instruments. Nothing like that.' He understood that he could've come across as a wannabe musician, but this wasn't in his plans.

Brad wondered what he wanted, other than making a polite introduction.

'I just wanted to welcome you to Snow Bells,' Mark explained. 'Obviously, folk are talking about you opening a new recording studio here in town, and wondering...well, what brought you here.'

Brad noticed that Mark kept glancing at the open door, clearly itching for a look inside the studio. 'Would you like to step in for a moment?'

The spark of interest showed in Mark's deep blue eyes. 'Yes, that would be great.'

Brad pushed the door open wide and led the way inside. He flicked the lights on, illuminating the front reception that was sleek and totally quiet. Two guitars, one acoustic, one electric, hung on the wall along with a classic saxophone, creating a silent musical welcome.

A black and white poster–size photo of Brad playing his guitar in his recording studio in New York was framed on the wall. With Brad's leading man appearance, it looked like a scene from a movie instead of an insight into his working world in the city.

'The main recording rooms are through here.' Brad led him through to the back of the two–level premises, and thumbed upstairs. 'I store equipment up there.'

The quietude followed them through, indicating that the walls had been insulated against the noise of the outside world. Carpeted flooring silenced their footsteps in the long, narrow hallway until they reached the main control room with its polished wooden floor.

Windows were surplus to requirements, and the sunlight shining through the front window was soon left behind as they ventured into the heart of Brad's new premises.

The entire studio was darker than Mark had imagined, but the styling was impressive. Everything was new. No makeshift equipment or furnishings.

A slight scent of cedar hung in the air, coming from the new fittings, and would no doubt fade when the fanfare of music and activity breathed real life into the studio.

Brad switched the lights on in the main control room. He gestured to the glass partitions showing the two studios. 'Studio one and two are where singers and musicians perform.' Then he referred to the control room. 'And they're recorded here. This is where the music is mixed, edited and adjusted until it's right.' It was a simplified version of the complicated process.

Mark scanned the array of technical equipment from the multi–track mixing decks to the microphones and headphones. A piano, keyboards and more guitars peppered the surroundings.

'It's a terrific looking recording studio,' Mark assessed. 'Are you offering it to outsiders, or is it for your personal use only?'

'I'm planning to record new songs for my forthcoming album. Once I've written them,' Brad added with a wry smile. 'But other artists, professional singers and musicians will be welcome to use the facility. I won't be offering it for teaching purposes or anything like that.'

Mark nodded. 'It all sounds exciting. I wish you every success with it.' He hesitated before adding, 'Are you planning on announcing your new studio? You know, letting local folks know what you're doing? Maybe some publicity?'

'Yeah, sure. I haven't figured it all out yet. My manager usually takes care of the marketing side of things for me, but he's busy helping to keep the studio ticking over in New York and with other business.' Brad took a deep breath and gazed around. 'I guess I'll put a notice in the front window that I'm opening in a few days, and what I intend doing, mainly using the facilities for my new music and for other recording artists, including people I've worked with in the past.'

Mark bit his lips and nodded.

Brad picked up on the contradictory reaction. 'Something on your mind?'

'No, well...I was just thinking that if you need any help with your marketing, you should talk to Robyn.' Mark smiled, unable to hide the admiration he had for her. 'She's lightning in a bottle. If anyone can smooth things for you here, get your launch right. It's her.'

'Lightning in a bottle, huh?' Brad grinned. 'That's quite a recommendation. She must be something special.'

'Oh, she is,' Mark was quick to tell him. 'If it wasn't for Robyn, I'd probably be back in New York working as a lawyer instead of being mayor of Snow Bells.'

Brad frowned, crossed his arms and leaned against the consol waiting for Mark to elaborate.

'She eh...turned everything around for me like that.' Mark snapped his fingers. 'Long story short — I'm the youngest mayor this town has ever had and people were understandably concerned that I wouldn't be as good as the previous mayor. He was very popular. I had big shoes to fill. At first I thought I'd show them that I was young, energetic and appeal to the younger demographic in town. That didn't quite work. So then I changed lanes and tried to appeal to the more mature members of the community. That didn't work either.'

'So you hired Robyn to help you?'

'No, I was floundering, that's for sure. To tell you the truth, I was this close to leaving and heading back to the city.' He squeezed his fingers together. 'But I was complaining about my predicament to Greg. He owns the local cafe and he's a real nice guy, good listener. Robyn overheard and she said to me, 'Stop trying to be what you're not. Be the mayor of the whole town. And you're a lawyer. Start dressing like one.' He smiled, remembering the slight edge to her tone, and how he took her advice to heart.

Brad eyed the lawyer–style coat Mark wore with a white shirt and tie. His light brown hair was neat and tidy. He was clean–shaven and looked like he could be both a lawyer and a competent mayor.

'I'm guessing you took her advice,' said Brad.

'I did. And I asked for more advice from her, hired her to sort my image. She's a plain talker. Doesn't pull her verbal punches, but that's what I like about her. And everything she told me to do worked so well that now I feel like I've been mayor of this town for years instead of only a few months.'

Brad heard the extra admiration in Mark's tone. 'You really like her, huh?'

Mark looked flustered. 'Sure, she's great.'

Brad smiled.

'She's not interested in dating me, if that's what you think.'

It was what he thought. 'You sure about that?'

'Yes, definitely, sort of. We're just friends. I don't think I'm the type of guy that a woman like Robyn needs.'

'She needs a lightning conductor?' Brad joked.

Mark smiled. 'Probably, and that's just not me. But you should talk to her about presenting your recording studio so that the town gives you a real, warm welcome.'

Brad nodded thoughtfully. 'I'll keep that in mind.'

Mark dug into his pocket. 'I should still have the card she gave me. Yes, here it is.' He handed it to Brad. 'She works from home.'

Turning the card over in his hand, he read the details and then pocketed it in his jeans.

'Okay, I won't take up any more of your time.' Mark started to head out. 'Thanks for the tour, and eh, if you want to sweeten Robyn up, she loves the gingerbread cupcakes that Greg makes.' He pointed to the cafe across the street and then headed out.

Brad waved him off, closed the door and glanced out the window at Greg's cafe. It looked inviting with pretty yellow and white gingham drapes tied back with ribbons. It seemed busy too.

'What can I get for you today, Robyn?' Greg said as she sat down at the only vacant table in the cafe.

The striped canopy shaded the bright sunlight from pouring in, but there was a warm glow from the gingham drapes and touches of yellow and white in the decor. The air was filled with the tempting aroma of cakes baking and pancakes being cooked for the breakfasts. Locally produced maple syrup sat on every table.

'Coffee and one of your gingerbread cupcakes.' Robyn settled down, unbuttoning her fashionable, business–style jacket that she wore with a white blouse and slim–fitting dark trousers. Her shoulder–length blond hair was freshly washed, dried silky smooth, and her makeup flattered her pale, attractive features, especially her light blue eyes with long, dark lashes. At thirty, her fresh appearance made her look a few years younger.

'Sorry, I'm sold out of the gingerbread cupcakes,' Greg told her. He was a good looking guy, in his thirties with dark brown hair, brown eyes and a friendly manner.

Robyn sighed. She loved the gingerbread cupcakes. She'd a ton of work to tackle and had popped in to treat herself before getting on with her day.

'Can I tempt you with a blueberry muffin? I know you like those.'

'Yes, I'll have that instead. Thanks, Greg.'

His assistants, Dwayne and Herb worked behind the counter, baking cakes and wrapping customer's takeaway orders. Dwayne, the taller of the two assistants, dealt with an order of cupcakes, carefully placing six in a box so as not to mess up the generous topping of buttercream frosting. Customers often phoned in their orders in advance and then popped into the cafe to pick them up.

The cafe was busy with all of the tables taken with customers enjoying breakfast there. It had recently had an extension added to accommodate extra customers, and a cake counter where Greg displayed his specialist cakes, including wedding cakes.

Robyn listened to the music playing in the background and frowned. Music? In the cafe?

Greg served up her coffee and blueberry muffin.

'Since when did you start playing music in here?' Robyn said to him.

'Just a couple of days ago,' Greg explained, seemingly unsure about it.

A customer walked in to pick up their order.

Dwayne served him. 'Here are the gingerbread cupcakes you ordered.' He handed the box of six cupcakes to Brad.

Robyn glanced round with longing at the handsome stranger's box of cupcakes, and then continued her conversation. 'I enjoyed the calm atmosphere in here, the ability to think without music playing in the background,' Robyn said to Greg as Brad paid for his order.

Brad looked over his shoulder. 'Music is good for the soul.' A hint of laughter lines ran upwards from the corners of his eyes, mapping in preparation where they'd take up permanent residency a couple of decades down the road.

'So is a relaxing ambiance where conversation doesn't have to vie against background music,' Robyn retorted. 'Though I suppose it drowns out eavesdroppers.' He'd stuck his nose in, so she snapped at it.

Brad jerked back as if he'd taken a hit. 'It was just a comment. I couldn't help but overhear. And music creates a relaxing *ambiance* too.'

Greg went to respond, but Robyn was quicker off the mark. 'Maybe you should go and listen to more music and relax rather than butt into other people's conversations.' She glared enviously at the box of cupcakes. 'And hum to yourself while you eat the last of the gingerbread cupcakes.'

'They're not for me. I bought them for someone else,' Brad told her defensively.

'To sweeten them up?' She was adept at sussing people. She'd met his type before. He was a looker. A real handsome type. Those cupcakes were to smooth the way for something he'd done wrong, or something he needed help with.

Her correct assumption jarred him. He didn't have an immediate reply.

'Music plays in lots of stores, in the local bars and restaurants, you can play it in your car,' Robyn elaborated. 'Plenty of music. We just don't need it *everywhere*.'

'And we're giving all our customers a free toffee apple cupcake. It's Greg's new recipe.' Dwayne bagged it and handed it to Brad.

Accepting the free sample, Brad buttoned his lips from further fraught comments. The young woman was lovely. Sexy beautiful. A dangerous mix. He'd met her type before and it never went well for him. He left the cafe without another word.

Herb peeked out from the kitchen area. 'Can we turn the music off now, Greg?'

'I prefer to have my coffee and pancakes without the music,' a woman commented to Greg.

Another two customers agreed.

'Yes, turn it off,' Greg told Herb. Then he spoke to Robyn. 'You're right. I thought I'd try it. But I like it better without the music.'

Robyn smiled at Greg and then enjoyed her coffee and muffin. She tried not to think about the interloper with those come–to–bed blue eyes and sexy smile like he knew the effect he had on women. But her feathers were ruffled and although the blueberry muffin was totally delicious, she resented that over–confidant man sticking his beak in where it wasn't wanted.

Leaving the cafe, she headed next door to Nate and Nancy's grocery store to buy the ingredients to make her own gingerbread cupcakes when she got home. She wasn't an expert baker like Greg, but she could whip up a culinary storm when she felt like it. And she certainly did today.

Checking her phone for the list of ingredients from an online recipe, she selected the flour, brown sugar, spices, butter and other items and put them on the counter.

'Making a gingerbread cake?' said Nancy.

'Gingerbread cupcakes. I had a notion, and Greg was sold out. Some guy bought the last of them, so I thought I'd bake my own when I get home,' Robyn explained. And then she frowned and listened to the song playing in the grocery store. 'Music? You don't usually play music in here.'

Nate was working at the back of the store and overheard her comment. 'I keep telling Nancy that if she wants music, I'll sing to her.' There was laughter in his tone, and then he teasingly started to sing a few notes as he waltzed through to join his wife and Robyn.

In their fifties, Nate and Nancy were a long-married couple and had owned the grocery store for years. It was a hub of the community.

Nancy bagged Robyn's items and handed them to her as Nate wrapped his wife in his arms and started to hum a song.

'Okay, okay,' Nancy conceded to Nate, smiling and making no effort to unwrap herself from his playful embrace. 'I heard Greg playing music and thought I'd play some too,' she explained to Robyn. 'But I suppose it's nicer to chat to customers without it.'

'It is,' Robyn agreed, picking up her groceries and then jolted when she turned around and bumped into Brad as she was leaving. 'Are you following me?'

He gazed down and gave her a languid smile. 'I've no intention of following a music grinch. I only came in for milk.'

She felt momentarily drawn to his lips, the only thing about him that wasn't lean. Those highly kissable lips had the luxury of vying against his gorgeous blue eyes as his sexiest feature.

Robyn walked briskly away, hackles up, heading to where she'd parked her car nearby.

He quickly paid for the milk and followed her out.

'Nice meeting you!' Brad called after her. He wasn't entirely sure this was true. She'd riled him even though he tried to pretend otherwise. But there was something about her that made his heart beat quicker, and not because she'd irked him.

Robyn kept on walking, pretending not to hear his parting shot at her.

Getting into her car, she drove off, deliberately ignoring him as she drove past him, but she could feel those intense blue eyes of his watching her.

Taking a steadying breath, she told herself to calm down. She'd a busy day ahead, various clients to deal with for their marketing campaigns, and cupcakes to bake.

Robyn's house was a short drive from the heart of the town. Set in a leafy niche of pretty houses in an idyllic locale, it was painted white and bordered with trees and greenery. Flowers clambered for attention around the porch — pink roses, blue cornflowers and yellow jasmine added splashes of vibrant hues and fragrance. Butterflies, bees and dragonflies were regular visitors.

Since moving in, she'd made it the home she'd always wanted after leaving her apartment in the city behind. Working in New York had yielded many benefits for her career as a freelance marketing consultant, but scored low on the personal side of her life. All work and very little play had finally caused her to up sticks and move to one of the prettiest towns she'd ever seen.

Snow Bells Haven was a real haven for the career-driven marketer. Plenty of local work, and she still dealt with clients in New York and elsewhere. But nowadays she had balance in her life. A home with a garden where she could grow flowers, bake cakes and relax after a busy working day.

She'd decorated the house herself, learning new home decor skills and putting her creative attributes to full use. The house was homely, with light cream and pastel tones, touches of classic chic and a vintage vibe. The kitchen was bright, airy and functional.

This morning it smelled of ginger and spices as she mixed the recipe in a bowl.

She prepared a tray of cupcakes and had just popped them in the oven when the doorbell rang.

'I'll be there in a moment,' she called through from the kitchen while setting the timer on the oven. She had a habit of burning things. Correction. She used to until she learned to always set the timer.

Hurrying through, she wiped her hands on her floral apron that was tied around the waist of her trousers, and opened the door, anticipating a delivery from the postman. Instead, she gasped, seeing the last person she expected to be standing on her doorstep.

'You!' she exclaimed.

Brad's reaction matched hers. 'You!'

'What are you doing here?' she demanded, eyeing him up and down. Her heart felt in danger of betraying her. This annoying man was undeniably handsome. Sexy handsome. But maybe the thundering of her heart was sheer aggravation. Yes, that's what it was, she concluded, uneasy that she could be in any way attracted to him.

He wielded the box of gingerbread cupcakes like either a gift or a guard. Those eyes of hers were challenging him and he wasn't accustomed to being on the receiving end of such a look. Friend of foe? The latter scored top marks.

Robyn put her hands on her hips and glared at Brad, defying him to explain himself.

Brad took a deep breath. Lightning in a bottle? More like tinder ready to explode at him.

'Look,' he said, trying to calm their predicament. 'We clearly got off on the wrong note. How about we draw a line right here, and start afresh?'

His tone seemed reasonable, and tussling with someone was more tiring than getting along. Not that she needed a new friend. She'd made plenty of those since moving to Snow Bells. The townsfolk had welcomed her, not only making her feel like she belonged, but that she'd always belonged. And for someone who'd never had a settled home life, that was quite an achievement.

'Okay.' She dragged out the agreement, and then tagged on a couple of stipulations. 'If you promise to stop prejudging me.' The music grinch. That niggled at her.

Brad nodded. He'd have held up his hands in surrender if he hadn't been holding the box of cupcakes like they were precious.

'Let's pretend like I hadn't overheard you in Greg's cafe and the grocery store,' he said.

Robyn amended his suggestion. 'Let's pretend you *did* overhear me in Greg's cafe and the grocery store, but you buttoned your lips and kept your remarks and your insults to yourself.' She folded her arms across her white blouse and defied him to disagree.

'I preferred my version of things, but...okay,' he agreed. A frown creased his smooth brow where a few unruly strands of blond hair were inclined to fall. 'But I don't recall insulting you.'

Robyn looked up at him and shot back a clear reminder. 'Music grinch.'

'Ah.' He jolted again like he had in the cafe from her verbal swipe. But she was right. He was wrong. 'I'm sorry.'

'Accepted,' she said brightly, without weakening her stance, facing him off on her front doorstep. Even from her height advantage of two steps up, he was still taller than her. She'd kicked her heels off when she'd arrived home and padded around in comfy socks while baking. But her heels wouldn't have helped compete against him in the height stakes.

The aroma of home baking wafted out from the doorway, adding to the feeling he got that caught him off-guard. Seeing her in town, he acknowledged that she was attractive, but here he saw a glimpse of her world, the flowers in her well-kept garden, the light and airy sense of her house. And he felt his heart squeeze.

'Why are you here?' she said plainly, having waited for him to explain away the cupcakes and the reason why he was standing there.

'The mayor of Snow Bells recommended I talk to you about helping me with the marketing of my new music recording studio. I'm Brad.'

She blinked in quick succession. First blink, he knew Mark. Second, he wanted to hire her. Third, this was the new music guy!

She'd heard all sorts of gossip and rumblings about him opening up a new recording studio in town. She'd seen the transformation of the former hardware store.

But the studio's front window was always shaded, nothing on show to hint at what was coming at them. Snow Bells was a small town with a big heart and welcomed folks hoping to make a new life there and settle into the flow of things.

A music recording studio akin to the one he owned in New York threw up all sorts of concerns about disrupting the balance of the community. The town was deceivingly quiet, while being lively. A mix that had taken her by surprise. She'd expected to relax more in Snow Bells than in the city, but the opposite was true. Albeit in a pleasant way. Plenty of work, so she was busy most days helping create marketing plans for small businesses to larger companies outside the town. Other towns nearby provided a steady income too. And she still had clients in New York that added to her list.

But the main differences were the people and the pace of things. Social events were a regular treat, something she loved joining in with, like the local dances, or the quilting and craft events. There was always something going on.

So where did that leave the new guy and his music studio? She hadn't figured that out. Now here she was trying to figure him out. The last man she expected to find dropping by her house offering sweet-tasting gifts.

Brad read the recognition of him in her eyes and waited on the welcome mat being ripped from under his boots. Any second now...

CHAPTER TWO

I'm a city guy
Singing a small town song
Trying to figure out
Where I belong

The timer sounded from the kitchen. 'The cupcakes!' Robyn exclaimed, and ran off to the kitchen to check on them.

Brad casually followed her in, bringing the sunshine with him. Leaving the front door open wide, it streamed in.

Above her gasps and mutterings, he heard the sound of his boots on the light wood floor. Scatter rugs were doing their job, cast around the open plan hallway, throwing tones of sky blue, primrose yellow and strawberry pink on to the white walls of the lounge and another room with a desk, presumably her office, where the sun highlighted them.

He felt the need to tread carefully so as not to mess up her lovely home, and because he'd invited himself in. But the cupcake chaos seemed to merit him backing her up in case her cupcakes were on fire. That was his excuse. He had it locked and loaded if she glared at him for daring to walk into her kitchen uninvited.

Standing for a moment, he looked around at the white cupboards and pastel tones of everything from the cookie jars, coffee mugs and other kitchen accessories. It was coordinated, styled two levels down from a magazine photo–shoot. Lovely but lived in. Yeah, that's how he'd describe it. He didn't feel entirely out of place. Neither did he feel he belonged.

He waited on her scolding him for being there. But having him casually leaning on the dresser that displayed dinner plates and fancy teapots was the least of her interests.

Brad took second place to her immediate priority. Too many baking mishaps made her dash to the stove.

Robyn grabbed a pair of quilted mitts, opened the oven door and checked the tray of cupcakes. 'They're not ready yet. I must've set the timer wrong in my rush to answer the door.' She sighed in exasperation.

Brad stepped closer, craned down and assessed the cupcake catastrophe. 'I'd give them another five minutes in the oven. Then check them again.'

Robyn looked round at him while holding the tray with the mitts. 'You can bake?' She didn't even try to disguise the disbelief in her tone.

'Don't sound so surprised.' He sat the box of cupcakes down on the kitchen table.

She put the half–cooked cupcakes back in the oven and set a timer for five minutes. Then she looked at him for some sort of explanation into his baking knowledge.

'My grandmother taught me how to bake cookies and cupcakes when I was a kid,' he said. 'I used to spend the holidays with my grandparents, especially at Christmas. I don't bake these days but...' He shrugged his broad shoulders. 'I bet I could still rustle up my special chocolate cupcakes.'

Was that a challenge she perceived?

'Careful, I'll hold you to that challenge if your five minute tip doesn't work,' she warned him playfully.

And that's the thing that took her aback. She was joking with the guy who'd annoyed her, insulted her, and was the cause of her cupcake chaos because he'd invited himself to her house. Now, he was standing in her kitchen looking cocky and telling her how to bake cupcakes. She needed to give her head a wobble. Things were not playing out as she'd planned. Her day was scheduled for work, not entertaining Brad.

He stood to full height as he responded to her remark. 'I never back down from a challenge.'

Robyn tilted her chin up in cheerful defiance. 'Neither do I.'

'Something else we have in common.' His deep voice resonated in the kitchen, and for the first time she heard the quality of his tone that probably gave him the singing voice that people loved.

'The *only* thing we have in common,' she corrected him.

He tilted his head to one side and gave her a look like he didn't agree. 'We both like cupcakes.'

She dismissed his suggestion. 'Lots of people like cupcakes.'

He nodded slowly, and then gestured for her to come with him to the front door that was still open wide. 'There is something we do have in common.'

Curiosity made her follow him.

He stood in the doorway and pointed to a house diagonally across the street. 'See that house over there, further along the road? The one with the apple trees at the side of the property?'

'Yes, what about it?' It was larger than her house, but just as quaint, a traditional property.

The look he gave her made her jolt.

'No!' she said as the penny dropped. 'You're the night owl?' Someone had moved into the house recently. She'd yet to see or meet them, but she'd noticed the lights were on most evenings until late at night.

'The night owl?' There was laughter in his voice mixed with surprise.

'Yes, the lights are on in that house, presumably your house, at two in the morning. Don't you ever sleep? It shines like a beacon in the night.'

'You would have to be up that late as well to notice them,' he said with a smirk.

'Sometimes I have to work at night to finish a client's marketing plan if I need it ready for the morning. Like this morning. I had to have the new menus promotion plan for Penny at the local lodge. That's where I'd been before I headed to Greg's cafe.'

A shrug of those broad shoulders again.

'There's no comparison,' she argued.

A smile played on his sexy lips, and he looked pensive as he viewed the close proximity of his house to hers. 'I guess this makes you the girl almost next door.'

The timer pinged, saving her from saying something she'd later wish she hadn't. She ran through to the kitchen again, burning up the floor with the socks she was wearing. They looked like they were hand–knitted, made from various scraps of yarn.

Brad followed her. His busy lifestyle kept him fit. He wondered if her penchant for pandemonium was part of her workout.

She pulled the tray of cupcakes out of the oven. 'These look ready to me.' Her anxious expression urged him to give his opinion.

He nodded and breathed in the gingerbread aroma. 'They smell delicious too.'

Robyn put the cupcakes on a wire tray to cool, while aware that she still had Brad roaming around her kitchen, taking up more space than was good for her heart. He certainly had an effect on her. She hoped he didn't sense the attraction she was trying to deny. It was probably due to it being an unsettled day, and now knowing that Brad was practically living next door.

The houses on the street were scattered between the trees and greenery, creating a beautiful verdant niche. Technically, his house was the nearest to hers. So maybe that did make her the girl next door. Sort of.

His attention was drawn out the window overlooking the back yard. There were more flowers there than out front.

He squinted against the sunlight shining in. 'Is that a herb garden you're growing back there?' He noticed the parsley and other dainty plants in pots and pretty containers. Did she sell flowers as a sideline? And what was with those potted rose trees sitting outside the back porch?

'Yes, I've gone all–out on cultivating my garden,' she admitted. 'In New York I lived in an apartment. I always wanted a garden, so...'

'You've developed green fingers. Taken the whole small town country lifestyle to heart.'

She didn't deny it. 'I'm embracing my creative side, doing things I've dreamed of but never thought possible. I've even joined the local quilting bee in the community hall. Nancy invited me when I first arrived.'

He looked round at her, pulling his attention away from the rose trees that looked like they needed planting before the sun wilted them. 'You're a quilter?'

'Hobby quilter, learning from the other ladies at the bee.' She picked up the oven mitts. 'These were a recent effort at patchwork.'

'Very nice.' He meant it.

She ran her hands down the apron. 'This is ninety percent my work. Nancy and Jessica helped me mitre the pockets and stitch the straps.'

'Impressive. It looks shop bought.'

She perked up at the compliment.

'Jessica, one of the other quilting bee members, owns the quilt shop on the main street. I've been helping her with her marketing, and she's teaching me how to sew a patchwork quilt for my bed.'

'Snow Bells sounds like a close–knit community where businesses help each other,' he noted.

'It is. That's why there's gossip about your studio tipping the balance.'

'I've no plans to upset anything,' he assured her.

She saw no hint of a lie in his eyes.

Taking a steadying breath, she pressed her back against the dresser and threw a question at him. 'Did Mark really recommend me?'

'He did.' Brad smiled and then revealed what Mark said. 'He told me you were responsible for helping him become accepted as the new, young mayor.'

'I just gave him a few tips. He'll make a fine mayor. He's trustworthy, reliable and a good person.'

He could hear in her tone that she set great value on those assets. Did his character come up to scratch he wondered.

Before he could prejudge himself, she added, 'Snow Bells is a very friendly town. But it needs reassurance that its trust in newcomers is warranted.'

Brad nodded. 'I get that. It's fair.'

'What type of help would you be looking for regarding your marketing? Not that I'm saying I'll take on the job.'

'Letting people know that I've set up the studio and intend to record new music there. I guess.' He threw his arms out wide. 'But I'm open to suggestions. Mark's recommendation was of the highest level when he told me I should talk to you.'

Robyn frowned. 'What did Mark say?'

'He said that you were lightning in a bottle.'

She laughed, flattered.

Brad continued. 'I knew I had to meet you. I had to see what a woman like that was like.'

'And so you knew who I was when you saw me in the cafe?'

'No. All I had was the card Mark gave me with your details. I noticed the address, saw that we lived on the same street, but that was it. When the mayor suggests I buy you gingerbread cupcakes, who am I to argue?' There was a straightforward tone to his complicated explanation that she found refreshing.

A question popped into her head. 'Are you insulted that I didn't know you, the successful singer and songwriter?'

'No. Not everyone knows me.'

'Half the town at least does. I've never even heard any of your songs.'

'Oh, you have.'

She shook her head. 'No, I don't think so.'

He insisted she had. 'In the grocery store. The song that was playing was one of the hits from my last album.'

Her eyes widened. 'That was you singing?'

'Yes, and playing my guitar.'

'Your music is contemporary with a little bit of country,' she assessed.

'That about sums it up,' he agreed. 'Some songs are a bit more country, some less so. But overall, that's a fair assessment.'

'I've never done any marketing for a music artist before,' she warned him.

'I've never dealt with a marketer before,' he countered.

That thing she did when she took in all the different parts of a client and their business started to play around in her mind like pieces on a chess board. She was already starting to have ideas how to promote him. Fast, no fuss. She had to rein in her ideas before they got ahead of her even agreeing to market his studio.

'Is it you or your new studio that you'd want me to market?' she said.

He hesitated. 'I kinda think the two aren't easily separated.' He sighed. 'I guess I don't know.'

'Come through to my office for a moment.' Robyn marched out of the kitchen and through to the room with the desk.

He kept up with her, hopeful that she would help him.

She accessed his New York website on her laptop, skimmed the surface and then pointed to the studio's introduction. The *about the studio* editorial.

Brad leaned close to view the screen alongside her as she indicated what she thought he needed to highlight.

'This editorial here describes all about your studio in New York,' she said. 'And there are plenty of photos of you with captions explaining about your songs, your success. We could siphon off the relevant parts. Make a scaled–down edit to get the message across about your new studio.' Her eyes were in close–up to his as she glanced directly at him for his reaction.

His reaction was two–fold. He nodded at her suggestion to glean all the information she needed from his website bio. But his private reaction caught him way off–guard. His heart felt like it was thundering loud and strong enough to match whatever lightning capacity she had. He forced himself to gaze at the screen instead of into the depths of those sexy, intelligent and trusting eyes of hers.

Robyn's mind was in creative mode, sparking with ideas faster than she could tell him, so she kept storing the excess, planning a promotion that would work to his benefit.

'I'm assuming you won't be having an open–day for your studio. No inviting local folk to nosey around inside?' she surmised.

'I wasn't planning to. The studio in New York is only available with prior booking and to professional musicians only. It'll be the same for the Snow Bells studio. As I said, it's not a teaching facility.'

'Which means what we're looking at is a *soft launch* for your new studio.'

'Soft launch?'

'A little bit of publicity in the local paper, just to explain that you're here, the studio is where you'll be recording your new music, and tactfully making it clear that it's a closed–door facility.'

'That sounds ideal. Do I need to phone the newspaper?'

'No, I have a good relationship with the editor. I'll call the paper about this. It's a weekly paper and their deadline is tomorrow around closing time, so we'll need to be aware of that. And there's no guarantee that your news will be included this late in the week. It could be featured next week. Unless...'

'Unless what?'

'Are you willing to pay for an advertising feature in the paper? That would ensure that it would make the next issue.'

'Yes. I'm happy to pay. Money isn't an issue.'

She blinked, momentarily forgetting that Brad was wealthy. She was so used to having to work to clients' tight budgets.

'I'll write the editorial for the feature myself,' she said. 'That way, it'll save time arranging for one of the reporters to interview you. And it'll allow us to include exactly what we want to say.'

Brad was impressed at how fast she was piecing the plan together. He let her run with it.

She pointed to a couple of the photos of Brad playing guitar and keyboards in the city studio. 'We could use these, but I think new pics would be more interesting. Keep the news feature fresh.'

'Okay. Do I need to hire a photographer, or will the newspaper send someone?'

'I'll take the photos.' She didn't even look at him as she said this.

Brad nodded. Another notch on Robyn's belt.

She stood back from the laptop seemingly finished with her research. 'I'll need to see your studio...soon. I've work to tackle this morning and this afternoon.' She checked the time. 'I'm way behind schedule.' Baking cupcakes, dealing with Brad. It had eaten up her time.

'Is there anything I can do to make up for the time I've cost you?' he said.

'Unless you can rewind this morning, I don't think so.' She wasn't intentionally being facetious.

'What was your schedule today?'

She listed each item off, adding some asides. 'Buy rose trees and other flowers from the flower market real early. Then give Penny the publicity plans at the lodge. Indulge in a gingerbread cupcake at Greg's cafe for breakfast. Not buy ingredients from the grocery store to bake my own cupcakes. Come home, sit down at my desk and start work, answering emails and dealing with clients until almost lunchtime. Plant the rose trees and flowers in the garden. Have lunch. And pop down to the main street in the afternoon to give Virginia the leaflets I had printed for her dress shop promotion.'

'A busy day.'

'It was. It is.'

'What if I could help you catch up on your schedule by planting the rose trees and the flowers while you work in here,' he offered.

She folded her arms and grinned at him. 'You're an expert gardener now too? Don't tell me, your grandmother taught you.'

'My grandfather. My grandparents owned a farm. I visited often from the city. He taught me to mend fences, I helped him repair the barn, feed the chickens, grow flowers.'

She laughed. 'Is there anything you're not adept at?'

'Lyrics.' Any hint of a smile faded from his face.

'Song lyrics?' she said tentatively.

He nodded slowly.

'But, correct me if I'm wrong, it says here that you write all your own material — music and lyrics.'

'I do. The music comes fairly easy to me. The lyrics...that's what I get stuck at.'

'You sound like you've got a way with words to me.'

'Was that a compliment?'

'A statement.'

'Well...song lyrics have to come from the heart to sound great. Mine often sound okay, until I work at them.' That shrug again. 'I've never been a guy who could express deep emotions easily.' He pressed his hand to his chest. 'I kinda keep it all bottled up inside. I feel them, but I just can't say them well.'

'What do you do?' she prompted him.

'I keep writing, then I show my manager and a couple of close musician friends to give me reliable feedback. I continue until the words are what they need to be. But I'm not *adept* at writing lyrics. I find that part of the music process hard. I'm just not a writer at heart. I'm a musician, a singer.'

'Why don't you hire someone else to write your lyrics?'

'I tried that a couple of times, but...' he interlaced his fingers. 'The music and lyrics coming from different directions didn't merge well. Maybe I've always had the wrong lyric writers.'

'Could be.' Her tone was soft, thoughtful.

'So what do you say before I take up any more of your time? Want me to take care of the rose trees and flowers while you push on?'

'Deal.' She untied her apron and sat down at her desk.

He started to walk out of her office, then turned back. 'Does this mean you'll help me with my marketing?'

'It does.'

Inwardly, he cheered. 'But I'm going to need coffee before I start tackling the gardening.'

'I'll make it for you.' She went to get up from her desk.

He held up his hand. 'No, I'll make us coffee. You do what it is you need to do. Let some of that lightning out of the bottle.'

She laughed as she watched him stride away to the kitchen.

Tucking aside wayward thoughts of Brad making coffee, she took advantage of his help and started dealing with her work, replying to emails, catching up on everything she'd aimed to do.

Chunks of Brad's life were spent on the road, travelling to venues, staying in expensive hotels, handy motels, self–catering lodges in towns he'd never heard of, so finding his way around an unfamiliar kitchen was second nature to him. He'd likely used every mainstream coffee maker going, and had become accustomed to not being at home. Robyn's well–designed kitchen was a breeze, and soon he had the coffee brewing and was serving up a cupcake on a plate for her to go with it.

He carried the coffee and one of Greg's cupcakes through to her office and sat them down at the side of her desk.

She smiled up at him while listening to a message on her phone. 'Thanks, Brad.'

'Enjoy.' He breezed back out, leaving behind him a feeling that warmed her heart, and warned her heart too.

Brad was likeable. She'd promised herself not to get involved romantically with any man until she'd firmly established her life in Snow Bells. A broken heart could ruin everything. She was happy with her new life in the town. The last thing she needed was heartbreak. And Brad was a heartbreaker — with bells on. Besides, he was surely the type to date models and other singers from his musical world, not a small town marketing consultant. She reckoned plenty of women would easily fall for him. She didn't want to add her name to the list.

Biting into the cupcake, she pushed on with her work, determined to clear the decks so she could deal with Brad's business. A soft launch was a breeze. She'd write his feature, ensure it was in the paper, and that would be the end of her marketing work for him. No big deal. Of course, they'd still be living near each other, but with them both having busy lives, they weren't likely to cross paths that often. And he'd be away a lot of the time on his music tours.

Brad found the tools he needed beside the flowers on the back porch. He figured from where she'd left the rose trees that she'd planned to put them near the middle of the garden, and the flowers at the side. So as not to interrupt her work, he made an executive decision and planted the rose trees closer to the house where they wouldn't be so exposed to the elements. He'd read that Snow Bells had white Christmases, and from his experience she'd be better shielding the roses from the colder weather.

Breathing in the fresh, bright morning, he thought how much he enjoyed working in the garden. He'd barely had time to work on his own garden, but he planned to, that's for sure.

He'd just finished planting the trees and the flowers when Robyn came out and joined him.

'I'm all caught up on work,' she said chirpily.

'Great.'

She admired the garden. 'I love where you've planted the rose trees.'

He explained what he'd done.

'I hadn't thought about the colder months,' she admitted. 'I appreciate your expertise.'

'Glad to help.'

'I called the newspaper about your feature. They're delighted to run it in the next issue. I've booked a half page of advertising space and they've offered to extend it to a full page of editorial and pics.'

'That sounds wonderful. Get them to bill me for the cost. And tell me what I owe you too.'

She nodded, estimating it would be her usual fee. Fair but affordable. 'You won't have to hire me for long. All you need is a feature in the paper. Once that's done, we're done.'

'Okay.' He tried to sound upbeat, but something in him had hoped that their connection would be longer. But he guessed that the mayor was right. Robyn didn't waste time. She cut to what needed done, and did it. Fast, efficient.

'I'll pop into your studio late this afternoon to have a look around, get a feel for the place and take some photos,' she told him.

'Perfect.' He gave her his number. 'Call if I have the studio door locked and don't hear you knocking.'

'Is your music that loud?'

'I wear headphones,' he explained.

'I'll bring my camera and take notes for the feature. It won't take too long.'

'I'm in no rush.'

'But I'll need to get the editorial written and the pictures taken,' she reminded him tactfully.

'Yes, of course.' He tried to sound casual about the whole deal. Brushing the soil from his hands, he smiled at her and then started to walk away. 'See you later.' He took the side route through the garden rather than enter her house again.

Robyn watched him walk away, and something in her heart made her call out to him. 'You're welcome to stay for lunch.'

He stopped and looked round. 'You sure?'

'It's nothing fancy, but...' It was her turn to shrug her shoulders.

Taking her up on her offer, Brad walked towards her, running his hands through his blond hair that looked a fair match for hers in the sunlight.

He followed her inside and washed his hands while she started to prepare the lunch.

'What can I do to help?' he offered.

'You make great coffee,' she told him as she popped a pizza in the oven and set the timer.

'Coming right up.'

'Tell me about your music,' she said, starting to prepare a crisp green salad with cherry tomatoes to go with their pizza.

He glanced round at her while he made the coffee. 'What do you want to know?'

'When did you get into music?'

'My grandparents bought me a guitar when I was eight. I loved it from the start. Spent all my time learning to play it. I listened to everything I could get my hands on — from blues to jazz, picking up the nuances of the different styles and learning what made each of them great.'

'You're self–taught?'

'Yes, but I can read and write music. I taught myself that too.'

She threw him an impressed look. 'Quite a motivated kid.'

'Music just always sat easy with me. I would happily spend hours playing my guitar, trying to improve my technique to make the guitar sing.' He smiled as he said this and she felt his enthusiasm.

'And the actual singing?'

'That came later.' He paused and remembered writing his first song. 'When I started writing my own songs.'

'A true talent.'

'Talent and hard work. And perseverance. Especially the latter. In my business, you've got to take a lot of criticism on the chin. A lot of no thanks.'

'But that clearly didn't deter you.'

'I'm the determined sort.'

'It's got you where you are today.' She meant his career.

'Having lunch with the lightning lady.' He gave her a warm smile.

She laughed, but her heart fluttered, flattered, feeling he wasn't spinning her a line.

It was true. She hadn't even invited Mark into her kitchen, never mind let him help her to make lunch, and she considered the mayor to be a good friend. Mark had been in her office a handful of times. But she hadn't ever been to his home, and he lived four houses down from her. Now here she was at excited ease with a successful stranger in her kitchen. Life sure could throw some wild curve balls.

CHAPTER THREE

She's springtime in my mind
Summer in my heart
Falling for her in autumn
Winter when we're apart

Robyn served up the salad on two plates while the aroma of the pizza filled the kitchen.

The timer on the oven was due to ping any minute. Brad poured their coffee and sat it down on the table ready for their lunch.

As they worked around each other in the kitchen, he'd continued to fill her in with glimpses of his musical past, and she planned to cherry pick a few details to add interest to the feature she'd write.

The doorbell rang.

'That'll be the delivery guy,' she said, expecting the leaflets and other items she'd had printed for clients. She hurried through and opened the door.

'Mark! What a surprise.' Robyn smiled at him standing there smiling back at her.

'I just wanted to tell you that—'

The timer pinged on the oven, sounding clear through to the hallway.

Robyn rushed away, beckoning Mark through to the kitchen. 'I'm making lunch.' Her words trailed behind her, and Mark followed suit, keeping pace with her.

As they hurried into the kitchen, Brad was wearing the oven mitts and lifting the pizza out of the oven.

Mark stopped and stared seeing Brad there.

'The pizza is ready,' Brad announced, and then glanced over his shoulder expecting to see Robyn. And only Robyn.

Mark forced a tight smile. 'I'd advised Brad to contact you,' he said, finishing what he'd originally dropped by to tell her. 'But I can see that you know this.'

Brad picked up on the slight edge to Mark's tone quicker than Robyn. She was interested in checking the pizza wasn't burned. Satisfied it was nicely cooked, she looked at Mark. He was still forcing a smile, clearly taken aback that Brad looked like he'd moved in with Robyn. And he thought Robyn was a fast worker!

'You were right about Robyn,' Brad told Mark, filling the stunned silence that permeated the air. 'She's great. She's already arranged a feature in the local paper for me and is planning a soft launch for my new studio.'

Mark forced himself to nod as if he was delighted, yet somehow, even though he knew he wasn't the man for Robyn, seeing Brad move in on her so fast jarred him to the core.

Robyn saw the look exchanged between the two men, and smiled brightly at Mark. 'Would you like to join us for lunch?'

It was on the tip of Mark's tongue to say no, but something in him decided to take her up on her offer. 'Thanks, the pizza looks delicious. I haven't had lunch yet.' He took his coat off and hung it on the back of one of the kitchen chairs, claiming his seat at the table.

Robyn quickly grabbed a third plate, added salad and placed it down in front of Mark.

'Want me to slice up the pizza?' Brad offered, while she poured a cup of coffee for Mark.

'Sure.' She tried to sound chirpy. And shame on her, she started to smirk at the situation. Maybe she was overtired, easily amused, but as the awkward threesome sat down to enjoy a convivial lunch, she sensed fireworks sparking in their midst.

Mark took a gulp of his coffee to wash down any snippy remarks. 'A feature in the paper, huh? That'll help make you real popular, Brad.'

'Robyn thinks it's an easy and efficient way to introduce me and my studio to the town.'

'I've never known her to be wrong,' said Mark. 'I'm sure you'll be a wild success.'

Brad washed his comments down with a sip of his coffee. He wasn't aiming to be a wild success, just ease himself into the town.

Mark sidelined Brad's business to talk to Robyn about something else. 'Tickets are available for the dance at the community hall.'

'I bought one,' she told Mark. 'Nancy was selling them in her grocery store.'

Brad ate his pizza, but glanced at Robyn for an explanation about the dance.

'It's to raise funds for repairs to the hall's roof,' she told Brad. 'Whenever the town needs fixing, we hold a dance or some sort of event.'

'The roof repairs are minor,' Mark added. 'Ticket sales should raise enough to pay for them. Folk like to get involved.'

'You should come along,' Robyn encouraged Brad.

'When is the dance?'

'A couple of nights from now,' she said.

'That'll be the day the feature comes out in the paper,' Brad calculated, unsure if attending the dance when he was a main topic of local news was a smart move or not.

'Yes, the paper comes out in the morning,' Robyn told Brad. 'Maybe you'd prefer to keep a low profile while the feature is hot off the press.'

'What do you suggest?' Brad said to her.

'We'll know the reaction to the feature by midday. Decide then,' she advised.

Brad nodded. 'Okay, but I'll buy a ticket in case I need it.'

Mark had one in his pocket. 'I have one here.' He placed it on the table. 'I bought two. One for you,' he said to Robyn. 'With you being so busy I thought you might not have had a chance to buy one.'

Brad took the ticket and put it in his wallet. He offered to pay for it.

Mark wouldn't hear of it. 'The ticket's paid for. Take it.'

'Thanks,' said Brad. 'But I'll make a contribution to the fund later today.'

They ate lunch exchanging tense pleasantries.

Robyn cleared their plates away and offered Mark a cupcake. 'Brad bought these from Greg's cafe. They're gingerbread cupcakes. He dropped by with them. It turns out he lives in the house diagonally opposite mine.'

Mark accepted a cupcake, but he couldn't hide his surprise. 'You live around here?'

'I do,' said Brad.

'I live a few houses down from Robyn,' Mark told him.

'Brad's house is the one with the apple trees in the garden,' Robyn said brightly.

'That's a nice house.' Mark didn't sound delighted. He bit into his cake and said no more about it.

Brad downed the remainder of his coffee and stood up. 'Well, I'd better get back to the studio. Thanks for lunch.'

'I'll see you out,' Robyn offered.

Mark decided he'd leave too. 'Look at the time. I have a meeting to attend.'

The three of them walked to the front door.

'Will you still drop by the studio later?' Brad said to her.

'Yes, late in the afternoon,' she confirmed.

'Brad gave me a tour of the studio,' said Mark. 'It's impressive.'

Nodding acknowledgment to Mark's comment, Brad started to walk to where his car was parked.

Mark headed away too.

Robyn waved them off then went inside and closed the door. She leaned against it and took a deep breath. The tension between Mark and Brad had eased a little from their initial reaction, but she was glad to draw breath and relax.

The doorbell rang, causing her to jump.

Opening the door, she took delivery of the parcel she'd been expecting. Carrying it through to her office, she started to get everything ready for her work that afternoon.

The sun shone brightly as Robyn walked along the main street after handing in the leaflets to Virginia's dress shop — and buying one of the lovely bargain dresses for the dance. A pretty pale blue dress that flattered her slender figure. She put it on the back seat of her car that was parked nearby. It was such a fine, sunny day that she wore only a classy dress and heels. She hadn't intentionally dressed up for her meeting with Brad. She always wore smart clothes for business.

Next stop on her to–do list was to pop into the lodge further along the main street. Penny had called to say that she'd had a chance to discuss the new menus promotion plan with her nephew Kyle, and they wanted to chat about the marketing ideas for the lodge's new restaurant.

The family–run lodge, owned by Penny and her husband, was the main place to stay in town. Her husband was away on business to events, promoting the lodge for vacations.

Kyle had a reputation for wanderlust, but having come home to Snow Bells in the spring to attend a wedding, he'd decided to stay and work at the lodge as their head chef. Kyle, thirties, trained as a chef in New York, but now intended to help run the catering for the lodge.

Guests staying at the lodge had their meals in the dining room, and there was a function room facility for parties.

But recently the premises was extended to include a restaurant for local people to enjoy lunch and dinner. Set at the rear of the lodge, it extended into the garden, and large windows with pretty scalloped shades allowed plenty of light in during the day. Lovely lighting in the evenings created a welcoming atmosphere, and the restaurant had a floral garden theme.

Zack, a local architect, had designed the extension. When the work was finished, Robyn had been hired to advise on the marketing of it, including planning the opening launch that had proved to be a success.

Robyn headed into the lodge's reception.

Penny, in her fifties and smartly dressed, welcomed her. 'Thanks for coming back to discuss the restaurant.' She called through to the kitchen. 'Kyle, Robyn is here.'

Moments later, Kyle strode through, tall, slim, dark blond hair, wearing his chef's whites, and smiled at Robyn. 'Aunt Penny showed me the promotion ideas for the new menus. I think they're great. But I wanted to ask your opinion on a couple of other ideas I have for the restaurant.'

'Yes, I'd be happy to help,' said Robyn. She'd done the marketing for numerous restaurants and hotels in New York and it was one of her main areas of expertise.

'I thought we could chat through here,' said Penny, leading the way to the office.

Robyn spent time discussing Kyle's latest ideas for the restaurant, offering advice, and agreeing to write an editorial for their website to update customers on the new menus and promotion.

'Zack and Sylvie's wedding will be the first bridal function we'll cater for at the new restaurant,' said Kyle. 'They're getting married here soon.'

Robyn had met Sylvie at the quilting bee, but didn't know her too well. Sylvie was a fabric designer. Nancy had mentioned that they were getting married in a small, intimate ceremony for close friends in the lodge's garden, and then having a meal at the new restaurant, followed by a dance party in the function room in the evening. Robyn, being a member of the quilting bee, had received an invitation to the wedding dance at night.

'They're keeping the ceremony small and sweet,' Penny told Robyn. 'Are you coming along to the wedding dance?'

'Yes, it was nice of Sylvie to invite me.'

'I've had a peek at Sylvie's dress,' Penny confided. 'It's beautiful. With her being a fabric designer, she's created a white silk fabric with a fine white floral print. The dress was made by our local dressmaker, Virginia.'

'It sounds lovely,' said Robyn.

'Zack and Sylvie are happy for their wedding photos to be put on our website to promote that we cater for weddings at the lodge,' Kyle added.

'That will be handy,' Robyn agreed, and then continued to chat to them about their marketing.

After leaving the lodge, Robyn walked back to her car, picked up her camera, put it in her shoulder bag, and headed to Brad's studio, phone in hand in case she needed to call him.

She knocked on the door and waited.

Moments later, Brad opened it, smiling to welcome her in.

'Can I take a couple of pictures of you standing outside the studio?' She dug her camera out of her bag. 'The lighting is great.'

'Yeah,' he agreed, tucking his thumbs into his jeans and standing happily outside it, all casual stance, thick blond hair, and blue eyes that vied against the cloudless cobalt sky for vibrancy.

Robyn snapped a shot and then studied the preview. 'Could you hold a guitar? It would help give more context to the image.'

He stepped inside, disappeared and then emerged with a gleaming red electric guitar. 'Will this do?'

'Ideal.' Her tone didn't begin to describe how great he looked standing there in the afternoon sunlight, hands on the guitar like he was playing something special. No doubt he could. No doubt he would once he got her inside the confines of the studio. Or would he? Would Brad play just for her? Hmmm...

Hands poised in a player's position on the frets and strings, standing upright as if facing an audience, he held the pose while Robyn took several pictures.

'This could be the lead photo,' she told him, explaining why she was being fussy about getting the right shot.

But he was patient, in no rush. She didn't know that he was admiring her — firstly for her professionalism in capturing the pictures, and thinking how lovely she looked caught in the glow of the sunlight.

Passers–by on the other side of the main street stared over at them, interested to see what was going on. Was Brad giving an impromptu performance? Was the studio open?

'We should go inside now,' Robyn told him, quickly leading the way before anyone ventured over to interrupt their business.

Brad didn't linger. He followed Robyn in, closed the door and locked it.

The silence surprised her. She'd imagined it would be hard to talk to him over the music she thought would be playing in the background. Instead, she couldn't remember the last time the air felt so quiet. Even the hush of night had notes of faraway traffic, the distant burr of the countryside. But here there was nothing except the beating of her heart. Excitement made her heartbeat quicken, and she wondered if he could hear the thunder of it in the quietude.

He took in her reaction to her first glimpse of his world. He saw her glance at the two guitars and the saxophone on the reception wall, then linger thoughtfully on the black and white poster. He'd have paid a lot more than a penny for her thoughts.

'Would you stand in front of the guitars and the sax?' she said.

He stood where she directed him.

Peering through the lens, she made sure she had everything in the frame and clicked her camera twice. Then checked she'd captured the look she wanted. She nodded, satisfied.

He led her along the hallway through to the main control room. The lights were on, but set to spotlights rather than a full overhead glare.

The air smelled of cedar and potential. She breathed it in.

A blue electric guitar sat on a chair beside a small table where a music manuscript notepad and pen were lying, giving her the correct impression that he'd been playing and taking notes before she arrived.

Musical notes were written on the lined paper, but no words, no lyrics.

'I'm working on new songs for the album,' he explained, seeing her piece together what he'd been doing. 'No lyrics, as you can see.' He gestured to the notepad, showing her something she'd never seen before. Real music, written in its rawest state, note by note.

'It's rough,' he said.

She noticed the headphones that were plugged into the main console, and started to figure out his writing process. She didn't need to understand it all, just an outline of his talent, a rough, like the musical notes.

'This would be a fascinating glimpse into your writing,' she said, adjusting her camera. 'Unless this is too private for public view.'

'No, it's fine, but don't show the music clearly.'

'I won't,' she assured him.

He sat with his guitar as if working on a new song.

Robyn viewed the shot and then paused.

'Something wrong?' he said.

'Do you have another shirt you could put on? The dark denim shirt is a good look, but you're going to be wearing the same thing in all the photos. Maybe we could mix it up a little.'

He put the guitar down. 'I have a change of clothes upstairs.' He strode off, leaving her to wander around, fascinated by the technical equipment, lots of buttons that the minx in her wanted to press, but she wouldn't.

The aroma of freshly made coffee mingled with the scent of cedar, and on the table beside the notepad and headphones was a pot of coffee, still hot, and two clean cups. Musical notes adorned the cups.

Stepping back, her heels caught on a cable running along the floor from the console to the blue guitar. Teetering slightly, she saved herself from tumbling by grabbing on to the edge of the console and touched an audio control by mistake, activating the sound system that played his recording at high volume.

Frantically fumbling with the knobs, she managed to silence it again.

Wide–eyed, she wondered if Brad had heard her. She'd have been surprised if the entire main street hadn't heard.

Brad was shouting down to her, but he didn't sound angry.

Her ears were still buzzing from the burst of guitar playing at full volume, and she heard him call her name and was sure he was beckoning her to come upstairs.

She headed up, leaving her bag behind, but kept a grip on her camera. Maybe he wanted her to take photos of him upstairs.

Walking in on him, seeing him half–dressed, wearing a pair of smart black trousers instead of the jeans, and very little else except his boots, she gasped and almost dropped the camera.

His back was towards her, and if she hadn't gasped she could've sneaked away without him knowing she'd seen him.

But her gasp was loud, and was followed by her looking flustered, especially when he turned around to expose his smooth, golden chest that made him look like a cover model for a fashion shoot. Brad was fit. Really toned. Broad shoulders tapered to the leanest waist she'd seen in close–up. And he was closer now, walking towards her, frowning.

'Is everything okay?' He couldn't think why she'd want to walk in on him unless something had happened and she needed his immediate attention.

No, everything was not okay. Not in her world. Not in her heart. Or the way her flustering made her feel like a total fool. It's not like she hadn't seen a guy without his shirt on before. Just not a guy like Brad. Phew!

'Yes, no,' she told him confusingly. And then started to run away. Running seemed the best option.

'Robyn, wait!' he called to her as she made a dash for the stairs.

She waited, but kept her gaze anywhere except his bare torso. Tempting as it was to look.

'Sorry,' she said. 'I thought you shouted on me to come up.'

A sexy smile formed on his lips. 'I said to help yourself to the coffee. To pour yourself a cup.'

'Oh.'

'But, seeing as you're here...' He walked over to a rail with a couple of changes of clothes including shirts and a waistcoat. He lifted a check shirt and a pale blue one on two hangers and held them up. 'Print or plain?'

'Go with the pale blue one,' she advised in an instant, trying to sound casual, but knowing she was failing.

'I like blue,' he said, putting it on and buttoning it up, but leaving the top button undone.

'It matches the dress I bought this afternoon for the dance.'

He hung the check shirt back on the rail, unhooked a stylish, deep blue, silk backed waistcoat and shrugged it on.

'You going with anyone to the dance?' he said.

'Like a date?'

He nodded and looked right at her.

His towering height and raw masculinity made her stomach do all sorts of flips that she didn't even have names for.

'No, I'm not dating anyone right now,' she said. 'I'm concentrating on work, establishing my business in Snow Bells.'

He took a step towards her. 'What about love?'

'Well, I love my work.'

The look he gave her made her explain. 'I plan to make time for romance once I feel totally settled and secure in town.'

His pale blue eyes deepened as if a storm was brewing in them. 'Make time for romance? There's something way wrong with those words.'

'Not ideal for lyrics.' She tried to make light of it. But she knew what he meant. And she agreed wholeheartedly. But she was stuck in the moment of her own making.

He didn't agree. 'A lot of songs are about heartache.'

'I don't have a broken heart. I've endured a bad break up in the past. Never going down that route again.'

'Just going to sidestep romance?' he said.

'Waltz around it for now,' she said, adjusting his summary.

He took one step back, stood upright and tugged on the edges of the waistcoat. 'Buttoned or undone.'

'Buttoned up. It'll highlight your broad shoulders and lean waist. Show your fit physique.'

He smiled at her. 'You think I look fit?'

The flustering kicked off again. 'It'll be a tidier look for the photos. I'll meet you downstairs.'

And off she went, almost running down the wooden stairs and back to the control room.

She heard his footsteps hurry after her.

If he'd heard her switch on the music by mistake, he didn't say a peep, so neither did she, and continued to suggest where he should pose for the next round of photos.

He sat with the blue guitar and pen in hand, pretending to strum and scribble simultaneously. The nearest visual representation to the truth where he'd try out a few notes, write down the ones he liked, and kept going as he created his songs.

Robyn checked the images, making sure the spotlights were enough to show the details while still capturing the atmosphere of the studio.

She photographed him with the whole studio background, and in close–up as the shadows and light showed the handsome contours of his face. When he glanced up at her with those eyes while playing a few chords a spotlight glinted off the guitar.

She finished and checked the images.

Brad stood up and looked over her shoulder, impressed by the quality of the shots that captured the mood of the studio, and him. 'Where did you learn photography?'

'Self–taught, to begin with. Then I took a course to brush up my skills. I like to offer clients a full range of services. From writing the features myself and taking the photos, to designing their logos, posters and promotional material, and creating their websites.'

'Multi–talented.'

'A multitasker.' She preferred her version.

Those lips of his smirked, not entirely agreeing. 'I read your website,' he confessed. 'The samples of articles you've written. Features for magazines and newspapers. You're a talented writer.'

She blushed, but was happy that he'd read some of her work.

'It makes my marketing work easier, more efficient. And I've always enjoyed writing. And meddling in other people's business, which makes me the ideal person for this type of job.'

'What about your writing? Ever considered taking that talent further?'

'I thought about it years ago before I set myself up as a marketing consultant. The latter made me feel more secure. That I could pay the bills, afford a fairly comfortable life for myself.'

'Maybe when you make time for love, you'll make time for your writing too.'

'Never say never.'

'I never do.'

She walked around admiring the decor of the premises and instruments on display.

'You play all of these?' the incredulity in her tone was clear.

Brad nodded. He played multiple instruments, but his heart belonged to his guitars with keyboards runner up.

He gestured to a black electric guitar on the wall. 'I played that one on my last tour for the best part of a year.'

She noticed the slight wear on it, though this seemed to add to its merit.

'I like to retire instruments on a high note.' He grinned. 'Pardon the pun. When I've played a successful tour, I'll often relegate a guitar to the sidelines.'

Her fingers itched to touch the smooth surface of the hardworking guitar that would now be forever silent. But her fingers didn't belong there.

'Everything goes out on a high note,' she murmured, replaying his remark and liking that nothing he owned was easily cast aside.

'Do you play any instruments?' That question again, but he needed to know. She walked around looking at the keyboards and drums. Everything told her something about him. And the things that were missing added to her assessment of his character.

'No, I'm not the type to sit and twang a guitar.' She heard herself say something that would set her up for being mocked, but it was out there. She couldn't retract her comment.

'*Twang?*' He laughed.

She raised a carefree hand to disguise her faux pas. 'Whatever the technical jargon is.'

'Twang's fine. Descriptive. Gets the message across. And how you feel about twanging.'

She threw him a barbed look that he tried and failed to dodge. It hit him right in the heart, giving him an unexpected jolt. He knew in an instant that he didn't want to upset her. He liked Robyn. He liked that she challenged him.

CHAPTER FOUR

I see you shine across the way
You brighten my night, you make my day
We live nearby, but it breaks my heart
Our two worlds are galaxies apart

Robyn wandered through to one of the studio rooms and looked at the large treble clef music symbol painted in black on the light cream wall. From floor to ceiling, it added a classic touch to the decor.

'I had Luke, owner of the local art store, create it for me,' Brad explained.

She had an idea. 'Did you hire any other local businesses to work on the studio?'

'Yes, local builders, Zack an architect, and I did a lot of the work myself. But I hired everyone locally.'

'We should include that in the feature,' she said. 'Give them a mention. People would appreciate that.'

'I'll give you a list of the names.'

Smiling that she now had another element to highlight, she looked at the keyboards that were sitting in front of the music clef.

'I should take a picture of you playing keyboards too. And drums.' A drum kit was over by the other wall. 'Let people know that you're multi-instrumental.'

Brad sat down at the keyboards. He didn't play a note, just positioned his hands over the keys for effect.

Robyn stepped back so she could get the artistic symbol in the background and snapped a few shots.

She showed him the images while he was still sitting at the keyboards. The only time she'd felt taller than him.

'I like this photo,' she said, pausing at one of them.

He leaned close to see it and nodded, then glanced up at her, causing her heart to jolt with attraction that was off the scales.

She immediately stepped back and walked over to the drums.

'Want to have a go at playing them?' he offered, heading over to join her.

She was tempted. 'No, I don't have a musical bone in my body. I've never even held a musical instrument in my life.'

'You've never held a guitar? Not even lifted one up out of curiosity?'

'Nope.'

'Take a seat.' He took the camera off her and insisted she sit down at the drum kit. He handed her the sticks. 'Hit a few beats.'

She hesitated.

'Go on.'

Ignoring the drum pedals action, she tapped lightly with the drum sticks, and smiled up at him, feeling mischievous.

'Hit them harder. They can take it.'

So she did, finding the nearest thing to rhythm that she could muster. Feeling feisty, she hit the cymbals as a finale.

Brad clapped his hands. 'You've got the rhythm in you, Robyn.'

She gazed at him wide–eyed. 'You think?'

'Sure do.' He beckoned her over to the keyboards. 'Sit down and just let your fingers run across the keys.'

She did, laughing at every note sounding wrong. 'Maybe the keyboards aren't for me.'

'Maybe not. How about guitar?' He picked one up and handed it to her. A beautiful acoustic guitar.

'It feels...daunting. I don't even know how to hold it properly.'

Brad stood behind her, leaned over and adjusted her hands on the frets and strings. 'Relax.'

Relax? Was he kidding? With him leaning so close she could feel the strong muscles in his arms and chest. His clean, masculine scent interrupted her concentration. And he'd rolled up the sleeves of his shirt, revealing the long, lean muscles in his forearms. But she pretended to be fine with him instructing her.

With Brad guiding her hands, she strummed her first guitar, feeling the rich tone, the resonance charging through her. Or maybe that was just the effect Brad's close proximity was having on her.

He pressed a plectrum into her hands. 'Use this to isolate the strings.'

She tried. 'How am I doing?' It sounded slightly better.

Brad stepped back, letting her take charge of the guitar on her own. 'Keep strumming. It's good for the soul.'

'Where have I heard that remark before?' she teased him.

Smiling, he moved further back and without her noticing, he used his phone to take a picture of her, adding it to the ones he'd secretly snapped of her playing the drums. His intentions were all good.

'I love the feel of this guitar,' she said, playing notes that sounded right and sounded wrong.

'Want to try an electric guitar?'

'Nope, I like this one.' She admired the lovely wood that it was made from, and the workmanship.

'Keep it if you want,' he said, meaning it.

She stopped playing and almost dropped the plectrum. 'No, I couldn't.'

'It's got some history to it. I played it on my last two albums. It's travelled thousands of miles with me. I find that my acoustic guitars improve with age.'

'A bit like some people.'

'I certainly have. You wouldn't have approved of me when I was younger. I was often described, even by my grandparents, as *wild and strong–willed.*'

'Snap. So was I. Still am sometimes.' As if to prove her point, she started strumming the guitar again.

She made him smile, and his heart felt another wave of warmth for her.

Putting the guitar aside, she looked around. 'I've probably got everything I need to write your feature.' She picked up her camera and shouldered her bag.

'When will I get to read it?' he said eagerly.

'As soon as I've written it. I'll head home and start writing.' She checked the time. 'It should take me about an hour.' She was used to writing features like these and knew from experience what was required.

'Do you need to go home? You could write it here while I work on my music. That way I could be on hand if you needed to ask me any other information for the feature.'

She had her laptop in her bag and supposed she could but... 'I need quiet to write. I can't write with music in the background.'

He held up his hands. 'I'll be working in the control room. You can work here in this room. It's soundproof, so you won't hear me.'

The idea instantly appealed to her. It would save time having to drive home, phone him if she needed more information, or email a sample to him. She could do it right here. 'Okay.'

He brightened. 'Great. You can use this table.' He wheeled a chair over to it. 'There you go. Would you like a coffee?'

'No, I'm fine.' She set up her laptop and settled herself down.

'Right, I'll let you get on with it. Shout if you need me.'

'You won't hear me.'

'I can hear you, if I want, but you won't hear me.' He gestured to the glass partition separating the two rooms. 'Or wave and I'll see you.'

She smiled and nodded.

He headed out and closed the door, effectively shuttering her studio room in complete silence. There was something so appealing and relaxing about the quietude. She settled back, fingers poised over the laptop keys, thinking how to start the feature with several ideas vying for first position.

Glancing up, she saw Brad enter the control room, pick up his guitar and continue where he'd left off before she'd arrived. She watched him strumming his guitar. Total silence. Not one pluck. No twanging.

He sat side on so as not to look like he was staring through to her, but enough that she could catch his attention if she wanted.

Picking up her camera, she took a few photos of him from her vantage point through the window that separated them, unintentionally capturing herself reflected in the glass. She viewed the image, and felt a thrill charge through her, seeing herself with Brad, a reflection of herself on the edges of his world. Was it a hint of her future she'd glimpsed?

Shrugging off such fanciful thoughts, she started to tap at the keys, writing the feature, getting the main points down before she honed it into the feature she had in mind.

She checked the photos on her camera, tying in the editorial with some of the pictures, and adding notes for the captions that she'd include with the feature so that the newspaper had the correct information.

'Concentrate,' she muttered to herself when she found her attention drifting through the window to watch Brad. She saw him pause intermittently from playing to write the music on his notepad. And peered with added interest when he seemed to be writing something else on the pad too. Lyrics?

Forcing her attention back to the feature, she found it fairly easy to write, mainly because she felt she knew what Brad and his studio needed for the feature. And the photos spoke volumes by themselves. His reputation as a successful recording artist helped too. She didn't need to elaborate on his fame. Instead, she explained about his new studio and his aim to write music for his latest album there in town.

As the feature started to shape up, she read it through and nodded to herself. This would work. She made a note to add the names of local businesses in the feature which she hoped the newspaper would include.

Clicking on the word count, she saw that she had plenty of editorial for the feature without going over the usual limit. For this particular feature, she wanted more photos than text. And she had a few winning photos to select from. It would be up to the sub–editor at the paper to decide the layout of the page, but she whittled down the pictures to the ones that showed the studio, and Brad, at their best.

Once this work for him was done, she planned to take a step back from him. Falling for a guy like him would be too easy and far too complicated.

Besides, she'd had a look at news articles online that confirmed he dated models and other glamorous women in his industry. She wasn't his type. He wasn't her type either. She'd finish the marketing for him as agreed, and then get on with her own life while he got on with his. It was a big small town. They wouldn't encounter each other too often, even if their houses were close by. Their worlds were galaxies apart.

Waving through to him, she indicated that she'd finished writing the feature.

He put his guitar down and came through, smiling with anticipation. 'That was fast and efficient.' Those words again kept circling her, but they were particularly apt.

She stood up and offered him her seat. She'd left the feature on her laptop so he could scroll through and read it. It wasn't too long.

'I'll leave you alone to read it,' she said, taking her bag with her through to the control room, effectively swapping rooms.

Watching him lean close to the laptop, she sensed his eagerness to read every word, to see how she'd portrayed him.

Sitting down where he'd been writing his music, she couldn't help but be tempted to read the scribbled lyrics beside the musical notes. She skim–read them once. Then read them again, finding words and phrases jumping into her mind to replace what he'd scribbled. Dare she write her words down for him to read? Or was that too presumptuous?

She dug out her notepad and grabbed her pen.

Casting caution to the wind, a tact she often used, she wrote another version of his lyrics, feeling the words flow with more depth and top notes of clarity. Maybe even some rhythm.

She wrote more words down for the chorus. She'd never written lyrics before, but words were words. Writing was one of her skills.

Steeped in the lyrics, she didn't notice Brad walking through with her laptop after reading the feature.

'Having fun?' His deep voice resonated in the quiet.

Robyn jumped, fumbled with her notepad and pen, knowing he'd seen what she'd been up to.

'Can I take a look at what you've written?' He peered at the lyrics, catching a few that instantly piqued his interest.

'Caught red–handed.' She sounded uneasy.

'Write–handed more like,' he joked with her.

The fact that he was joking with her calmed her concern that he was offended by her rewriting his lyrics.

'These are great. Better than mine,' he conceded after reading them.

She let out the breath she hadn't noticed she'd been holding. 'I was just messing around while you read the feature.'

'The feature is great too. I wouldn't change a word of it. It's perfect.' He looked at her sitting there while he said this, causing her heart to beat wildly.

She went to stand up.

'Hold on there, I want to go over these lyrics with you.' He pulled up a chair and sat beside her.

'I have a tendency to overstep sometimes.' She wished she could pull the new lyrics out from under his nose and just deal with the feature.

Brad's strong hand kept a grip of her notepad as he studied the words. A frown broke across his forehead and he ran his hand through the front of his hair, pushing it back as if to clear this thoughts.

'You wrote these lyrics without hearing my music?' He needed to clarify this. Had Robyn figured out how to replay what he'd recorded? In the soundproof room he wouldn't have heard anything. And he wouldn't put it past her to figure out which buttons to press. She just kept on taking his breath away with her abilities. He'd never met a woman like her before.

'I didn't need to hear the music,' she said.

'That's not the way it usually works.'

She shrugged.

'Could you write more lyrics like these?'

'I don't know. I could try.'

'Do try. Write lyrics and then I'll set them to music.'

'Is that your usual method for creating songs?'

'No, the music comes first with me. Then the lyrics. But a lot of successful song writing is done from the lyrics first.'

'Hmmm, I don't know.'

'Give it a try,' he insisted.

'Okay.'

'If I use any of your lyrics, you'll be paid and credited,' he assured her.

'I don't want my name in lights. I really don't want to be infamous.'

He smiled.

'Really,' she said. 'I prefer to be a background person, free to go around without being noticed and asked for my autograph or pose for a picture.'

He understood. 'Sometimes, I'd like that too. But it comes with the territory, and I appreciate my fans.' He lowered his tone. 'If I use the lyrics, you will be paid. No argument on that. But your identity will be kept a secret.'

'Promise?'

'You have my word.'

'And you'll have mine, if I can think up some to string together for your lyrics.' She extended her hand.

He shook her hand.

She took a deep breath. 'So you're okay with the feature and the photos I've selected to go with it?'

'Yes,' he confirmed. 'This is a list of the local businesses I hired.'

'I'll email the feature to the paper.' She opened her laptop, added the information about the local businesses, attached the images and pressed send. 'Done. The editor will confirm if it's okay once they've read it. And I'll let you know when they do.'

Brad nodded. 'Efficient.'

She sent another mail and then closed her laptop. 'I've emailed you a copy of all the photos I took of you. You're welcome to put them on your new website.'

'I don't have a new website.'

She looked at him like he was missing a trick. 'Then add them to your New York studio website. You surely want to highlight that you've opened up a second studio.'

He seemed slightly flustered. 'Yes, I just haven't got around to doing that.'

'Well, you should. Announce the new studio so that it chimes in with the feature coming out in the paper,' she suggested.

'That's a good idea. I'll contact my manager to take care of it. And you'll be paid for all the new photographs.'

Robyn shook her head. 'They're included in the cost of my marketing work for you.' She'd gone the extra mile for him, but wasn't looking for extra money.

He blinked, surprised that she wasn't angling for more. 'That's very amenable of you.'

'My work is all–inclusive. I took extra photos to make sure I captured what I needed for the feature. As I said, I've never worked with a recording artist before. Anyway, you're welcome to have the extra pictures.'

He was still taken aback.

Checking she had everything in her bag, she smiled and got ready to leave. 'I should get going.'

'Remember about the lyrics.'

How could she forget? 'I will. But no promises that I'll be able to come up with what you need.'

'Try anyway.'

Her sweet lips smiled again at him, causing him to wish that she wasn't leaving.

He walked her out, blinking against the bright sunlight as they emerged from the seclusion of the studio.

The stores in the main street looked inviting in the afternoon glow. Flower baskets filled with summer blooms hung from the street lamps and store fronts. The forthcoming Snow Bells market fair was advertised on one of the archways, welcoming participants to hire a stall, or townsfolk to visit the event. Brad noted it. There always appeared to be something inviting going on in the town.

'I'll keep you updated on the feature,' she said, walking away.

'Thanks again, Robyn,' he called after her.

He closed the door and watched through the glass as she headed across the street, feeling like she was taking a part of his heart with her.

Then he remembered. The photos he'd taken of her! Hurrying out, he ran after her.

'Robyn!'

She jolted and looked round, seeing Brad running towards her.

He had his phone in his hand. 'I have photos for you too. Please don't be mad at me for taking these.'

She peered at the images as he scrolled through them on his phone.

'You took pictures of me playing the guitar, keyboards and drums!' There was laughter in her voice, seeing herself giving all three instruments a real go.

'I'll send a copy to you.'

Her phone sounded that she'd received them. She scrolled through them and paused at herself playing the guitar. Even she could've been fooled into thinking she was genuinely playing it.

And he'd captured her playing the keyboards looking like a pro. This made her laugh. As did the two of her playing the drums. Especially the one where she'd hit the cymbals.

'I'm not the only one adept at taking photos,' she quipped.

'I'd like to keep a copy for posterity,' he told her. 'These are precious.'

'Why? Because they highlight how not to play musical instruments?' she said jokingly.

'No, because you're the first person to play keyboards and drums in the new studio,' he told her.

'Me? Surely you've played them,' she reasoned.

He shook his head. 'Only the guitar. I've been so busy getting the studio ready, I haven't had time to play the keyboards or drums.'

'The music grinch lands a first at your new studio.' She said this as if it was a banner headline.

Brad opened his arms wide, shrugged, gave her a winning smile, and then headed back to his studio.

Robyn shook her head and continued to walk to her car.

Nate came running out of the grocery store and waylaid her. 'Nancy and I saw you go into the music studio. What's it like? All fancy?'

'It's stylish. A professional studio.'

'Are you doing his marketing?'

'I am. I'm writing a feature for the local paper. It'll be out in the next issue.'

'I'll tell Nancy to order in extra copies of the paper. Customers will be eager to read about it.'

The paper sold copies direct, but most people bought their weekly copy when they picked up their groceries.

Nancy overheard as she came out to join them. 'Nate, could you deal with the customers? I need to talk to Robyn.'

'Yes.' Nate smiled as he hurried inside the store, leaving Nancy to chat to Robyn.

'What did you think of Brad?' Nancy said eagerly.

'He's a nice guy. Talented. Wants to write his music here in town,' said Robyn.

'You look flushed,' Nancy observed.

Robyn brushed a hand across her rosy cheeks. 'I was busy trying to write the feature for his studio.'

'He's a handsome one. Don't you think?'

'I hadn't noticed,' Robyn lied.

Nancy threw her a disbelieving look.

'Okay, so he's a looker. But I'm only interested in dealing with his marketing.'

'I hear he made you pizza for lunch.' Nancy spoke in a confiding tone.

Robyn didn't even bother asking how she knew. Gossip in Snow Bells circled fast. Instead, she described what happened.

'Brad lives in the house nearest to you?' This was news to Nancy.

'He does, but once I've finished his marketing, we won't be seeing much of each other. We'll be like ships that pass in the night.' She kept the lyric writing news to herself for now. She wasn't sure she could write new lyrics for him.

'Brad having a house could solve a huge problem.'

Robyn frowned.

'We always make a newcomer a welcoming gift,' Nancy explained. 'If he's moved into a new house, do you think he'd like a quilt? The quilting bee could make one for him.'

'Yes, that would be the perfect gift.' For the man who probably had plenty of everything else. 'Everyone loves a beautiful new quilt.'

'Come on, let's tell Jessica.' Nancy then shouted into the grocery store to Nate. 'Robyn and I are just heading along to Jessica's quilt shop. I won't be long.'

'Okay, Nancy.'

Nancy linked her arm through Robyn's and hurried her along to the quilt shop. 'We'll have a quick look at the fabric. If you've met him, maybe you could help select it.'

'Yes,' Robyn agreed. 'He said that he likes blue. And he has a liking for musical notes and instruments.'

'Jessica has a fine selection of quilting fabric.' Then Nancy looked thoughtful. 'Is Brad going to the dance?'

'Mark gave him a ticket he'd bought for me. But Brad wants to see how people react to the feature. It comes out on the morning of the dance night.'

'Everyone will love the feature,' said Nancy. 'You wrote it. Tell Brad he has to come to the dance. No excuses accepted.'

Robyn laughed. 'I'll tell him.'

Nancy frowned. 'Did you find out why he moved here? Why Snow Bells Haven?'

'Brad said he wanted to open a second studio in a small town that wasn't too far from New York,' Robyn explained. 'He drove around the countryside looking for a suitable town. Some he'd been to before that he thought were nice. Then Snow Bells Haven showed up on his map. He'd never heard of it, but liked the name, so he headed here. He told me he loved the town the moment he drove down the main street. It was quaint, but thriving. Busy, but calm. And he saw the hardware store had a for sale sign.' Robyn paused. 'I've included all of this in the feature that'll be in the paper.'

Nancy squeezed Robyn's arm. 'It's so exciting to have him here in Snow Bells. I can't wait to read your feature.'

Hurrying on, they approached Jessica's quilt shop. The window display was filled with a wonderful selection of handmade quilts to buy and fat quarter bundles of fabric tied with ribbon ready to be sewn into quilts or other items.

They paused outside the window under the shade of the canopy.

'Jessica told me she's had a delivery of new fabric,' said Nancy.

Robyn pointed and smiled. 'I love those bundles of quilting weight cotton with the pretty floral designs.'

'I've got my eye on those ditsy rose prints. Come on, let's go in and talk to Jessica.'

'And try not to buy everything in the shop,' Robyn joked.

Giggling, they walked in to find Jessica folding fabric behind the counter. A customer had just left and she was tidying up the shop.

Jessica was in her forties, wore a lovely handmade dress, and had her hair pinned up in a chignon. She was married to the town's sheriff.

The shelves were brimming with rolls of cotton fabric suitable for quilting. And fat quarter fabric bundles. There was an assortment of haberdashery items, including pincushions and thimbles, ribbons and trims, and a thread display.Jessica smiled as they walked in. 'Here comes trouble.'

Nancy and Robyn didn't correct her.

'Robyn is doing the marketing for Brad's new music studio,' Nancy announced, getting straight to the point.

Jessica's interest perked up. 'What's he like, and why did he move to Snow Bells?'

'It's all coming out in the newspaper feature that Robyn's written,' Nancy said calmly. 'But now we know that he's moved into the house next door to Robyn.'

'Diagonally across the street,' Robyn clarified. 'So technically—'

Jessica laughed and cut-in. 'You're the girl next door!'

They all giggled at the situation.

'Yes,' said Robyn. 'Nancy has suggested that the quilting bee make him a welcoming quilt for his new house.'

'Robyn knows his tastes. He likes blue,' said Nancy.

'He likes musical note artwork too,' Robyn added.

Jessica grinned and clasped her hands with glee. 'I have new fabric that has musical notes on it. And one with a musical instruments pattern.' She dashed from behind the counter over to one of the shelves packed with rolls of cotton quilting weight fabric.

Robyn and Nancy hurried over to see the designs.

'I loved the music theme fabric samples and ordered them in with the other new designs,' Jessica explained. 'I thought they would be suitable for people that love music.'

'The black and cream musical notes fabric is so classy,' said Robyn, thinking that Brad would like it.

Jessica gave them a look of triumph and reached up to a higher shelf. 'Take a look at this though.'

'It's pale blue tones with a musical theme,' Robyn said, feeling that they'd found the perfect fabric for his quilt.

Jessica opened her arms. 'Or we could make a patchwork with all of these fabrics.'

'A subtle blend with a lovely blue backing fabric,' Nancy suggested.

Jessica and Nancy were both experienced in quilt making, so Robyn took their advice.

They helped Jessica lift the rolls of fabric over to the counter where she unrolled them so they could see the full effect.

They looked at Jessica's pattern folder too and decided on a modern classic design.

'Oh, this will work beautifully,' said Robyn, pleased that they were going to make a quilt for him. This would surely make him feel welcome in the town and part of the community.

'We use the money in the quilting bee fund to pay for all the welcoming gifts,' said Nancy.

'I'll handle the transaction,' Jessica assured them.

With Nancy and Jessica being two of the main members of the quilting bee, the sale of the fabric, and the batting for the quilt, was settled.

'Now all we have to do is make the quilt,' said Jessica, getting her cutting mat and rotary cutter ready to prepare the fabric.

'You're the experts.' Robyn didn't expect she'd have a hand in the quilting.

Nancy and Jessica smiled at her.

'Everyone in the quilting bee will stitch a part of the quilt,' said Nancy. 'And that includes you, Robyn.'

CHAPTER FIVE

Our love is strong in all seasons
Against all reasons
No matter our past
Years on, we're still together
Smiling that they said...
It would never last

'You walked in on Brad when he was half–naked!' Nancy exclaimed. 'No wonder you looked flushed when I saw you coming out of his music studio.'

Robyn had revealed what happened earlier at the studio, while helping Jessica and Nancy cut the quilting fabric in the shop. Jessica was showing Robyn how to use a rotary cutter to precision cut the fabric.

'Brad was half–dressed,' said Robyn, wishing she hadn't confided this to them. 'Almost fully–dressed. The only thing he wasn't wearing was a shirt.'

Jessica pretended to fan herself with a piece of fabric. 'I've seen pictures of him and he looks gorgeous.'

'He looked...very fit,' Robyn conceded. 'But don't tell anyone about this. I don't want him thinking that I'm talking about him.'

'We won't say a word,' Nancy assured her.

'Not a peep,' Jessica added.

'Did he sing for you?' Nancy said to Robyn as they continued to share the task of preparing the fabric for the quilt.

'No, not a note.'

Nancy and Jessica exchanged a disbelieving look.

'What?' said Nancy. 'He didn't sing or play his guitar the whole time you were in his studio?'

'No, I staged the photos of him playing,' Robyn insisted. 'And when he was playing his guitar to write a new song, I was working on the feature in a soundproof room so I could concentrate on my writing. I couldn't hear him play or sing a note.'

'We won't tell anyone about this,' Jessica told Robyn.

Nancy nodded, and together they made short work of preparing the fabric ready for sewing into a quilt.

'I'll make a start on it,' said Jessica. 'And bring it along to the next quilting bee night at the community hall.'

Leaving the fabric in the shop, but armed with the fat quarter bundles of floral fabric they'd both succumbed to, Robyn and Nancy walked back along the main street.

They paused at Robyn's car. A message came through for her.

'It's the paper,' Robyn said to Nancy. 'They've confirmed that Brad's feature will be in the next issue.'

'I'll be sure to order extra copies for customers,' Nancy told her, sounding excited.

Waving, Nancy hurried back to the grocery store, while Robyn sat in her car and sent a message about the feature to Brad.

He was working in his studio. He read the message and called her. 'Thanks for letting me know. I'm looking forward to seeing it in the paper.'

The rich tone of his voice on the phone had an immediate effect on her, but she forced herself to push this aside.

'Nancy and Nate at the grocery store are ordering in extra copies for customers,' she told him. 'Oh, and, Nancy says to tell you that you have to go to the dance night. No excuses accepted.'

'In that case, I'd better go.'

'And do you have a quilt in your house?'

'Yes. On my bed. Why?'

'Don't tell anyone.'

'Why not?'

'It's a secret. Just trust me. You don't have a quilt for your bed. Or any quilt. The quilting bee members will be at the dance. They'll probably ask you if you have a quilt.'

'I'll cross my fingers when I deny it. Are they planning to make me—'

'Don't ask,' she cut–in. 'And I never mentioned this to you.'

'Got it.'

After the call, Robyn drove home with a lot on her mind.

Later that evening, Robyn sat in her home office dealing with work for some of her other clients.

She concluded her business by emailing Brad with the fee for the marketing work she'd done for him. Pressing send, she closed her laptop, and headed upstairs to bed, taking the laptop and a notepad and pen with her.

Her marketing of his new studio was finished, but...there was the issue of writing lyrics.

She sat up in bed with her laptop, trying not to gaze out the window. The lights were ablaze in Brad's house again. She guessed he'd be working on his new songs. And that brought her back to the lyrics. If she was going to attempt to write some for him, she'd have to at least listen to his music to get a feel for the type of songs he wrote and performed.

On her laptop were clips from his previous performances, some live, others recorded and set to a video showing Brad at his most handsome and appealing. This could be horribly bad for her as she was trying not to fall under his spell. Then again, perhaps it would show her even more that their worlds were at opposite ends of the universe.

Settling back, she clicked play and saw him on stage about to perform to a huge audience. He played a few chords on his guitar to warm up, and the lighting dimmed in the auditorium while he was spot–lit standing with an electric guitar and the microphone in front of him.

The anticipation in the audience was palpable, and she found herself holding her breath, waiting on him bringing the song to life and igniting cheers from the audience.

She didn't have long to wait. It was obvious that the audience knew the opening chords and were about to be treated to one of his popular hits.

Here we go, she thought...

His voice resonated out along with one of the most intense starts to a song she'd heard in a long time. And suddenly, she got it. She saw what the audience saw. Felt what they felt.

The rhythm, the crescendos, the way he performed, Brad nailed it. No wonder there was such a buzz surrounding him.

She rewound, having been so absorbed in the performance that she hadn't fully taken in the lyrics. There was a version of the lyrics online, and she pulled that up too so she could grasp every word.

This song was about being heartbroken, something he'd told her that many songs featured. Was it written from the heart? And if so, who was the woman who'd broken Brad's heart so bad he'd written a song about it?

'Come on, concentrate on the song lyrics,' Robyn chided herself, finding her interest drifting in the wrong direction.

She listened to the words. Could she write words that sounded so personal without revealing her own attraction to Brad? That was the conundrum.

Gazing out the bedroom window at his house, she continued to listen to him singing while wondering what he was up to.

Brad was on a video phone call with his manager in New York.

'Check out your website, Brad. It's been updated with the news about your new studio and those great pictures of you. Terrific idea of yours to put them on the website.'

'It was Robyn's idea,' Brad told him.

'The small town marketing consultant?'

'Yes, she's originally from New York. She's done the same as me, left the city behind to set up in Snow Bells Haven.'

'And she really took all those photos of you earlier today?' His manager sounded impressed.

'She did. The town's mayor recommended her to me.'

Brad opened his laptop while he continued the call, and smiled when he saw the updated website. In the latest news section, several of the photos that Robyn had taken of Brad in his studio were highlighted, along with details of the Snow Bells studio.

'This looks great,' Brad said, scrolling through the editorial and pictures.

'The photos really sell the new studio. There are a couple that could be contenders for the cover of your next album. They're a fresh take on you. As if she sees you in a different light. I like them.'

'So do I.'

'And I love the sample you sent of your new song, especially the lyrics. They really pop and they're so expressive. Moving to that small town has certainly brought out a fresh creative spark in you.'

Brad took a deep breath. 'Robyn rewrote my original lyrics.'

'She rewrote them?'

'Yes, without even hearing the music.' Brad explained what had happened.

'Is Robyn signed with anyone? Another studio, recording artist or agent?'

'No, not as far as I know.'

'If she can write more lyrics like these, sign her up before anyone else snaps her up. There's real talent there.'

'I've asked her to try and write more lyrics for me. She's not sure if she can do it, but I think she can.'

'Encourage her. Tell her she'll have her name on the credits.'

'Robyn doesn't want her identity to be known. I promised her that if I used her lyrics, her name wouldn't be on the credits.'

'Okay, so she doesn't want her name known. But everyone likes money. Assure her she'll be well paid,' his manager insisted.

'I've told her that.'

'Fine, let's see what she comes up with for you.'

Brad glanced out the window of his living room and saw that a light shone from one of the upstairs windows of Robyn's house. She was still awake. He wondered what she was doing.

Robyn sat up in bed, having heard another one of Brad's live performances from a few years previously. Then she decided to take a peek at Brad's New York website. She wanted to see if it listed his latest hits so that she could listen to a couple of them before getting some sleep.

His last album was highlighted at the top of the website, but as she went to click on it, she gasped, seeing one of her pictures of him headlining a news update on his new studio.

Scrolling through the news, she noticed that several of her photos were now on the New York website. She smiled, delighted that Brad had done as she'd suggested.

Playing the first song from his last album, she viewed him in the pictures, and lyrics started to come to mind.

Grabbing the notepad and pen by her bedside, she wrote them down while they were fresh in her mind. The words flowed fast, fluent and she scribbled them down at a swift pace. This wasn't a new experience. When she got an idea for marketing, she often had to grab a pen or type like blazes on her laptop as the sparks of inspiration ignited.

She stopped and read the words she'd scribbled down. They needed work. Some rhymed, others didn't, but she was sure she could make them into a chorus and a verse for a song. Late at night was often when she found inspiration, and she always kept a notepad and pen handy for jotting them down in the midnight hours.

The lyrics weren't about heartbreak. They were about love, finding it when you were busy trying not to. Was she talking about herself a little bit? She dismissed the notion as soon as she thought about it. Writing song lyrics were often about love, romance, feelings reciprocated or thwarted.

Another verse sprang to mind, and she wrote it down too. Maybe she should learn how to formulate lyrics. Or maybe not. Sometimes writing from the heart without boundaries of how many lines were needed, not really knowing what a stanza was, kept the lyrics fresh and exciting. Brad would soon let her know either way. If he liked them, fine. If not... She mentally shrugged. She hadn't set out to become a song lyric writer. So she wouldn't be upset if it didn't work out for her in that arena.

Brad's manager remembered to tell him something before they ended their chat.

'Oh, and, Aria called me. She saw the news on the website about your new studio.'

'I've told you before, I don't want to get involved with Aria.'

'She's modelling again in New York, but she's split up with her latest guy, the actor.'

'Aria's love life is of no concern of mine.'

'I just thought you'd like to know that your ex is interested in dropping by your new studio.'

Brad sighed with exasperation. 'Aria is not my ex–girlfriend. We never dated.'

'Okay, you're right, but she kinda sees things differently. Especially the dinner date.'

'I was having dinner, alone. Aria joined me, uninvited. I didn't even make it to the main course. I walked out. She followed me, and the paparazzi took those photos of us coming out of the restaurant. The story was slanted.'

'Well, just so you know, she's back on the scene.'

'Thanks for the heads up, buddy.'

'Sure. If Aria calls again, I'll tell her the score.'

'I don't need any more complications in my life right now. That's why I'm grateful for the help Robyn's been to me.'

'You like her, don't you?'

'She's efficient, makes things happen. Does what she promises to do. I like that.'

The manager smiled at him.

'What's that look for?' said Brad.

'Nothing,' He smiled again.

'It's strictly business, though I am going to a local fundraising dance. The mayor gave me a free ticket, but I've made a small, private donation to the fund. Robyn will be there.'

'You taking her to the dance?'

'No, we're both going alone.'

'Robyn's single then?'

'She is, but she's made it clear that she's not looking for romance right now. She's concentrating on her marketing business. She's fairly new in town too.'

'She must be something a little bit special though if the town's mayor recommended her.'

Brad smiled. 'He said that Robyn is lightning in a bottle.'

'Is she?'

'Yes, take a look at the updated photos on the website. The song lyrics. She's written the feature that's coming out in the next issue of the town's local newspaper. And that's just what she's achieved today.'

His manager laughed. 'It sounds like Robyn's lightning won't be easy to contain in that bottle. Especially if she writes more song lyrics for you.'

'I've an idea how to credit her, without giving away her name.'

'What's your idea?'

'I'll email it to you. It's something visual. You'll see what I mean.'

'I'm intrigued.'

'And I'm exhausted. We'll talk again in the morning. I'd better get some sleep.'

'Yeah. But remember to send me that idea.'

'I will,' Brad told him before ending the call.

A fresh, sunny morning drifted through Robyn's office as she replied to emails and forged on with her day's work. She wore a white broderie anglaise dress that was pretty and comfortable with a pair of neutral, low-heel pumps.

She'd just taken a sip of coffee when the doorbell rang. Peering out the window, she saw it was Brad and went through to the hall and opened the door.

He was standing there wearing jeans, an ice blue shirt and a warm smile. A sort of sheepish smile, like he wanted something.

'Could I talk to you for a few minutes?' he said, peering over her shoulder to check that she didn't have a client in her office.

'Yes, come on in.' She stepped aside and he entered the hall.

'I understand that you're probably busy with work.'

She led him through to her office. 'I've caught up on everything. I made an early start to the day,' she told him. What she didn't tell him was that she'd woken up a couple of times in the depths of the night with more ideas for lyrics that she'd scribbled down and then went back to sleep again.

He glanced around, looking like he had something weighing on his mind.

'Is everything okay?' she said.

'Yes.' He sounded edgy.

'You don't sound very convincing.'

He took a deep breath. 'Here's the situation. After you left the studio yesterday afternoon, I played around with the lyrics you rewrote. The words created a spark in me, and I changed the music for the chorus. I hadn't been able to get it right, but suddenly, I improved on it. I made a recording of the song and sent it last night to my manager in New York. And he loves it. He thinks, as I do, that it's one of the hit songs we need for the album.'

'That's wonderful.'

He nodded, but still looked edgy. 'I've been working on the album for months, writing and recording the songs in the New York studio. It's almost finished, but I got stuck for any standout hits. All my albums have at least two hit songs. In the city, I just wasn't feeling it.'

'And that's why you came to Snow Bells?'

'Yes, a fresh start, inspiration. And I've found it. At least for one song. We're definitely putting it on the album. You'll be paid for the lyrics.'

Robyn brightened. 'Great!'

'I told my manager that you don't want your name on the credits. He understands, but he wants to know if you're signed with any other studio or recording artist. And if not, and you write more lyrics for me, he wants to sign you up to my label.'

Robyn laughed. 'I told you I've never done any marketing work for a music studio before.'

'Yes, but this wouldn't be for the marketing, though I'd still like to talk to you about that too. This would be for the lyrics. If this song becomes the hit we think it has the potential to be, we'd want you signed with us.'

Robyn sat down on her chair. 'What would that entail? I mean, I'd still want to continue my marketing work here in Snow Bells.'

'You would. Nothing would change in that respect. The lyric writing would be separate. If you're amenable to that idea.' He paused. 'Though I understand that it'll depend on whether you feel you can write any more lyrics for me for other songs.'

The notepad with the night–time lyrics scribbled on them was on her desk. She pushed it towards him. 'I kept waking up with ideas for lyrics. They're unfinished. I'd need to tidy them up obviously.'

Brad picked up the notepad, eager to see what she'd written.

She didn't say a word while he read them.

He nodded and smiled as he read them all.

'I don't even know it they're verses or choruses,' she said.

'I love these. I could work with these right now.' The enthusiasm in his voice sounded clear.

She pointed to the notepad. 'There's more on the next page.'

Brad's interest notched up another gear. 'You wrote these last night?'

'And some this morning while I was making breakfast. I scribbled them down in the kitchen.'

There was a mix of delight and surprise in his tone. 'You're incredible.'

'It's just words. You'll need to create the magic to make them into a hit song.'

'Two songs. These subjects are both different. Heartfelt and heartbreak.'

'I wasn't sure what type of angle you're aiming for.'

'I'll let you hear the songs on the new album so far. It'll give you a feel for the theme.'

She nodded.

He read the lyrics again and held tight to the notepad. 'Can I take this with me, and call you later?'

'Yes.' She stood up.

'Oh, and I emailed the payment details for your first song lyrics.' He gestured to her laptop.

Robyn checked her mail while Brad walked out of the office.

'I'll let you get on with your work,' he said, hurrying away.

She gasped when she read the payment deal. 'Wait! Brad!' She called after him, but he was already bounding across the street to his car. He drove off to his studio in town.

Robyn smiled to herself. He had the notepad with the lyrics. But he had her grocery list too. She hoped nothing else private was scribbled on the pad.

Forcing herself to concentrate on her marketing work, she dealt with clients as usual, while in the background, her mind was thinking up lyrics. This was a good bad thing, she assured herself. The excitement of the deal, having her lyrics made into a song, sung by Brad on his new album, would fade once she was over the initial elation.

By the afternoon, she was still buzzing, but she'd torn through the day's marketing tasks. A win–win day, she told herself.

A mellow, end of day glow filtered through her office like liquid amber.

She heard someone pull up in her driveway and saw Brad stepping out of his car. He had his guitar with him, her notepad, two bags of groceries, and a broad smile on his face.

She hurried to open the door, anticipating that he'd been working on a new song.

He had, but he'd something else to show her that was due to ignite her excitement levels again.

'Have you had dinner?' He held up the bags of groceries he'd bought from Nate and Nancy's store.

'You found my grocery list.'

'I did. Nancy seemed to know you're tastes.' He left his guitar in the hall and carried the bags through to the kitchen and put them down.

'No, I've been working,' she said. 'I'm about to make dinner.'

'I'll make us dinner while you listen to the songs on the album,' he suggested.

'I could handle that.'

He escorted her through to her office and gestured to her laptop. 'Check out the private links I've sent to you. The new songs I've recorded in the Snow Bells studio for the album are on there. And the one with your lyrics.'

Robyn sat down and started to scroll through the links, looking for the song that had her lyrics, eager to listen to it first.

In the background, she heard Brad rustling around in the kitchen, and then the sound of dinner being made faded as the music began.

Her heart beat along with the rhythm, feeling the excitement, hearing his voice sounding deep, strong and vibrant, singing the words she'd written.

'This song sounds like a winner, Brad,' she called through to him.

Mistaking what she'd said, he replied from the kitchen where he was making a pasta dish, stirring the tomato sauce mix while the pasta cooked. 'Yeah, I'm making pasta for dinner.'

Robyn smiled to herself and continued to listen to the music links.

And then she saw a link that wasn't to any of the songs. It was a mock–up of the album cover, with a note that said: *Rough layout of the new album cover. Photo of Brad in his new Snow Bells Haven studio.*

She blinked. There was Brad playing his guitar, looking handsome and moody and... It was one of the photos she'd taken of him, cropped and made into the cover shot. There were words written on it in a bold but artistic font. Love & Lyrics.

She sat there gazing at the cover...and Brad. It was striking, atmospheric, and captured Brad at his artistic best. It was the type of image she would've advised if she'd been handling the marketing. The songs were great, and the cover image really helped create a feeling of love and romance.

And then she noticed that there was a second image showing the back cover of the album. The credits included a little bird, a robin logo, beside the credit for the lyrics and the cover art photo.

Brad had kept his promise not to name her in the credits. But he'd secretly named her with the robin logo. She nodded and smiled. She'd take that. A hint at her name. And she loved robins.

She felt her world shift to a slightly different path, not too far from the one she was on, but taking a side route to an exciting and adventurous road filled with love and lyrics.

'Dinner's ready,' Brad called to her.

She went through to find him serving up two plates of his delicious pasta.

'Take a seat,' he said, insisting on serving everything. He'd set the table with napkins and poured two cups of coffee.

'This looks tasty. I've barely eaten anything all day. The time whizzed by,' she told him.

He sat down opposite her. 'Tuck in.'

She smiled across at him. 'I saw the album cover.'

'What did you think? From a marketing consultant's view?'

'I know I took the photo, but putting that aside, the cover is a winner. I love it.'

'I do too. So does my manager. He had our cover designer put a mock–up together so we could see what it would look like for the album. I had other words in mind as part of the cover art. But seeing those photos you took, well...I thought love and lyrics sounded a whole lot more...romantic. And at the heart of this particular album, is romance.'

Brad gazed across at her, causing her to blush.

'You're blushing,' he teased her.

'I'm just flabbergasted and flummoxed from hearing the song with my lyrics and seeing the cover.' She pointed to the pasta. 'And that you've cooked dinner.'

'I enjoy cooking. Besides, I wanted you to hear the songs and see the cover design.'

'I love the robin logo.'

He threw her a sexy grin. 'I thought it would be a way to acknowledge your work while keeping your identity a secret.'

'Any other surprises you have in store for me tonight?' she said.

'I brought my guitar with me. That's a subtle hint.'

CHAPTER SIX

Dance with me tonight
Let's fall in love within the song
When I hold you in my arms
It's where we both belong

'You're not thinking of giving me a guitar lesson,' Robyn said to Brad as they went through to her office after dinner.

He smiled. 'No, I want to talk to you about melody and rhythm.' He tapped her notepad before handing it to her. 'This is filled with gold dust. Those lyrics you wrote are wonderful.'

She sat down at her desk and flipped through the pages, eager to see that she hadn't scribbled anything too personal on the notepad.

'And filled with my grocery list,' she said.

'Plus a load of phrases that I couldn't figure out,' he told her.

Robyn immediately started to search through the notepad wondering what he was referring to. She stopped when she saw what he meant and held up the page listing items and notes for her quilting and knitting.

'You mean this?' She reeled off some of the items. 'Fat quarter bundles, two sets of number sevens, size nine circulars, Fair Isle, rotary cutter, hexies and English paper piecing, with notes on fussy cutting and dealing with dog ears.'

He jokingly glanced around. 'You have a pet?'

'No, those are my quilting and knitting notes.' She closed the notepad and looked at him. 'Did you see anything that mentioned about a particular quilt for a particular person?'

'Was that under the fabric stash notes?' He tried not to grin.

'Yes.'

'I never saw anything about a quilt,' he lied. 'But I did see something about a log cabin. Is that one of the cabins at Snow Bells Haven cove?'

'No, it's a quilting pattern term.' She felt like they were teasing each other and continued to play along.

'So a quilt sandwich shouldn't have been on your grocery list.'

She laughed. 'You really have read through all these notes.'

'I was searching for all the musical inspiration I could get.' He leaned forward. 'What is a fabric stash? That seemed really important to you.'

'It would be easier to show you than to explain. Come on through to the lounge.'

He followed her, curious to see a further glimpse into her life.

The lounge with its pastel decor was comfortably furnished and in one corner there was a white painted cupboard.

Robyn opened the doors wide and stepped back. 'This is my fabric stash.'

Shelves were stacked with bundles of neatly folded fabric. Some were tied with ribbons, like the floral bundle she'd bought from Jessica's quilt shop. Others were divided into prints and solid shades.

'That's a lot of fabric.'

'This is tame in comparison to some of the other members of the quilting bee. Nancy has two cupboards full, but she's built that up over the years.'

'What are you going to do with it all? I mean, I assume you'll use it to make quilts.'

'Maybe. Sort of. But not entirely.'

'Could you translate that for me?'

'My fabric stash will be used for making quilts and other sewing. I'd like to make a skirt from this fabric here. Once I learn how to put a zip in. But some of it is so pretty and too precious to cut, so it's there to be admired, saved as part of the uncut stash and cherished.'

'Like collector pieces,' he said.

'Exactly. I like looking at it, and it's relaxing to sort through it and imagine what I'll make from some of it — one day.'

'Maybe. Sort of.'

'Precisely.'

She closed the doors and turned to face him with a triumphant smile. Then she opened a pale pink painted dresser beside it. 'This is my yarn stash.' It had a lovely selection of various types of yarn.

Brad grinned. 'You have a lot of yarn too. Though the fabric edges it.'

'I haven't decided if I'm more of a quilter or a knitter. Maybe even a dressmaker.'

'That's a lovely dress you're wearing,' he commented on the classic white design.

'It's vintage broderie anglaise.'

Brad looked none the wiser.

'Whitework–type cotton fabric with a decorative effect. I bought it from a vintage store in New York. It becomes softer and more beautiful the more it's washed and worn.'

'Like well–loved jeans,' he said.

'Yes. It was such a warm day I thought I'd wear it. I tend to dress for business even when I work from home. My wardrobe is filled with my city–style clothes. I haven't yet relaxed into more casual wear since moving here. But I'm sure I will.'

'The business–style suits you.'

She smiled at him, trying not to blush at his compliment.

'But with all this fabric and yarn, you'll be able to make plenty of casual items,' he said.

She closed the dresser on the yarn stash. 'I'm having a lot of fun with it. I find it relaxing after a day's marketing work.'

'And now lyric writing.'

'Which brings us back to you wanting to talk to me about melody and rhythm,' she reminded him, and started to wander back through to her office.

'Wait.' He paused in the hallway. 'I have an idea.'

She glanced round at him.

'Grab your laptop and the lyric notes.' He picked up his acoustic guitar.

'Where are we going?'

'My house. I'd rather play my electric guitar to let you hear the music I've come up with for your lyrics.'

Eager to hear this, Robyn gathered her things and hurried after him.

She breathed in the clear, night air as they walked across the street to his house. 'I love nights like this. There's an energy to the evening air, an atmosphere of excitement that I've always loved.'

Brad nodded. 'I feel the same. It's the reason I bought this house instead of one of the cove's cabins. I checked a few properties, and then I saw this one — and I loved the garden out back. I was sold on it.'

'You bought it for the garden rather than the house.' She sounded intrigued.

'For both, it's a beautiful house,' he explained. 'But the garden reminds me of when I was a boy and I'd take my guitar out into a clearing in the trees on my grandparents' farmland. They didn't mind me playing within earshot, but when I was trying to learn something, to get it sounding just right, I preferred to be on my own. The evenings on the farm felt so free, miles from the city. The clear night skies were filled with stars, and after I'd played my guitar in my special spot, I'd lie back on the grass and gaze up at the night sky and imagine my future. In the stars, in my music, becoming a singer and songwriter, doing what I loved, and for others to love along with me.'

They reached the house and he welcomed her inside, turning the lights on to illuminate the downstairs rooms, the pale neutral decor, wide hallway and lounge that had glass patio doors opening out on to the garden at the rear of the property.

Brad put his guitar down and opened the doors wide, letting in the calm night air.

'Come on out, Robyn. Take a look at this.' He stood on the lawn. It was bordered by tall trees that created privacy, even though the nearest house was Robyn's.

She put her things down and joined him outside. Breathing in the air that mingled with the fragrant scent of the flowers, greenery and trees, she felt herself understand why he'd bought this house. She loved her garden too, but the thick trees here were a borderline forest stretching into the outskirts of the town.

A blanket was draped over a two–seater garden swing chair. He shook it and laid it down on the grass. Then he relaxed on it, arms folded behind his neck and gazed up at the star–sprinkled sky.

Robyn joined him.

Light poured out from the lounge, but stopped short of them lying there. She imagined they looked like a scene from a movie. Maybe an end scene where the characters had found where they both belonged and would live happily ever after.

Shaking the thought from her overactive imagination, she let herself become lost in the moment. 'This is beautiful.'

'Yeah. I loved it the moment I saw it. I knew I'd found a place that I could call home.'

She sighed happily. 'Snow Bells is a wonderful place to live.'

'People will think we're running away from New York. Running away from the worlds we used to belong to.'

'People can think what they like,' Robyn retorted. 'I prefer to think of it as running *to* somewhere new.'

'I admire that in you,' he said.

'What?'

'Your strength of character.'

'It often gets me into trouble,' she said.

'And I like that you're not a *no person*.' He went on to explain. 'When I've suggested you give things a try, from helping me with my marketing, to letting me rewind time for you, and then having a go at playing musical instruments when you'd never even held a guitar. And writing lyrics. You've always said — *yes*.'

'I have a headstrong and unruly streak in me. And a competitive streak. You are a challenge.'

'Me?'

'Yes, you. Don't pretend otherwise.'

He laughed.

They lay there for a moment gazing up at the night sky.

'Can I ask you something about the lyrics you wrote?' he said.

'Ask away.'

'When you wrote the words down, did you hear the melody and sense the rhythm of the tune?'

'No, I didn't hear anything. I could never write the music for a song. But I suppose I sensed the atmosphere that the words created, the meaning behind them.'

'I'm the complete opposite. When I read your lyrics, I start to hear the music.' He stood up. 'I wrote an opening riff for the first set of lyrics. I think it's one of the best I've created in a long time.'

Robyn stood up too. 'That sounds exciting. I'd love to hear it.'

'Let's go inside and I'll play it for you.'

They went into the lounge, closing the patio doors against the night.

While he set up his electric guitar, she admired the decor. Pale neutral tones and stylish furnishings. Lamps created pockets of light. But the lounge didn't look lived in. It looked like it was waiting to be lived in by someone with time to devote to it rather than an expensive show house.

A gold disc was framed on one wall. Brad saw her notice it.

'It's the first one I ever received so it's a bit special,' he told her. 'The other discs are in the New York studio. But I didn't want to put this up in the new studio.'

'Why not?'

'Because the new studio reminds me of the past, when I first started out in the music industry, in a tiny space in New York. I like that feeling. It's like a second fresh start. If this album does well and I receive another disc, I'll put it up in the new studio.'

'I like that idea.'

His electric guitar was set to play and she sat down ready to hear the riff.

'Before I let you hear this, there's something else I'd like to tell you,' he said.

Robyn nodded.

'When I ran off this morning with your lyrics, you told me you hadn't finished writing them.'

'Yes, I planned to go over them, polish them, improve the lyrics.'

'I understand, but I was so eager to get to the studio with them. You and your lyrics have lit a spark in me that I haven't felt in a long time. I feel like I did when I was first starting out in the music business. I wrote fresh, from the heart. I think life kinda tamed that flame out of me a little. That's what was missing when I was trying to write new material.'

'And now you feel that spark again?'

'Yes, and I like how that feels. Your lyrics, although unfinished, felt like three separate songs. I don't know if that's what you were aiming for.'

'I woke up twice during the night and scribbled down two different sets of lyrics. One set was about finding love, the other about losing it. The third set was written in the kitchen while I was cooking breakfast. There's probably a buttery thumb print on the paper to prove it.'

He smiled. 'The thing is, with a little bit of work, making the lyrics less raw, we've got the makings of three potential hit songs. Because I can hear the music every time I read your lyrics.'

'The perfect partnership. Working partnership,' she clarified.

He lowered his eyes, getting ready to play his guitar, but there was a secret smile playing clearly on his lips.

The air in the room felt electric as he played the opening riff to the first song.

Whatever Robyn had been expecting to hear, Brad blew clean out of the water. The room resonated with one of the most beautiful and exciting pieces of music she'd ever heard. Tingles ran though her body, sensing she was hearing a piece of the future before anyone else heard Brad play the song.

And then he started to sing the lyrics, doubling the effect.

She let herself become lost in the song, the melody and the rhythm.

The power of Brad's singing and playing was sensational. Not only did she think he'd written a hit song. He'd created a musical masterpiece. A song that people would dance to, fall in love with, make memories from, and remember as something special.

When he finished, she stood up, gave an involuntary cheer and applauded.

The relief that she loved it as much as he did showed on his face.

'I think we've done it, Robyn.'

'You've done it. I could never write music. It's not in me.'

'But the words are. And that's where the spark in me ignites.'

'What will you do now?'

'I made a recording of the song in the studio. But I wanted to let you hear it first before I sent it to my manager.'

'Another first for the music grinch,' she joked, still buzzing with excitement.

Brad put his guitar down. 'I'm going to send it to him right now.'

Robyn looked around the lounge while he did this.

'There,' he said firmly. 'Let's see if he likes it too. He loved the rewritten lyrics I used for the previous song. But this one soars a lot higher.' He gestured to Robyn. 'Because all the lyrics came from you.'

She blushed. 'I still can't get my head around you making music from my words.'

'We're just getting started. Tomorrow, I'm going to focus on some of your other lyrics. With any luck, I'll feel that spark to write again.'

'The feature comes out in the newspaper tomorrow,' she reminded him. 'I'm in town early to chat to Penny and Kyle at the lodge. I'll pick up copies of the paper and drop them off to you at the studio in the morning around ten.'

'Thanks, that would be great. I'll be locked in the studio writing the new songs, so remember to—'

'Phone if you don't hear me knock on the front door,' she cut-in, feeling like they were slotting into an easy working rhythm.

He smiled at her and nodded.

Her heart felt a warmth towards him that she just wasn't ready for. She ran her hands through her hair to brush away unwanted thoughts of how easy it would be to fall in love with him.

'Are you okay?'

'Yes,' she said, pretending her heart wasn't racing, challenging her to give into her feelings for Brad. Wandering over to the gold disc, she brought the conversation back to safer ground. 'How many songs will there be on your new album?'

'I have eight in the can. Now these two new songs. They could be hit singles. Hopefully, I'll write another two from your other lyrics. We're looking at twelve tracks. Most of my albums have ten to twelve tracks on them.'

Her heart started to calm, and then she pictured her involvement with the potential success of his album and it began to soar again. Her emotions were riding on a rollercoaster that she wasn't used to. She could usually contain and control her feelings quite well. Brad was the wild card that changed the game.

She wasn't sure if she liked feeling on the edge of a new romance. She wasn't sure if she didn't.

'A penny for your faraway thoughts.' Brad's deep voice cut–in before she could make up her mind.

'Do you want me to polish the lyrics, so that they're up to scratch for tomorrow?' she offered.

'Yes, that would be great. How about I make us hot chocolate. It always helps me to relax and think clearly.'

'I'll go with that excuse to have hot chocolate. But any reason is fine by me.'

'Two hot chocolates with whipped cream coming up.'

She watched his tall, lean, sexy frame head through to the kitchen, leaving her to rewrite the remainder of the lyrics. And maybe rewrite a few of her own steadfast rules about not mixing business with romance.

Hearing the sounds of Brad making the hot chocolate in the kitchen faded into the background as she worked on the lyrics. Remembering some of the ideas she'd had earlier, she added those, deleted extraneous words, replaced others with words that sounded like poetry, creating deeper meaning to the lyrics.

The second set of lyrics resonated with her current mood. Was she prepared to put her heart on the line and risk it being broken? Or would she hide the love that was building up every time she was with Brad?

'How much whipped cream do you like with your hot chocolate?' Brad called through to her.

'Yes, please,' she shouted through to him, while adding the finishing touches to the lyrics.

She heard him laugh, and then the background sounds faded again while the last line of the second chorus that had eluded her sprang to mind. She was still scribbling it down as he walked through carrying two mugs of hot chocolate brimming with lashings of whipped cream.

It was her turn to laugh. 'Is there any hot chocolate in those mugs of whipped cream?' she said teasingly.

Brad pretended to peer into the mugs. 'I don't know. We'll just have to take a sip to find out.'

Robyn put the notepad and pen down, lifted up her mug and took a sip. 'Mmmm, very chocolaty.'

He laughed and gently brushed a cloud of whipped cream from her nose.

This intimate gesture sent shivers of attraction through her. She was sure he hadn't intended having that effect, just being friendly, but she couldn't help blushing.

'I didn't mean to embarrass you,' he said, thinking this was the cause of her rosy cheeks.

'It's fine. I was too eager to drink it. I love hot chocolate, even on warm evenings.'

He held up his mug in a collaborative gesture. 'To drinking hot chocolate whatever the season.'

'Or the reason.'

He laughed. 'Now you're talking in rhythm.'

'I shouldn't do that all the time.'

He smiled and sat down opposite her. 'I'm glad we get along.'

'I've finished writing the lyrics for your song.'

'Stop it!' He grinned at her.

She smiled playfully and then drank her hot chocolate.

The notepad with the lyrics lay on the table, and he tried not to look at it.

Robyn pushed the pad closer so he could read it.

Brad held up his hand to shield his eyes. 'No, don't show me the lyrics. It's late. I plan to work on them in the studio tomorrow.'

'Are you sure I can't tempt you to take a peek?' She pushed them even closer.

He tried not to laugh. 'If I read them, I'll start hearing the music and then...well, I'll be up half the night songwriting.'

She started to read the opening lines. '*Dance with me tonight...*'

'You minx!' He shook his head, grinning at her, picked up their half empty mugs and hurried through to the kitchen to top up their hot chocolate.

'I guess I'll just have to write the music myself,' she joked, and went over to where he'd left his electric guitar. It was still set up to play. While he was in the kitchen, she picked up the guitar, put the strap around her neck, and started plucking it with a plectrum, and attempted to find the chords.

She could hear him laughing from the kitchen, and didn't know that his manager had called and they were talking on another video phone call while she played in the background.

Searching the strings for any sort of right note, without success, she didn't notice Brad walking through while taking the call.

'Is that someone twanging a guitar?' his manager said to him.

She stopped immediately. *Twanging*? She mouthed to Brad.

'Robyn's here tonight. We're brainstorming music and lyrics,' Brad told him. He turned the phone to face her, showing his manager that she was playing around with his electric guitar.

'Hi, there, Robyn. I love the latest song. I was just telling Brad that it's a surefire single release from the album. Your lyrics are terrific.'

Robyn smiled tightly, squirming at being caught playing around with Brad's guitar. 'Thanks. And nice to meet you.'

'I'm looking forward to meeting you in person when you come to New York,' his manager announced to her.

Brad instantly turned the phone away from Robyn as she stared wide–eyed.

'I haven't actually had a chance to tell Robyn about our trip to the studio in New York,' said Brad.

His manager got the message. 'Oh, well, I'll let the two of you get on with your creative process. And again. The song you sent tonight is great!'

Clicking the call to a close, Brad hurried away to the kitchen and came back with two fresh mugs of hot chocolate topped with another lavish layer of cream. He handed one to Robyn.

'A trip to New York, huh?' she said.

'I was going to tell you about that tomorrow.' He took a gulp of his drink, swallowing down his excuse.

'Why would I need to go to New York?' She pushed for an explanation.

'Because I'll make the final recording in the studio there with some of the session musicians I work with.'

'Are they your band?'

'No, I don't have a band. I record a lot of my tracks on my own, singing, playing guitar, then layering on keyboards or whatever else I play. The session musicians are hired to back me up in the studio when needed, and play with me on tour. And sometimes a song needs a few tweaks and I thought that it would be wise to have you there in case the lyrics need changed.'

'Right. Well, I suppose I could go with you.'

'I'll give you plenty of notice so you won't let any of your marketing clients down. You'll be paid of course too for your time.'

'You wouldn't need to do that.'

'I certainly would. It could be a whole day and an evening of your time. If the recording runs late, we'd probably have to stay overnight, or drive back to town well after midnight.'

She could hear the tension in his voice. 'It's okay. I'll go. I'm used to New York.'

'We both are, but I know we'd rather be here in Snow Bells.'

'Yes, but once the album is recorded, our work would be done.' She sipped her drink, managing not to get any cream on her nose.

It felt like a cold breeze blew through is heart every time he thought about their work being finished. He wanted her in his life. This concerned him in two ways, both of them tugging him in different directions. Falling in love with Robyn wasn't in his plans, but he could feel himself in jeopardy of tumbling down the rabbit hole of romance and falling for her hard. He was right on the edge. But deep down, he knew that the one he risked hurting was Robyn. Getting romantically involved with him could turn her world inside out. He needed to keep things on a professional level until he figured out what to do. He liked her too much to cause her heartache.

'A penny for your thoughts this time,' she said.

He shook his head. 'Nothing. Just churning stuff over in my mind.'

'Oh, look!' She sounded excited and pointed outside. 'There's a shooting star. And another one.' Running over to the patio doors, she pulled them open and dashed out in time to see the second one trailing across the night sky.

Brad followed her out and stood behind her, watching her gaze up and then make a wish.

'I hope whatever you wished for comes true for you,' he said. His rich, deep voice sounded wistful in the night air.

She smiled round at him. 'I didn't wish for myself. I wished for something for you.'

His heart felt in jeopardy again. 'For me?'

'I obviously can't tell you what it was, or the wish won't come true.'

He breathed in deeply and held out his hands to her. 'Dance with me tonight.'

She laughed lightly. 'Those are my lyrics.'

He took her in hold and she didn't resist as he began waltzing with her under the starlight.

'We're dancing without any music.' She felt the strong muscles in his arms and shoulders as they danced.

'We have our own music.' He began singing her lyrics...

'Dance with me tonight, let's fall in love within the song, when I hold you in my arms...'

'That sounds so beautiful.'

'I glanced at your lyrics,' he explained. 'And there was that spark. This melody sprang to mind and I think it has the makings of a real romantic number.'

'Very romantic.' She gazed up at him and then clarified. 'The song.'

'Yeah. I imagine people could fall in love with a song like this.'

'I'm sure they will. Another potential hit for you.'

'For us.'

Her heart was pounding so hard she eased herself out of his arms, ending the moment. 'It's late. I should head home and get some sleep. A busy day tomorrow.'

He nodded firmly. 'I'll walk you home.'

'No, it's fine. I'll see myself out.' She smiled at him.

Feeling like she was leaving a part of her heart behind, she walked back home, breathing in the excitement of the night. A night to remember.

CHAPTER SEVEN

I'm letting you go
Because I love you
I care too much
To hold you back

I'm letting you know
Because I love you
That I'll be here
If you ever come back

Brad reneged on his promise to himself to get some sleep. Instead, he played his guitar until the edge of dawn, working his musical magic in tune with Robyn's lyrics.

He sat outside on the swing chair making a new melody in harmony with the poignant words she'd left on the notepad.

Seeing the stars fade behind the approaching pink and blue dawn, he went inside, and after putting his guitar down in the lounge, he picked it right back up again as another spark of inspiration ignited in his musical mind.

Finally, the shadows of the tall trees outside the patio doors began to look less like dark silhouettes against the lightening sky, and he put the guitar on the stand and trudged reluctantly upstairs to bed.

In the past, he'd have played on until the sun was shining through the morning sky, but he needed to be fresh and alert for working at the studio — and dealing with any possible fallout from the feature in the paper.

Hopefully, the folks in town would understand that he wasn't there to cause ripples on the calm and assured waterline of their daily lives.

In the remaining nightglow shadows of his bedroom, he stripped his clothes off, eased the tension in his weary shoulders, and shook off the remnants of the melodies that mixed with images of Robyn's sweet smile. Jeez, she melted his heart in ways he'd never felt before.

Lying down on the cool, silk sheet, he pulled the quilt he wasn't supposed to own up to his lean waist. He saw the last twinkle of a star shining through the window, the brightest one left in the sky, and then it was gone, like the night itself.

Brad closed his eyes and fell into a deep sleep, hearing the latest song lyrics...*I'm letting you go, because I love you...*

It was going to be a scorcher of a day in more ways than one.

Robyn peered out the bedroom window at the azure sky. Another warm day dawned, but so did a challenging one. She hoped that the newspaper feature would work well to introduce Brad and his new studio to the town. She planned to pick up copies of the paper from the grocery store after chatting to Penny and Kyle at the lodge about the editorial and updates for their website.

Rummaging through the dresses hanging in her wardrobe, she needed a sure–fire number. She unhooked the red one, a fashionable little red dress that always made her feel confident and classy.

She put it on, stepped into a pair of heels and looked at herself in the full–length mirror. The dress was sleeveless with a nice neckline and skimmed her slender curves, flattering her figure. It was eye–catching, but this wasn't a day for blending in.

People were bound to stop and talk to her about Brad being in the paper. She needed to up her game for the day.

Her blonde hair hung smooth around her shoulders, and after adding a touch of rosy red lipstick to her otherwise subtle makeup, she hurried downstairs to pick up her bag and get ready to drive to the lodge to meet with Penny and Kyle.

Stepping out into the sunshine, she looked across at Brad's house, still feeling the effects of the previous evening with him.

There was no sign that he was up, and she wondered if he was still asleep. His lights had burned a hole through the long night.

She'd woken up once in the depths of the night, jotted down lyrics, noticed his house lit up, and then snuggled down to sleep again.

But she'd slept well. Probably due to all the fresh night air the previous evening while dancing under the stars.

Shaking away thoughts that would cloud the clarity she needed for dealing with business, she got into her car and drove to Snow Bells main street.

Parking across from the music studio, she grabbed her bag and her camera. The main street looked picturesque and summery in the sunlight, and she took several stock photos of it. Up–to–date images where handy for her clients' websites, features and other literature.

She included Brad's studio in some of the shots, but noticed that the lights weren't on. This didn't mean he wasn't in. It didn't mean he was. He could be tucked away through the back of the premises making music.

Putting her camera in her bag, she walked the short distance to the lodge, enjoying the feeling of the warm sun and bright energy of the morning.

Brad unlocked the front door of his studio and went inside, armed with Robyn's notepad. He checked the time as he went through to the control room. Early enough. Robyn said she would drop by around ten. That gave him ample time to try out the song he'd been working on the previous night. It had sounded great at home, but everything sounded ten times better when it was recorded in the studio. Besides, he planned to add accompaniments, playing keyboards and extra layers of guitar to the soundtrack.

He should've looked and felt tired having had only a few hours of snatched sleep. But years of not living by the clock, and playing evening gigs, had made him accustomed to working long hours. Music always filled him with energy, and this morning he couldn't wait to try out the ideas for the new song in the studio.

And he was looking forward to seeing Robyn soon, and reading the feature in the paper.

Making himself a strong cup of coffee, he set up the studio, closed out the sounds of the world and started playing...

Aria followed the silence along the hallway until she saw Brad through the soundproof studio window playing his guitar and singing.

Her fashionable little black dress, worn with towering heels, enhanced her model–like figure and contrasted with her porcelain complexion. Titian red hair, like watered silk, skimmed her shoulders, and her green eyes flashed in recognition when she saw Brad. As handsome as ever, but wearing a white shirt, waistcoat and dark trousers. An upgrade to his usual jeans and denim look. It suited him, but unsettled her. He looked more confident than when she'd last seen him.

Shrugging away her doubts that she couldn't win him over, her self–assurance overtook her reluctance to knock on the window, deliberately interrupting his recording. He could always sing the song again.

Brad jolted, thinking he must've forgotten to lock the front door, but hoping it was Robyn.

His hopes were dashed when he saw Aria peering through at him.

'What the...' he muttered angrily. He stopped the recording and marched over and opened the door, but stood there, preventing her from setting one stiletto inside the room.

She had the audacity to try to kiss him and smother him with her unwanted arrival.

Although she was taller than Robyn, he still towered over her, and jerked his head back preventing her from kissing him. He knew her wiles only too well, and mentally kicked himself for not locking the front door.

She pretended not to notice that he wasn't enthralled to see her there.

'I called your manager,' she said, breaking the tense silence. 'He told me you'd opened this new studio. I thought I'd drop by and say, hi.'

'This won't work, Aria.'

'What do you mean?'

'I'm not interested in us getting together.' He refrained from being snarky, hoping she'd just leave.

'So now I'm not allowed to have a tour of your lovely new studio after I've driven all the way from New York.' She kept her tone light and flirty.

'Correct.'

Her confidence took a hit. She wasn't accustomed to being sidelined. Most guys tripped over themselves to gain her attention. Brad was the only one she'd never been able to win over. But she believed she could wear him down, especially as he was now hiding in a small town that she'd had to search for on the map. She'd always had a thing for him. And she was determined that one day he'd feel the same about her. Perhaps even involve her in his music. Include her in his world.

'I know you're not dating anyone.' She sounded so assured.

Brad shook his head. 'You're wrong. I am seeing someone.' It wasn't a total lie. He couldn't get Robyn out of his thoughts.

Aria's sensual lips smiled at him. 'You're lying. I can tell.'

He stood his ground. 'I've never met anyone like her.' No lie.

'You must've just met her. Is she from this small town?'

'She's from New York.' No lie again.

Aria's envious green eyes blinked in annoyance. 'New York?'

Brad nodded.

'Is she in my line of work, fashion and modelling? Or acting?' Aria demanded to know.

Under other circumstances he wouldn't have given her any details. His life, and the people in it, were none of Aria's business. But he decided to take his phone out and show her the pictures he'd taken of Robyn in the studio.

Aria couldn't hide her bitterness. 'She plays guitar, keyboards and drums!'

'She's incredibly talented.' True, just not when it came to playing musical instruments.

Accepting that Brad was seeing this woman, Aria turned to leave. 'You can walk me out.'

This was the only thing she'd said that he was happy to do.

Aria glanced unsmiling at the musical instruments and the framed picture of Brad on the reception wall. 'I don't understand why you'd want to hide away in this little nowhere place when you have your studio in

New York.' Her tone was snippy. 'Is it so you can be with her?'

Brad said nothing, opened the door and they stepped outside the studio into the sunlight.

Robyn bought two copies of the newspaper in the grocery store. Her meeting with Penny and Kyle at the lodge had gone well. Now, she was excited to see the feature in the paper and take a copy to Brad.

'It's a great write–up about Brad's music studio in the paper,' Nancy said to Robyn. 'Customers have been in here this morning buying copies. The town's starting to buzz with the news. We've all been wondering why he opened a studio here in Snow Bells Haven. The feature you wrote explains everything — and the pictures of him inside his studio are fascinating.'

Robyn couldn't resist having a peek at the feature page. Her heart soared. It looked impressive.

'I'm taking a copy over to Brad,' said Robyn.

Nancy looked out the grocery store window. 'There's Brad standing outside his studio. He's talking to a beautiful looking woman. I've never seen her before.'

Robyn glanced round and saw them standing together deep in conversation. The woman stood so close to Brad that she was practically leaning against him.

'Do you know her?' Nancy said to Robyn.

'No, perhaps she's a fan, or a friend,' Robyn suggested, trying not to sound upset. Seeing the woman effectively flirting with Brad took her aback. She'd no right to feel upset, but she couldn't help it.

'Why don't we have dinner tonight before I head back to New York,' Aria suggested, trying to persuade Brad.

'No, I have other plans.' True again. He planned to go to the dance, hopefully with Robyn.

And then it happened...

He saw Robyn walking out of the grocery store and heading straight across the main street to the studio. She looked gorgeous, he thought, feeling his heart react to seeing her.

Aria noticed the woman in the red dress too. The same woman she'd seen playing the guitar and other instruments. Only now she looked like she'd stepped off a fashion runway — and she was heading their way. Aria immediately moved closer to Brad and draped herself around him.

Brad untangled himself from Aria's clutches and stepped back, but he knew that Robyn had seen Aria's attempt to cause trouble. Had it worked? Did Robyn think he was involved with someone else? That he'd been lying to her all along.

Come on, Robyn! Don't jump to the wrong conclusion. Figure it out. Brad willed her to suss things out as the seconds ticked by as she approached.

To cloud the situation even further, Mark came out of Greg's cafe and waved across to him.

He nodded acknowledgement to the mayor, but kept his focus on Robyn.

Any second now...

Brad's heart soared as Robyn smiled at him while totally disregarding Aria.

'The feature is out in the paper,' Robyn announced to Brad as she walked up to him. 'It's wonderful. I bought a copy for you.' She handed it to him — and her eyes gave him the go–ahead to welcome her. Really welcome her.

Yes! Brad cheered to himself. Robyn had figured out the situation. Taking a chance, he accepted the newspaper and pulled her close, giving her a loving hug and sensual kiss.

His kiss felt like fire igniting in her heart. Robyn steeled herself, keeping up the act that they were a couple. That was her best guess. This other woman was a troublemaker. She'd met her type before in New York, and it never went well.

Aria stepped back from them. 'Call me if you change your mind, Brad.' Glaring daggers at Robyn, she strutted away.

Brad swept Robyn inside the studio and locked the door. 'Phew! That was awkward.'

'Do you want to tell me what just happened?'

'I'm sorry for kissing you.' This sounded like the worst lie he'd uttered that morning. He wasn't sorry. He loved every second of it. He'd kiss her again if he thought it was appropriate, but it wasn't.

'I'm guessing it was for effect. To make her think we're dating.'

'Nailed it. Yes. Her name is Aria and she's tried before to get involved with me.'

'Romantically involved? Or in your music business?'

'Mainly the first, partly the latter. Aria manipulates situations to get what she's aiming for.'

'It seems like she's aiming for you.'

He held up his hands. 'I'm not interested.' He explained about her phoning his manager and the restaurant date ruse.

'She sounds like trouble,' said Robyn.

Brad nodded.

'But let's not allow someone like her spoil our great news.' Robyn gestured to the paper. 'Check out the feature. Plus, the editor has given your studio a mention on the paper's weekly local news article.'

'Come on, let's go through the back to read it in private without anyone interrupting,' he said.

They went through to the control room and sat down, reading a copy each, commenting on the editorial and the photos.

'It's come out really well,' Robyn said, sounding delighted.

'You've hit the right note to introduce the studio to the town.'

She smiled at him.

His heart thundered in his chest. 'You look incredible this morning.'

She smoothed her hands down her dress. 'This is my sure–fire dress when I need a confident shield.'

'Your dress looks wonderful. But I think it's your own self–confidence, smarts and sensibility that's your real shield.'

The way he looked at her took her breath away. She could still feel his kiss on her lips.

Putting the paper down, he ran his hands through his hair, and stood up. 'Coffee?'

'Yes, breakfast was a rushed sip of coffee before I dashed out this morning.'

'I figured we'd both be running circles around ourselves today, so I bought supplies from Greg's cafe.' He headed away to make the coffee.

'Gingerbread cupcakes?'

'Nope,' he said without glancing back. 'I thought I'd mix it up a little with cookie dough cupcakes.'

'I can handle that.'

Leaving her alone while he made the coffee, she looked at her lyrics on the notepad. He'd added musical inflections under the words, and had obviously been working on another new song.

'Did you get any sleep last night?' she called to him.

'Not much.'

'I wouldn't know. You don't look tired.'

Her fingers itched to press the rewind and play buttons on the console to hear what he'd recorded. But she resisted, in case she pressed delete or sent it out into the wide blue yonder.

'You can play the song if you want,' he said, bringing through a tray with their coffee and cupcakes.

Robyn clasped her hands and sat them on her lap. 'I wouldn't dare meddle with your recording.'

But he knew she'd been tempted.

He sat the tray down on the table, and they helped themselves to the cupcakes and coffee.

'Tasty cupcakes,' she mumbled.

He nodded and pressed the replay button, then relaxed back while the song got its first airing outside of his own mind.

Robyn stopped eating and put her coffee down. 'This is a beautiful ballad.'

'Most of the album tracks are upbeat. But I like to add a few ballads to tug at the heartstrings.' She certainly tugged at his, and when he'd created the melody, he'd written it with Robyn in his heart.

There was knocking on the track, and then the recording stopped.

Brad sighed. 'Aria interrupted the final verse.'

'Do you think Aria will be driving back to New York?' The thought had played in the back of her mind, along with the song. She wanted to clear the air of any further issues with the ex that never was.

'Yes, there's nothing to keep her here now,' he assured her.

Mark did his utmost to comply with Aria's demands.

He'd waylaid her as she'd stomped away from the music studio, clearly perturbed, and asked if she was okay. As mayor, he didn't like to see visitors to the town anything less than happy. And Aria was feeling way less than that.

Thrusting her phone at him she demanded that he take pictures of her standing outside Brad's studio.

She struck a pose, making herself part of Brad's new venture. 'Does my hair look okay in this bright sunlight?'

'Yes,' Mark assured her. 'It looks very glossy.' He took a picture and showed it to her.

'Change the angle. You're casting shadows on my face.'

Mark stepped aside and approached the task from another angle, sans shadows. He clicked another two photos and then showed them to her for approval.

'Don't you know how to take a flattering photograph?' Those green eyes iced him to the core.

Ever biddable and willing to keep a tourist happy, he tried again. 'Sorry, I'm not a photographer. I'm Mark, the town's mayor.'

Aria ditched the frosty look and smiled at him. 'You're the mayor?' She sounded incredulous. 'Of...' she'd forgotten the name of the town.

'Snow Bells Haven.' He gestured around him.

Aria's bitterness swung to a sweeter notch on the fake pleasantry scale. 'I'm Aria. Is there anywhere nearby that you can take me for an early lunch?'

'I, eh, there's Greg's cafe right over there. They serve delicious pancakes with locally produced maple syrup.'

An icy breeze chilled the warm day, or perhaps it was just the look Aria gave him that flipped the weather.

Figuring that was a hard no, Mark suggested somewhere else. 'Or there's the lodge. They have a lovely new restaurant, and Kyle is a top notch chef.'

The temperature bar raised again into the warm zone. That was a taciturn yes.

Taking her phone off him, she scrolled through his efforts to capture her well. 'A couple of these are quite acceptable. My social media posts with pictures of me are very popular.'

He was prepared to believe her.

Tottering on her heels, she linked her arm through his. 'Is this lodge far?'

'No, it's just along here.' He pointed to it.

Aria noticed the archway sign advertising the Snow Bells market fair. 'Does anything exciting go on in this little town in the evenings?'

Mark sparked with enthusiasm. 'Yes, there's always something to enjoy. In fact, there's a fundraising dance on tonight in the community hall. It's back there. The quilting bee members are helping to raise money for the roof repairs.'

Aria glanced over her shoulder. She was clearly bored.

'The tickets are all sold out,' Mark added, trying to blow some puff into the popularity of the event. 'Everyone will be there.'

Aria's interest perked up. 'Everyone? Including Brad?'

'I think he'll be there.'

'With his new girlfriend — the woman in the red dress?'

'Robyn?'

Mark doubted that Robyn was dating Brad, but what did he know? The guy had been cooking pizza in her kitchen. They seemed to have hit it off from the get–go.

'So that's her name,' Aria mused. 'What does she do? Apart from being a multi–instrumentalist.'

Not wishing to correct her, and not underestimating that Robyn had hidden musical talents, Mark explained about Robyn's marketing business.

'What's a New York marketing executive doing in Snow Flakes Harbor?'

'Snow Bells Haven,' Mark corrected her.

Aria waved a dismissive hand in the air. 'Whatever.' She sighed wearily. 'Okay, I'll go to the dance.'

'But the tickets are all sold out,' he reminded her.

'You're the mayor. You can take care of that minor formality for me, can't you, Mark?' She smiled at him. 'I can go as your plus one.'

Aria was one of the most beautiful women he'd ever met, and although he knew she was trying to play him, he figured he'd play along anyway. He didn't have a date for the dance. Robyn was taken. So why not turn up with Aria on his arm. No ticket, no problem. He'd make a donation to the fund to cover his plus one. Besides, Aria was the only person he'd met that hadn't mentioned he was so young to be the mayor. Maybe she saw him for the mildly successful man he was. Or she just wasn't that interested in him. Secretly believing it was the latter, he tried to kid himself it was the former.

'I assume you're a fan of Brad's music,' said Mark.

'Not really. I know him on a personal level. Brad and I go back a long way, if you know what I mean.'

'Oh, right.' Mark didn't push for the details.

By now they'd reached the lodge and Mark escorted Aria inside, hoping that Penny and Kyle would help him tame the visiting vixen without causing a ruckus.

Penny welcomed Mark and Aria in.

'We'd like a table for lunch in the new restaurant,' said Mark. 'We don't have a prior booking.'

'That's fine, Mark,' Penny assured him. 'Come on through. We have a table right beside the window. The garden is looking so pretty.'

They were seated at their table. Guests dined at several tables, enjoying an early lunch, and other tables were booked with reserved cards, indicating the popularity of the new restaurant.

Aria looked impressed. A first, Mark thought. So far, so good.

Instead of studying the menu, Aria scrolled through her phone, looking at the pictures of herself outside Brad's studio.

Mark didn't chide her. She'd have to put her phone down to eat lunch.

Penny hurried into the kitchen to alert Kyle of the newcomer's arrival.

'The mayor is here for lunch,' she announced, and then whispered. 'He's brought a beautiful woman with him. She seems to be from out of town. From the city, I'd say.'

Kyle's eyebrows raised so high they tipped the edge of his chef's hat. 'I thought Mark had a thing for Robyn.'

Penny shrugged.

Kyle wiped the flour from his hands. He'd been making delicate choux pastry for chocolate eclairs. 'I'll take their order.'

Penny thought he would, and was glad to hand the task over to her nephew. There was a vibe from Mark's guest that she thought Kyle would handle better.

Aria was still scrolling through the photos on her phone, selecting one, and then reselecting another. She'd taken a furtive photo of herself in the music studio, capturing Brad in it without him even noticing. This was going to be her lead asset when she announced her visit to see Brad at his new studio.

'I think I'll reveal all and post this picture of Brad and me on my social media,' she decided, showing Mark the photo she'd selected.

Kyle approached Mark and Aria's table, overhearing part of their conversation, and catching a glimpse of the photo.

'Hi, Mark,' said Kyle. 'See anything on the menu you'd like? I can recommend the day's lunch special.'

'I'll have the special.' Mark handed back the menu.

'Have you had a chance to peruse the menu?' Kyle said to Aria.

Seeing Kyle standing there watching her scroll through her pictures, she glared up at him. 'No, come back in five minutes.'

Kyle didn't flinch. He'd met all kinds of diners, including dismissive ones. 'The special is popular. A French cuisine theme. But perhaps that's just not to your taste, so I'll leave you to study the rest of the menu.' Giving Mark a relaxed smile, Kyle walked away.

'No, wait,' Aria called to him. 'What's so great about the special?'

Kyle gave her a wicked grin. 'The name gives it away.'

'Okay, I'll have the French special. But I prefer to add my own seasoning.'

'Big mistake.' Kyle picked up her menu from the table where she'd barely glanced at it, and went to leave again.

'Fine,' said Aria.

Kyle winked at Mark, indicating that Aria wasn't getting everything her own way in his restaurant.

Mark tried not to smile too hard.

Kyle hurried back through to the kitchen, beckoning Penny to join him.

'Mark's out of his depth with his lunch partner,' Kyle told Penny. 'Can you find out what she's doing here in Snow Bells? She has pictures of herself standing outside the music studio, and one of her and Brad. He wasn't smiling. She's planning to reveal all on social media. Whatever that means, but I don't like the sound of it.'

Penny grabbed her phone. 'I'll call Robyn. She'll know what's going on.'

CHAPTER EIGHT

I love living in a small town
Between the country and the sea
It's filled with family and friendship
A great community

The only thing that's missing
Is someone to love
A heart that's kind, a smile that's true
A love to set me free

Could that someone be you?
Could your someone be me?

Brad played the latest melody, adding depths to the song with every note of his electric guitar. The tones were deeper with a mellow quality. Not quite a slow dance, but one that Robyn pictured couples wanting to get up and dance to whenever it was played. He'd captured the core of the romance.

Robyn sat there steeped in the resonance of the tune. Hearing a song played for real in a studio was such a wonderful experience.

A call came through for her from Penny.

Thinking Penny was phoning about the lodge business, Robyn stepped outside the recording room to chat while Brad continued working on the song.

'Hi, Penny.'

'Mark's here at the lodge having lunch with a woman named Aria.' Penny spoke in a confiding tone.

'Do you know anything about her? Kyle thinks she's up to something. He heard her say she's planning to put a picture of her and Brad on her social media and reveal all.'

Robyn's heart twisted hearing Penny explain the details of what was going on in the restaurant.

'Aria wants to date Brad, but he's not interested,' said Robyn. 'She turned up at his studio today. We thought she'd be driving back to New York by now, not having lunch with Mark.'

'Don't blame Mark. He's such a nice guy. Too nice in her case. Kyle is handling her wiles better.'

'Could Kyle get a photo of Mark and Aria together?'

'I'm sure he could. What are you planning to do with it?'

'Play Aria at her own game.'

After the call, Robyn went back into the recording room looking concerned.

Brad stopped playing. 'Something wrong?'

'Aria's still in town. She's having lunch with Mark at the lodge. Penny called to warn me that Aria has a private picture of you with her taken in the studio.'

Brad frowned. 'I never saw her take any photos.'

Robyn shrugged.

He sighed and shook his head. 'She's up to her tricks again.'

'I've suggested that Kyle takes a photo of Aria and Mark together.'

'What are you going to do with the photo?' said Brad

'Give it to your manager in New York. I assume he knows the score about you and Aria.'

'He does. He's already told her I'm not interested in her.'

'Well then, if Aria intends posting a picture of the two of you on her social media, I'm guessing she's going to slant things to make it look like the two of you are an item.'

'That sounds about right.'

'So what if someone had gossip that Aria has fallen for the mayor of a small town. That maybe she planned to settle into a small town life and leave the city behind. With a picture of them looking cute together.'

'Aria wouldn't like anyone thinking that.'

'I didn't think so. It's the only way to stop her posting a photo of the two of you in your studio. If she posts that she's in Snow Bells, it'll help to confirm that she's opted for a small town life.'

'Checkmate.' Brad smiled, fitting the moves together.

'Aria can't post anything about Snow Bells, especially your studio, without adding to the gossip that she's left New York.'

Brad took out his phone. 'I'll call my manager and let him know what's going on.'

Robyn listened while Brad explained the situation to him.

'Send me the photo of Aria with the mayor guy,' his manager told him. 'I'll speak to Aria, congratulate her on falling for him.'

'I think she'll back down from posting about me on her social media,' said Brad.

'So do I,' his manager agreed. 'Smart move to deal with a tricky situation.'

Kyle sent a photo of Aria having lunch with Mark. She was accidentally smiling at him.

'I have the photo we need,' Robyn told Brad. She sent it to him.

Brad looked at the picture, nodded, and then forwarded it to his manager.

'Got it,' his manager confirmed. 'I'll call Aria now.'

Aria looked at her phone. 'It's Brad's manager. I have to take this call,' she said to Mark.

He continued to enjoy his lunch while the verbal battle began.

'I'm not dating Mark,' Aria argued. 'This small town's gossip is ridiculous! I don't care if he's the mayor. I'm not in love with him, or leaving New York to move here.'

Brad's manager sent her the photo. 'The two of you sure look happy together. He's a fine looking guy. And he's the mayor.'

Mark lost his appetite. 'What's going on? Does this have anything to do with us going to the dance tonight?'

The manager overheard Mark's remark. 'It sounds like you're a happy couple Going dancing, having lunch...'

'Okay! You win, this time,' Aria conceded. 'I won't post the picture of Brad, if you won't spread gossip about me.'

'Deal.'

'And for your information, I'm leaving this town right now and driving home to New York,' Aria shouted and then clicked the call to a close.

She stood up. 'We're done here, Mark.'

Kyle and Penny stood in the wings listening to the drama unfold.

'Not staying for my chocolate eclairs?' Kyle said to Aria as she strutted past him.

Aria iced Kyle, and continued on her way out.

'I'll phone Robyn and tell her everything's fine,' said Penny.

Brad's manager had already called Brad to confirm what had happened.

Robyn spoke to Penny. 'Thanks for your help.'

'A bad situation avoided,' Penny told her.

'Is Mark okay?'

'Kyle's plying him with chocolate eclairs. He'll be fine,' Penny assured her.

'Could you tell Mark that he gets a mention in Brad's newspaper feature. Brad is quoted as saying that the town's new young mayor welcomed him to Snow Bells Haven and offered him advice on local businesses to contact regarding the launch of his new music recording studio.'

'I'll tell Mark,' said Penny. 'I'm sure he'll be delighted.'

After the call, Brad rewound the song recording and they both listened to it. Neither of them wanted to rewind the fiasco with Aria.

'This song has a great beat for dancing,' Robyn remarked.

'You think so?' Brad stood up and pulled her into his arms and began dancing with her in the studio.

Robyn couldn't dance properly for laughing.

In Brad's strong hold, he led her around the floor and dipped her in time to the music.

She squealed and giggled.

'I think this is going to be my latest method to test a song's viability,' he said, dancing to the rhythm of the beat.

'Is that a known method?' she said playfully.

'It is now.' Brad finished by almost lifting her off the floor and finishing in time to the song.

Breathless, mainly from the fun of it, Robyn shook her head at him. 'You are nothing but trouble.'

'That makes two of us. I guess that's why we get along.'

She nodded thoughtfully. They did get along. The music grinch and the songsmith.

'That was quite a workout,' she remarked, sweeping her hair back. 'You need to write more slow ballads.'

'I can do that. Someone has written real romantic lyrics for me to wrap my music around.'

The way he looked at her shot tingles through her.

For a moment, she thought he was going to lean down and kiss her.

For a moment, he thought he might.

Robyn's phone rang, helping her out of a tempting situation that would've been difficult to unravel herself from. Brad's kiss from earlier, real or not, had felt authentic and was sure to rewind in her mind for quite a while.

'It's Mark,' she told Brad, and then took the call.

'Robyn! Tell Brad thanks for giving me a mention in the paper. Penny just showed me a copy. I didn't expect to be included. It was a nice surprise.'

'I'm here at the studio. I'll tell him,' she assured Mark. 'And, I wouldn't have fried your reputation on social media with the Aria fiasco. I was bluffing big style.'

'That's okay. I trust you to always do the right thing,' he said. 'I've had a crazy day so far, but save me a dance for tonight.'

'I will,' she promised. 'See you at the dance.'

'Got a date tonight with the mayor?' said Brad, picking up his guitar and starting to play around with the chords.

'No, just one tick on my dance card. Mark phoned to thank you for including him in the feature.'

'You wrote it.'

'I wrote a direct quote from you.'

Brad smiled at her. 'So all's well with the mayor.'

'It is. Storm averted.'

'Does that mean you don't have a partner to take you to the dance?'

'It does. But I'm fine going on my own.'

'I'm thinking I'll go tonight. Follow through from the feature by meeting folks.'

'And enjoy the dancing.'

'Would the girl next door to me be free to go with me to the dance tonight?' There was a twinkle of mischief in those blue eyes of his.

'She would.'

'Pick you up at seven?'

Robyn lifted her bag. 'See you then.' She headed out of the studio into the sunshine to get on with her day.

Robyn put on the pretty pale blue dress she'd bought from Virginia's dress shop. She wore heels that she could dance in, and was looking forward to her night out. Checking she had her ticket in her purse, she turned the bedroom light off and went downstairs to wait for Brad. He was due to arrive soon.

Her heart fluttered even though she knew it wasn't a date.

Brad put a blue silk tie on with his white shirt. He couldn't remember the last time he'd worn a tie, never mind a full suit, but the occasion seemed to merit it. He wanted to look smart to accompany Robyn to the dance.

And he couldn't remember the last time he'd felt so nervous about going out on a date. Though it wasn't a date, he reminded himself. It was a dance. A chance to show the local community that he wanted to be part of their events. Going there with Robyn just happened to sweeten the night out.

He checked the time. Almost seven. Time to go and pick her up as agreed.

The evening air felt clear and calm, unlike him, as he stepped outside and walked to his car that was parked in the driveway.

Relax, he told himself as he drove the short distance to Robyn's house and parked outside.

As he walked up to her door, he sighed. He hadn't brought flowers or anything like that. It wasn't necessary, but it would've been nice to have given her a flower corsage to impress her.

Arriving empty handed, he knocked on the door.

Robyn had seen him pull up and was ready to leave. She opened the door and smiled at him, impressed that he'd worn a suit and tie. He'd really made an effort.

'Ready to go?' he said.

'Yes. You look really smart.'

'You look beautiful tonight.'

They walked to the car and he opened the door for her, then got in and drove to the main street.

'Did you manage to get any more songwriting done?' she said, making light conversation.

'I did. Your lyrics really inspire me. I got lost in the music, and suddenly it was time to dash home and get ready for the dance.'

'My day was a blur too. But I got a lot of work done.' She gazed out at the night sky as they drove along the main street towards the community hall. 'It'll be fun to unwind at the dance party.'

'I read the other local news in the paper. It seems there's always some event being held in the town.'

'That's true. The Snow Bells market fair is coming up soon. You should go, if you're still in town.'

He frowned. 'Where else would I be?'

'New York. Recording the remaining songs for the album in the studio there.' Maybe even taking her with him on one of his trips to the city.

'I've rearranged my plans. I'll explain later,' he said, pulling up to the community hall. 'It looks busy.'

Twinkle lights decorated the front of the hall and the doors were wide open, inviting in the warm night and everyone taking part.

The hall was buzzing with activity as Brad escorted Robyn up to the entrance, and music poured out into the evening air.

'It sounds like there's a live band playing,' said Brad. He enjoyed traditional country music.

'They invited a live band from one of the larger towns nearby. Nancy told me the band played here before and are quite popular at local events.'

The lively atmosphere pulled them into the heart of the community hall. A buffet was set up along one side, and Greg was there topping it up with snacks. He'd volunteered to help out in the kitchen, while Dwayne attended the dance with his wife, and Herb was there with his girlfriend.

Nate and Nancy were already waltzing on the busy dance floor, and the band played up on the stage. More twinkle lights were draped around the hall and the stage itself was well–lit for the four–piece band to play.

A few heads turned when Brad walked in with Robyn. He was used to being noticed, but tonight he wasn't sure if it was because of the feature in the paper.

Mark saw them and came over to chat. 'Hi, I'm pleased you could make it.'

'It seems like a great turnout for the fundraiser dance,' said Brad.

'Yes,' Mark agreed. 'I'm about to make an announcement about how much money was raised from the ticket sales — and a private donation.' He gave Brad a knowing look.

Before Robyn could question Mark, he walked away to make his announcement, taking the microphone to the front of the stage.

'Can I have your attention for a moment,' Mark announced, as the music faded to a lull. 'I'm pleased to announce that the money from the ticket sales for the dance tonight almost reached the roof repair target. But an anonymous donation of one thousand dollars came in, making up the shortfall.

People cheered and looked around, wondering if the person responsible was at the dance.

'It was you, wasn't it, Brad?' Robyn whispered to him.

Brad smiled and said nothing.

Mark finished his speech. 'Whoever made this donation, I'd like to thank them on behalf of the dance arrangers and myself. The repairs will now be done soon by a local company. So, enjoy your evening, and have a great night everyone.'

Applause and cheers filled the hall, and the music kicked up into a lively beat again.

'Would you like to dance?' Brad said to Robyn.

'I would.'

Dancing around the floor, a few couples smiled and nodded acknowledgment to Brad, making him feel welcome.

'That's Jessica and her husband,' Robyn told him. 'She owns the quilt shop. He's the town's sheriff.'

'I see Zack's here,' Brad remarked, noticing the architect.

'Yes, and that's his fiancée, Sylvie, he's dancing with,' Robyn added. 'They're getting married at the lodge.'

'I'm sure I'll soon get to know everyone.'

'You will.'

As the song came to an end, and another one started, Robyn paused from dancing with Brad.

'You should mingle,' she advised him.

'On my own?'

'Yes, otherwise people will get the wrong impression. We'll be seen as a couple.'

A stab of disappointment shot through him. But she was right. That didn't make the circumstances any easier.

'I'll go and get something to eat at the buffet,' she said. 'It'll give you a chance to circulate.'

'Okay.' He tried to sound like this was a sensible idea. They weren't here on a date, though when he was with Robyn, it was hard to separate his growing feelings for her.

Before they got a chance to go their separate ways, Mark approached them.

'Brad. The guys in the band are excited you're here tonight. They've asked if you'll come up on stage and join them for a number.'

Brad hesitated. It wasn't the first time he'd gone to a party or social event and been asked to give an impromptu performance. He always obliged. There was no reason why he shouldn't do it.

'They know all your hits, so you could sing anything you want. They'll accompany you,' Mark assured him. Then he looked at Robyn. 'And they're happy for you to join them too. You could play guitar or—'

'I don't play any instruments,' Robyn cut–in.

'Oh, right. Aria said you were a multi–instrumentalist,' said Mark.

Brad tried not to smile.

'No, not me,' Robyn insisted.

The band members were playing, but looking over at Brad.

'I'd be happy to join them for a number,' Brad confirmed. He smiled at Robyn and went over to the stage with Mark.

Robyn watched as Brad discussed with the band what song he'd sing.

Brad was given the use of an electric guitar from the side of the stage where they'd stored their spare instruments for different numbers during their evening's performance.

The smiles from the band members showed their delight that Brad was about to take the lead and sing.

The dancing slowed as people became an audience, standing looking towards the stage, anticipating what was about to happen.

The band's lead singer made an announcement. 'We're thrilled that Brad is going to play one of the hits from his last album.' He stepped back, letting Brad take the lead.

Without any fuss or introducing himself, Brad started playing the opening riff of the song, igniting cheers from the audience, most of them knowing the song and looking forward to hearing the live performance.

Brad played the borrowed electric guitar, making it sing with a level of expertise and talent that showed why he was such a popular and successful performer. But there was no ego there that Robyn could see. Only a man happy to share his talent. He nodded to the other band members, encouraging them to up their game as he started singing the song.

It was one that Robyn remembered from the night that she'd been brushing up on Brad's music. Hearing him singing it live was wonderful, and she felt the atmosphere in the hall rise with excitement as Brad sang...

I'm ultramarine, you're cerulean blue
Under a sky of cobalt hue
In my watercolor world I paint the two of us
We blend so well
In a love that's true
Just me and you
The art of us...

This would be a night she'd always remember, Robyn thought, splitting her view of Brad up there on the stage, filling the whole hall with vibrancy, and watching the delighted faces of the people enjoying his music. To think that she was going to be a background part of his world, writing lyrics for him, sent waves of mixed emotions through her. What an incredible world to be part of. But she already loved the world she'd made for herself.

'Brad's a wonderful singer, isn't he?' Mark commented, coming over and standing next to Robyn.

'Yes, he is,' she agreed.

As the song came to an end, Brad was encouraged to give them one more song. He smiled and started playing another number, a slower ballad this time.

'I believe you promised me a dance,' Mark said to Robyn.

'I did.' Robyn let Mark lead her in a slow waltz around the floor as couples took the chance to dance together while Brad performed.

Dancing with Mark felt fine, comfortable, but there was never any spark of attraction between them. At least not on her part. The way she felt when Brad held her in his arms ignited so many feelings inside her. Mark had never been the one for her. Or her for him.

'What are you going to do about you and Brad?' Mark said, wise enough to know what was going on.

There was no point in denying her predicament, so she spoke plainly, the way he'd always admired.

'I'm torn. Mixed up. I don't want to get involved in another life when I've just started making a happy one here in town.'

Mark nodded. Those deep blue eyes reflected her trouble. 'Whatever you do, nothing is worth a broken heart. There's no guarantee you'll ever completely mend it. But from my time as a lawyer, dealing with clients' issues, one thing was clear. It was the things people didn't do that cut the deepest wounds. Looking back over your shoulder at the chances you walked away from is a lonely view.'

She guessed he was speaking from his own experience too.

'Do you ever feel you've missed out on a better life in the city, working as a lawyer, rather than being mayor of this town?' she said.

'Not for a second. It's the best move I've ever made, and I'm sticking to it.'

Robyn smiled at Mark, and then they stopped talking and danced as close friends to the remainder of the song.

Brad's view from the stage made him note two things. One — he'd always stand out a little bit in Snow Bells Haven even when he eventually blended in. But that was okay. He was fine with that. Two — he needed to be extra careful to protect the contented life Robyn had built for herself in town. Even if that meant stepping back and letting her breathe a little without him making demands on her time and talent.

He'd never been adept at balancing life on a fine dividing line, but he'd have to learn, and learn fast. Since meeting Robyn, things had moved at a lightning pace. Storm warnings lay ahead, that's for sure.

Handing back the guitar, that he'd signed for them, and shaking hands with the band members, Brad joined in the dancing, taking Robyn's advice. Somehow, he ended up dancing with Nancy. And then with Jessica, Greg's girlfriend Lucie, Virginia from the dress shop, and Dwayne's wife.

Dwayne took a photo of his wife dancing with Brad. 'Thanks, Brad,' Dwayne said, beaming at him.

'My wife is a huge fan of yours. This has made her night.' And then off they went to show the photo to Herb and his girlfriend.

Greg saw snatches of Brad's performance as he dashed back and forth from the kitchen to the buffet, but he heard every note.

He piled more cupcakes on a stand and topped up a tray of sandwiches as Robyn approached the buffet.

'Gingerbread cupcake?' Greg said to her.

'Cookie dough. Blame Brad.'

Greg smiled. 'Actually, blame me. I was the one to suggest he try them this morning when he said he wanted something delicious for you.'

She smiled and helped herself to a cup of coffee to go with her cupcake.

'You and Brad seem to have hit it off,' Greg remarked.

'We're getting along fine.' She played down her feelings, and bit into the cupcake to prevent herself from saying anything she'd later wish she hadn't revealed.

'I thought you looked like a well–matched couple when I saw the two of you earlier. Like you were dating.'

She took a sip of coffee. 'No, it's just friendly business.'

'Okay, if you say so.' Greg grinned at her.

Someone came over to Greg. 'Do you have any slices of your apple pie left, Greg?' the man said hopefully.

'Coming right up.' Greg hurried through to the kitchen.

Robyn stood to the side of the buffet eating her cupcake and drinking her coffee while watching the evening unfold. Money had been raised and everyone was having a great time. Success all round. So what was eating at her? Her feelings for Brad, she admitted, looking across the hall at him mingling and getting to know folks.

As if sensing her watching him, Brad glanced round, looking right at her across the dance floor. He excused himself from the company he was talking to, and made his way towards Robyn.

Halfway there, Penny arrived with Kyle. Robyn remembered Penny said they'd be late due to having to tend to the lodge and restaurant earlier in the evening.

Kyle waylaid Brad, and Robyn saw them shake hands. Another acquaintance made. Then Penny accepted a chance to dance with Brad, leaving Kyle to head over to the buffet.

'Robyn!' Kyle's warm smile soothed her.

Ever astute, Kyle sensed that Robyn had been looking at Brad. 'Do you want to dance with me instead?'

Robyn put her coffee cup down. 'Yes.'

Brad and Penny smiled as they danced past Kyle waltzing with Robyn.

Two ships that pass in the night, Robyn thought to herself, happy to dance with Kyle. But as she glanced over her shoulder at Brad dancing away with Penny, she caught a glimpse of that lonely view Mark had mentioned.

CHAPTER NINE

I can't change the past
But I can change how I feel about it
The only thing I can't change
Is how I feel about you
I've loved you long, I've loved you true
The only one I love is you
For me, it's always been you

Brad and Penny stood at the side of the dance floor talking as Kyle waltzed Robyn around.

When they finished waltzing and joined Brad and Penny, Robyn heard part of their conversation.

'Yes, let me know the dates,' Penny said to Brad. 'I'll be happy to sort that out for you.'

Kyle didn't pick up on it, but Robyn wondered what was going on.

'Come on, Aunt Penny, time to dance with me,' Kyle said cheerily.

As Penny and Kyle headed away, Robyn frowned at Brad.

'This is what I wanted to talk to you about,' Brad began.

'Your change of plans?'

'Yes. I'm going to record the remaining songs for the album in the studio here in town,' he said.

'You're not going to the New York studio?'

'No. I've spoken to the session musicians that will be involved in the recording, and they're happy to make the trip here. I was talking to Penny about booking them rooms at the lodge for their short stay. She's going to sort out the accommodation as soon as I have the exact dates.' He shrugged. 'But I have to finish writing all the songs first.'

'That's ideal.' She wouldn't have minded the trip to New York, but she was happier to stay in Snow Bells. 'What made you change your mind?'

'I thought it over and decided that I want this studio to be great, and that won't happen if I keep running back to New York. I want to make this work here.'

She agreed.

'We can still take a trip to New York if you'd like to see the studio,' he offered.

'I have to go to the city sometimes to deal with clients from my past, so I'm sure we could work in a visit to your New York studio.'

'We'll do that,' he said.

'Can I steal Brad for a group photo with the quilting bee members?' Nancy said to Robyn.

Brad smiled as he was hustled away with Nancy.

Robyn tagged along, being a member of the bee.

The ladies, and Greg, a keen quilter, grouped around Brad while Jessica handed her phone to her husband.

The sheriff made sure he had everyone in the picture. 'Budge up folks, and big smiles.'

'Quilting!' they cheered in unison, resulting in a truly happy photo, with Brad in the middle.

After handing the phone back to Jessica, the sheriff took the opportunity to shake hands with Brad and welcome him to the town. Another acquaintance made.

Robyn watched as Brad was pulled into the hub of the community, truly welcome.

'Did I see someone having apple pie earlier?' said Brad.

'Come on over to the buffet and I'll get a slice for you,' Greg offered.

As everyone dispersed to continue enjoying the evening, Brad escorted Robyn over to the buffet.

'I think the feature worked,' Brad confided to her. 'You wrote everything that needed to be said to explain my intentions of opening the studio in Snow Bells.'

'Here you go, Brad.' Greg thrust a slice of apple pie topped with whipped cream at him.

'Thanks, Greg.'

Robyn helped herself to a sandwich.

'Tell me about the Snow Bells market fair,' Brad said to her as they enjoyed their food.

'It's a big deal here. All the local farmers, flower growers and businesses get involved. There are stalls selling everything from crafts to home baked cakes. This will be the first one I've attended, but I've heard it's really popular.'

'You said that I should get involved.'

'Yes, you'll meet more members of the community and it'll give them a chance to meet you. Once people have read the feature and word gets around that you plan to be in your studio working on your music, the extra interest in you will settle down.'

'I haven't been to a market fair since I was a boy. My grandparents used to take me to their local one. It used to be fun.'

'Nate is one of the event planners. Speak to him.'

'Speak to me about what?' Nate said, overhearing his name being mentioned.

'About Snow Bells market fair,' said Robyn.

'Are you two getting involved?' Nate looked hopeful.

'I'm planning to attend, and spend far too much at the craft and cakes stalls,' Robyn said to Nate.

Nate smiled at her, and then looked at Brad. 'What about you?'

'I'll come along too,' Brad agreed.

Then Nate viewed Brad with a keen eye. 'Do you think you could be persuaded to perform a song or two? We have a small stage set up where the mayor announces the opening of the fair and there are prizes presented for certain participants in fun events.'

Robyn's smile brightened and she nodded encouragingly at Brad.

'Yeah, sure. I'd be happy to play at your fair.'

Nate rubbed his hands together with glee. 'Wonderful. I'll tell the other members running the event, including Mark, and we'll get the ball rolling.'

Hurrying away to tell Mark and others, Nate left Brad standing with Robyn.

'Care to dance? Before you rope me into anything else,' Brad said jokingly.

Robyn took Brad's hand and let him lead her on to the dance floor where they danced to three songs in a row, getting lost in the music and each other's company.

At the end of the evening, Robyn and Brad said their goodnights to everyone, and stepped out into the still night air.

They walked together to his car, and she couldn't help feeling like it was a date night. A sense that the evening wasn't quite over.

She didn't know how strongly Brad felt the same thing, but he'd tucked his feelings away, not for ever, but for now.

Other couples drifted outside, and people Brad had met, like Jessica and the sheriff, waved over to him as if he was now a friend and not a stranger. He found that he liked fitting in more than he'd imagined. And he liked being there with Robyn. It offered him a fresh perspective of the type of life he could have, while still working on his music. The best of both worlds now seemed feasible. Something else he'd never imagined.

While on his last tour with the band, he noted that he was the only single guy left among them. He'd hear them back stage phoning their wives and fiancées telling them they'd be home soon and were looking forward to seeing them.

He remembered at the end of one particularly successful concert night when the crowd sang along to the final two numbers, knowing all the words to his songs, and he'd stood there on stage looking out at them. Thousands of them. All the smiling faces. All the voices singing. And thinking to himself that he'd never felt so alone.

It was something that was starting to bug him these days. Maturity no doubt. He was still in his early thirties, but lately he'd felt a pang of longing to find someone to love and settle down with. No one watching him up there on stage, successful, unattached, free to travel on tours without leaving the love of his life behind, would know how lonely it could be.

When he was younger, he could be happy spending time on the farm, out in the countryside, away from everyone while he played his guitar. He never felt alone there. Not once.

But there were increasing times when he walked unnoticed through the streets of New York and felt completely on his own.

On his last tour, where his concerts had been sold out, he'd come to the conclusion that the worst loneliness he felt was when he was in the heart of a crowd.

As they drove past the music studio, Robyn remembered she had more lyrics for Brad. She'd brought them with her to the dance, but in all the excitement she'd forgotten about them.

'These are the missing lyrics, the chorus, you wanted for that song you mentioned.'

He brightened from his deep thoughts. 'I was working on that today in the studio. I have the melody for the chorus, so I'd love to try out the words.' By now they were heading away from the main street and driving the short distance home. 'Are you up for hearing the song, with the chorus? I'd value your opinion.'

'Yes.' She gazed out the window at the night sky and the rolling hills, fields and trees as they left the busy hub of the town behind.

Lights shone from distant windows of houses dotted on the verdant landscape, including the farmhouses in the surrounding fields. She sighed to herself. Snow Bells was a haven she'd never want to leave.

Brad drove up to the leafy niche of properties that were scattered in the greenery. He parked in the driveway of his house and they went inside, through to the lounge where he opened the patio doors to let in the night air.

Eager to read the lyrics, he skim–read the words as he set up his electric guitar.

Robyn noticed that he used it more than his acoustic guitar.

'The verse goes like this,' he said, starting to play and sing the song.

She nodded, hearing the melody, thinking that it sounded different from the other songs she'd heard him creating recently, but it would be a tuneful addition to the album.

Brad sang her lyrics for the chorus. 'These really work with the melody.' He continued to play and sing, blending the verses and chorus together into one musical number that sounded like another potential hit.

Strumming his guitar, he smiled at her. 'Help yourself to coffee or anything you want to eat or drink.'

'I'll make coffee,' she said, heading through to the kitchen. She flicked the lights on and changed her mind about the coffee and made hot chocolate instead. She checked the fridge. Plenty of milk and whipped cream. His kitchen was pretty well–stocked. Probably even better than her own.

The aroma of chocolate wafted through from the kitchen to the lounge, giving the game away regarding what she was up to.

He smiled to himself and kept on playing, feeling more at home in his own house when Robyn was there.

Topping two mugs of hot chocolate with whipped cream, she carried them through to the lounge and put one down for him.

'I love the lyrics you write,' he said to her.

She sipped her hot chocolate. 'Lyrics keep popping into my mind these days.'

'Write them down.'

'I do.'

He played the chorus again, adding to the richness of the melody, enhancing it to suit the lyrics.

'That sounds even better,' she told him, wandering over to the patio to peer out at the night while sipping her chocolate. The scent of the garden wafted in. She flicked the lanterns on, curious to see what it looked like lit up. Quite magical, she thought.

He admired her, but still kept his feelings for her to himself.

'Snow Bells Haven seems to be buzzing with romance,' he commented. 'There were a few couples I met tonight that had only recently got together.'

'Maybe there's something in the air in Snow Bells that sparks romance,' she said lightly.

Robyn didn't see him nod in heartfelt agreement as she looked out at the garden. The lanterns cast a glow across the garden and illuminated parts of it. Several types of white flowers acted as their own highlights in the shaded nooks where the lantern lights failed to reach.

'This looks like a moon garden,' she commented.

'What's that?' He continued playing, and she felt the vibrations from the song drift over her shoulders and pour out into the evening air where they faded before anyone else could hear them.

'It's a garden that flourishes at night. The flowers, especially white flowers and silver foliage, can be enjoyed in the evenings when it's dark. They glow in the moonlight.'

Brad put his guitar aside and came out to join her. 'I see what you mean.' He pointed at some of the flowers. 'I didn't plant them, but I intend adding to the garden, so I'll keep your moon garden idea in mind and use plants that put on a show at night.'

She smiled round at him. 'Apt, for a performer like you.'

'Yeah.' He fought the natural urge to put his arm around her shoulders and pull her close so they could stand there together.

She breathed in deeply. 'It's so calm and quiet.'

'When I'm not twanging my guitar,' he said teasingly.

'That's not what I meant,' she said lightly.

'I was thinking I should let you hear the song I recorded in New York for the album that's the perfect foil for this new song. The lyrics for the chorus are perfect.'

'I'd like to hear it. I know you let me hear the songs you recorded in the studio here, but I've been wondering what the other songs for the album sound like. Are they similar or wildly contrasting to the new material?'

Brad walked with her inside the lounge as he explained. 'Every album of mine has a theme. It's a fine balancing act to make the new songs fresh while keeping them in line with fans' expectations. If I go too wild one way, or too safe the other, it won't work.'

'It must be hard to please everyone,' she acknowledged.

'I can't, but I try to keep the majority happy, and create new songs that give a successful range to the album.'

She understood.

'There are songs about the atmosphere of late nights. Getting happily lost in the excitement of the night. That feeling you spoke about. In the depths of the evening, wanting to find your way home, even if it's a place you've never been to or knew you needed.'

'Like leaving New York and coming to Snow Bells Haven?' she said tentatively.

'Exactly. The majority of the songs that will make the final cut on the album were written and recorded in New York. But I knew something was missing. I'd felt that for a while. My last album did well, but I wanted this one to do better. I needed to get away from the city, and find new experiences in a small town life, reset my heart to the way I used to feel when I was first starting out in the music industry.'

'A fresh start, like you mentioned in your interview.'

'Yes, and I believe I've found it.' He pressed his lips firmly together.

'What so secret that you can't tell me?' She knew he was holding something back.

'Everything and nothing.' Everything about her, and nothing he could tell her yet, if ever.

'Complicated.' She smiled gently and didn't press him for the explanation he clearly wasn't ready to reveal.

He handed her a set of headphones. 'Put these on while I try out this new chorus. It's one of the tracks from the album. When you hear it, you'll see what I'm getting at when I said this new song with the chorus lyrics you've written is the perfect foil for it.'

Robyn put the headphones on and listened to the first notes of a song she'd never heard before. It started to resonate through her. The opening stretched out mellow, before erupting into a number that made her want to dance. So she did. A little bit.

Watching Robyn move to the rhythm of the song made his heart secretly sing. And helped him to add another dash of excitement to the chorus. There was that spark again, he thought to himself, as she lit up his world with her carefree heart.

When the song finished, she took the headphones off. 'I liked that. I understand what you mean about it being an ideal pairing for the new song.'

'I'd planned to list it as the opening number on the album, but now I'm putting two of the new songs as the first and second tracks.'

Robyn was pleased that her lyrics were going to be on the lead numbers.

Brad handed her a piece of paper where he'd jotted down lyrics. 'I had these in mind, but I couldn't make them work. I wondered if you could try.'

She read the handful of words which were more like a list than lyrics. The dawn, the aurora, the night. But as she read them again, an opening line came to mind, and without saying anything to him, she picked up a pen and began to write it down. Followed by other lines, and gaps where she wasn't sure where the lyrics would go.

Brad quietly wandered outside and breathed in the night air while Robyn stayed in a bubble of creativity, scribbling the lyrics like lightning.

'I'm not sure if these work,' she said, finally walking outside to join him. She handed him the scrap of paper with a fortune's worth of lyrics on them.

'You've captured the idea that I was hoping for.' Smiling at her, he hurried inside and couldn't wait to pick up his guitar to start playing around with the song.

The opening notes were soulful and then led into a rock number. Another piece of potential gold dust.

She'd been right, she thought. The night hadn't ended at the dance. It wasn't a traditional date night, but she couldn't help but feel the romance in the air. Maybe it was coming from the excitement of the music, the way his playing resonated with her, or just being with Brad. The two of them, creating beautiful music until after midnight.

As he played, she filled the gaps in the lyrics, and they played around with the words and melody until she finally got ready to head home.

He walked her to the front door of her house, insisting that he accompany her.

She unlocked the door. 'I had a great night. The dance was a success.'

'So was our song writing. The ideas spark between us.' And sparks of deep attraction, he thought to himself, at least on his part.

'I'd better get some sleep. I'm working in the morning with the ice cream parlor. Creating a new website for them, promoting their latest range.'

'Sounds like a delicious marketing assignment,' he said, grinning at her. He'd seen the ice cream parlor in the main street, along from Greg's cafe and near the flower shop.

'It is,' she agreed, smiling at him.

'Thanks again for writing the feature for the paper and introducing me to everyone tonight at the dance.' He started to walk away, feeling that if he lingered he'd be tempted to kiss her goodnight and that was territory he didn't want to overstep into yet.

Robyn watched him walk away and felt a longing in her heart, but then went inside and closed the door. She didn't blame herself for being attracted to him. She'd seen the way the ladies at the dance had responded to Brad. Their excitement at meeting him would soon level out and then tone down. But she knew how she'd felt seeing him perform live up there on the stage, backed by a local town's band. And she'd just spent the latter part of the evening in his house, personally surrounded by his talent.

Upstairs in her bedroom, she hung her pretty blue dress on a hanger and got ready to get some sleep. Her real world beckoned in the morning. The quilting bee was on in the evening at the community hall, and she'd told Nancy she'd be there. The repairs to the roof wouldn't interfere with any of the events at night in the hall, and according to Mark, the work would be done soon with minimal fuss as the repairs were external.

Getting into bed, she saw the lights were still on in Brad's house, and pictured him working on his music.

Brad didn't have anything special planned for the following day, so it was one of those long evenings where he worked on, playing around with the new song, until the dawn nudged the night aside.

Messages had come through from his manager in the New York studio, and he responded to them, not expecting to get an immediate reply. But his manager phoned him.

'You're working late,' Brad said to him in a video call.

'This is the studio that never sleeps,' his manager reminded him jokingly.

'Do any of us?'

His manager laughed. 'I was going over the tracks for your new album with a couple of the guys in the studio. I got your message about changing the running order.'

'Yes, I'd like to open with two new tracks from the Snow Bells studio. Did you get the recordings I sent to you?'

'I did. They're terrific. And I agree. Let's open with the new studio material as the lead tracks, and then ease into some of the other numbers. How many new tracks do you think you'll introduce?'

'Three and counting. If we go over the twelve tracks we planned for the album, we'll tuck the New York surplus in our back pockets.'

'Sounds fine by me. The new material is the best you've written in years. And you've always written fast. It's like the music catches fire with you.'

'I've certainly felt the burn since coming here and teaming up with Robyn. She rewrote lyrics tonight that I'd been playing around with, and I think I've come up with a riff that'll make this one a standout song.'

'I'd still advise you to get Robyn under contract. She has a real gift for writing lyrics. You don't want anyone else enticing her away,' his manager told him.

Any mention of splitting from Robyn tore at his heart. 'I trust her to hang around with me.'

'Okay then.'

'Want to hear the song so far? I'll work on it some more in the studio tomorrow.'

His manager relaxed back in his chair. 'Play on.'

Brad sang the song and played his guitar while his manager listened and started nodding in time to the beat.

'Oh, yeah! That's outstanding, Brad. It's a contender for the last track on the album to finish on a high note.'

'I agree.'

'How did the dance go tonight? You told me you were hoping to make a friendly impression with the people in the town.'

'It went well. I met everyone from the members of the quilting bee to the sheriff. And I performed a couple of songs on stage, backed by a local band. I borrowed one of their guitars. I didn't expect to have to sing, but it went down well.'

'When did you ever go to an event and not get invited to sing?'

Brad laughed lightly. 'But I made some friendly connections at the dance. I spoke to Penny, owner of the local lodge. Tell the guys she'll have rooms for them there when they come to play at the studio. It'll be for a few days. Her nephew, Kyle, a top chef, has opened a new restaurant there. They'll enjoy this trip more than they expect.'

'I'll tell them. It sounds like a short vacation. I might even invite myself along,' his manager joked.

'You're more than welcome. Or you could stay at my house. I've got a spare room.'

'I like the idea of the top cuisine at the lodge. No offence to your culinary skills, Brad.'

'Hey, I cooked pizza for Robyn and we shared it with the mayor.'

'You're sounding more and more like your old self when I first took you on as a client. I'm getting that raw vibe you used to have that transferred so well to your music.'

'That was at the core of my plan to come here,' said Brad.

'I like the sound of the town.'

'Robyn's advised me to take part in Snow Bells market fair soon. It's a big event around here. Nate, one of the guys running it, wants me to sing a couple of songs on stage. I agreed. Robyn encouraged me.'

'You should do that.'

'When I was talking to Robyn this evening, she suggested that I could use it as a soft launch for the new album. Play a couple of the new tracks, hopefully with the guys as backup if we can arrange the timing of it. She called it a champagne move. Let a couple of bubbles out, before uncorking the full bottle. To gauge the reaction to the songs on a fresh audience. But not announce it until the day to prevent the town's market fair being inundated with outsiders.'

'I'm liking Robyn's marketing ideas. We should get her to help promote the New York studio too.'

'Yes, I'll talk to her about that,' Brad was eager to agree. Anything to keep Robyn in his world got his interest.

CHAPTER TEN

I'm sitting in the sunlight
Gazing at the sparkling blue sea
Feeling I'm falling for you
Hoping we were meant to be

The pastel tones of the ice cream parlor reminded Robyn of vanilla, strawberry and pistachio. The striped pink, cream and pale green canopy shaded the front window from the bright sunlight. It was another warm, sunny day, and even though it was mid–morning, the shop was busy with customers buying ice cream. Some were sitting in to eat fancy ice cream sundaes, and others left with their hands clasped around a cone.

Robyn went inside. She wore a classy floral print cotton dress and low heel shoes that created a summery look while still being smart for business.

The couple who owned the business smiled when they saw her and waved her through to the office behind the counter.

They were a couple similar to Nate and Nancy, and had hired Robyn to create an upgraded website for them. She'd already made it. Now she was here to present it to them, and sat down at the computer in their office, showing each of them separately what she'd planned, while the other tended to customers.

It didn't take them long to agree that they were happy with the website, so the whole process was done and dusted efficiently.

The owners had insisted Robyn sample their new selection of ice cream and she'd been delighted to comply.

Finally, she left with two extra large ice cream cones, and walked across to the music studio. The lights were on, and she knocked on the door.

No reply.

Managing to balance the cones and phone Brad, he came through and let her in.

'It looks like the marketing for the ice cream parlor was a success,' he remarked.

'It was.' She thrust a cone at him. 'I thought you seemed like a strawberry and cream with cherries on top type of guy.'

'I can be that guy, if I get to enjoy this treat.'

He led her through to the studio where he'd been working.

'I haven't had anything except coffee today,' he admitted, eating the ice cream.

'I'm probably a bad influence on you, tempting you with a cone.'

He nodded and mumbled. 'Oh, you are.'

They sat and listened to part of the song he'd recorded while finishing their ice cream.

'It sounds wonderful,' she said.

'I'm still working on it.' He turned the recording off. 'I feel I can improve on it.'

She glanced around the studio that was lit with spotlights. No windows. Nice and quiet, but she wondered if he needed a change of scenery to come up with fresh ideas for the song.

'You're missing a beautiful sunny day outside.'

He frowned. 'I'm working on the songs.'

'Don't you ever work outside in the sunlight?'

'I used to before I opened the studios. Now I'm used to not knowing whether it's a bright morning or stormy afternoon. I'm steeped in the work, the music.'

'That's a shame. I thought maybe you could head out, even for a short while. Grab your guitar. The acoustic one. And play and compose in the wild.'

'First the cone, now the outdoors. Is there no end to your troublemaking?'

She stood up. 'It's part of my job.'

'To haul me away from my work?' he said, grinning.

'To relocate your work, just for a little while.'

She started to walk away. 'But it's okay. I'm heading to the cove for some fresh sea air. Have fun.'

Grabbing his acoustic guitar, he ran after her. 'Wait for me.'

Robyn waited while he locked the studio door. Then they got into his car and drove off, past a pretty little knitting shop and Virginia's dress shop, to the nearby cove.

The narrow road leading up to the cove was edged with greenery and flowers. Robyn opened the car window and breathed in the fragrance of the flowers and lush countryside that then merged with the scent of the sea.

The cove felt like a hidden niche, with a view of the bay and a deep blue sea that was popular for swimming.

They parked on the edge of a grassy area where a few people were enjoying picnics, relaxing in the sunshine or sitting shaded by the trees.

There were several stylish cabins situated around the cove, and after getting out of the car, Brad carried his guitar and they wandered to an area away from the main hub where they had it all to themselves.

The sea sparkled in the sunlight, and they sat down on the grass overlooking the coast. Robyn breathed in the fresh sea air.

Brad was reluctant to play his guitar and disturb the calm atmosphere.

'Play, work on your song,' she encouraged him. 'If you don't, I'll be forced to play your guitar and sing and you certainly don't want to hear that.'

'It's all yours.' He handed her the guitar, not expecting she'd do anything with it.

Feeling mischievous, she started to strum the guitar and sang makeshift lyrics while trying not to laugh.

I'm sitting in the sunshine, twanging my guitar
Wondering if I've gone too far
He's giving me the side eye
But I think it's worthwhile
Causing trouble, to make him smile.

Brad laughed and then applauded.

She handed back the guitar. 'I warned you.'

'That was really—'

'Awful,' she cut–in. 'Badly played.'

He laughed again and didn't argue.

'You play,' she told him. 'I'll relax and enjoy the sea view.'

The view he had of Robyn, her blonde hair shining in the sun and blowing back from her beautiful face in the light breeze, made his heart soar.

He started to play and sing, feeling that she was right to get him out of the studio for a while.

'I don't see a future for me, playing guitar or singing off–key,' she said, unintentionally phrasing in rhyme, while listening to him.

'What about a future with me?' His words burned bright in the sunlight.

She blinked out of her easy thoughts and looked at him. Her heart jolted at his remark, initially mistaking the meaning.

'Being my lyric writer,' he clarified, though maybe deep down his remark meant more than he'd intended, giving away a hint of his feelings for her.

'Yes, I'm happy to do that, for now.' She gazed out at the sea.

For now. The time stamp bothered him, but he continued to play. Maybe this was their time. But like a summer romance, it would fade by the autumn and not make it into the cold heart of winter. He shook these doleful thoughts away and played cheerfully, smiling at her, as she smiled again at him. The balance of whatever they had together restored to enjoy the beautiful sunny day.

'Do you ever go swimming here?' he said.

'Not yet, but I plan to. It's on my to–do list when I'm less busy with work.'

'Is that the list where romance is scheduled?'

'It is. I'd like to say the list is getting shorter, but it's actually getting longer. Take tonight for instance.

I'm going to the quilting bee evening at the community hall. They're working on some guy's quilt and I've promised to add a few wonky stitches to it.'

'Lucky guy. And I'm sure your stitches will be precise, like everything else you do so efficiently.'

'My quilting is certainly far superior to my guitar playing and singing, so don't worry about any wonky stitches on the main part of your quilt. Mine will be hidden on the backing and the binding. Jessica says she's determined to show me her technique for hand stitching the binding on.'

'It sounds like the quilt is nearly finished,' he said.

'Jessica is a whiz at making a quilt. She's been working on it in her shop, with help from Nancy and a few other members dropping in to stitch it. The quilt should be finished soon. And tonight I'll be working on my own quilt too, so I'm looking forward to an evening of quilting and gossip.'

Brad continued playing, while Robyn relaxed in the sunshine, making progress with the song.

He knew he wanted to talk to her about marketing the New York studio, but decided to discuss this another time.

After a while, Robyn checked the time and stood up. 'I suppose we should get going.'

Brad stopped playing and stood up too. 'I feel the benefit of having been working on the song outdoors in the sun. Thanks for encouraging me.'

She smiled at him and they walked back to the car and drove down to the studio.

He parked outside and then opened the door of the studio.

'My car is parked over there,' she said, pointing across to the ice cream parlor.

'Enjoy your evening at the quilting bee,' he told her.

She smiled and walked over to her car, but became waylaid by Kyle.

'Robyn,' Kyle called to her as he came out of the grocery store carrying a selection of items that he'd run out of in the restaurant kitchen. 'Do you have a minute? I'd like to talk to you about a couple of things for the restaurant.'

Brad watched from the window of the studio as Robyn chatted to Kyle, and then they both got into her car and she drove off to the lodge.

Until recently, Brad wouldn't have thought he was the jealous type, but seeing Robyn with Kyle, he had to shake away the unfamiliar feelings. Mark wasn't the right guy for Robyn, but from what he'd heard about Kyle dealing with Aria, he was probably more suitable. And he was a chef. From his experience, women loved a man who could cook. The way to a woman's heart and all that.

Trying to shrug off the unwanted feelings that threatened to weigh him down, he made sure he'd locked the front door, and then went through to the studio to work on his music.

No sunlight to distract him. No sea view. Or Robyn.

Alone in the studio, he settled down and became lost in the music.

'Thanks for your help, Robyn,' Kyle said to her in the restaurant kitchen. 'I needed theme ideas for the new menus. I like to run these suggestions by you.'

'The themes sound tempting. I was glad to help.'

'You should drop by for dinner one evening, if you're ever free.' His invitation hung in the air. 'I'm guessing you and Brad are an item now.' It was more of a question than a statement.

'No, we're on a friendly business level.'

'When I saw the two of you today, I couldn't help noticing the way Brad looks at you.'

'There's really nothing going on between us. And he knows that I'm not interested in getting involved romantically with anyone at the moment. My priority is my business. Romance would complicate everything, and work is complicated enough right now.'

Kyle nodded, getting the message. 'Well, then...the offer still stands. Come for dinner one night. My treat.'

'Thanks, Kyle. I'll do that.'

Kyle walked her out. 'That woman, Aria, is she Brad's ex–girlfriend?'

'No, nothing like that. She'd like to be, and tried to hustle him, but she's gone back to New York. She's out the picture now.'

'I imagine Brad is used to women buzzing around him. I saw the reaction to him at the dance. I'm not envious, no way. I wouldn't like that type of attention and notoriety,' he said truthfully.

'He says it comes with the territory, but I think he handles things well. He's definitely concentrating on the music for his new album.'

'I read the feature in the paper that you wrote. It explained everything. I don't blame him for wanting to get away from the city. Though Snow Bells Haven is a busy small town. Aunt Penny says that Brad is inviting members of his backing band, guys that toured with him, to the studio here, and they'll be staying at the lodge.'

'Yes, that's the plan. He's sorting out the exact dates.'

'Will you be continuing to do his marketing? Or was writing the feature all that you were doing for him?'

'I'm going to be helping him from time to time.' She continued to keep the lyric writing a secret until she felt confident to reveal what she'd been up to. Perhaps she'd wait until the album was released to ensure that her lyrics were used on Brad's album. It still seemed like a dream come true.

Robyn waved to Kyle as she drove off home, driving by the studio, seeing the lights on, and rewinding their time at the cove. Going to the quilting bee would be a good distraction from work, and Brad. She planned to work all afternoon so that the time would whiz by until she headed to the community hall.

Jessica was working on Brad's quilt. Nancy sat beside her, and they'd kept a seat for Robyn in the community hall.

Robyn arrived around seven in the evening. She wasn't late. They were early, eager to set up their bee night for an evening of quilting and gossip.

Unfortunately, Robyn heard her own name and Brad's being chatted about. A couple of the members had seen them up at the cove. The gossip was slanted towards Robyn and Brad having fun — and a romance brewing.

The gossip stopped when they saw Robyn had arrived.

'Come and join us,' Jessica beckoned to Robyn, welcoming her into the hub of the bee.

The members, around twenty ladies, sat at two long tables where everything from fabric scraps, patterns, rotary cutters and cutting mats were shared. A few of the members had brought their sewing machines along and these were shared too. Robyn had recently bought herself a sewing machine, but she'd left it at home.

The ladies smiled tightly, knowing they'd been caught talking about Robyn and Brad. But she didn't mind, and spoke up to clear the air of any tension.

'I encouraged Brad to take some time out from the studio to enjoy the sunshine at the cove,' Robyn said to them. 'But there's no romance brewing. It's just business, while I'm helping him with his marketing.'

She almost let slip about writing the lyrics, but it still didn't feel like this was something she wanted to share when the whole situation was unsettled. Buttoning her lips, she unpacked her craft bag with the quilt she'd been working on. But she'd been so busy recently that she'd made little progress with it.

'We're such gossips when it comes to love,' said Nancy. 'Snow Bells Haven has a reputation for creating love and romance.'

With the air cleared, the atmosphere swept Robyn into quilting mode, and Jessica showed her the progress they'd made on Brad's quilt.

Robyn looked impressed. 'It's gorgeous.'

'Would you like to help sew the binding on?' said Jessica.

Robyn put her quilt aside. 'Yes, though don't let me sew any tricky bits. I don't want to spoil it. I've never sewn binding on before.'

'It's an easy slip stitch,' Jessica explained and then demonstrated what was required. 'I've used my sewing machine to attach the binding to the front of the quilt. We'll finish it by folding it over to the back of the quilt and hand–stitching it down.'

'I notice you're using a light neutral thread,' said Robyn.

'This shade blends with most fabrics,' Jessica explained. 'And the stitches are so small and mainly hidden.'

Robyn tried her hand at sewing a few stitches and was quite pleased with how neat it looked.

'The corners are the tricky bits,' Jessica told her. 'But I've already sewn the first corner and I'll show you what to do when you come to the second corner.'

'But you only need to sew so much,' Nancy told Robyn. 'We're all helping to sew the quilt.'

'Okay,' said Robyn, feeling the pressure ease as she didn't think she could tackle the whole quilt binding by herself.

While various quilts and quilted items were being made by the members, along with other sewing and crafts, the chatter continued and eventually came full circle back to the topic of Robyn and Brad...and romance.

'The thing is,' Robyn said to Jessica and Nancy, 'I've never been the starry–eyed type. When I first met Brad, I had no idea who he was. Unlike most people in town. I saw the reaction to him at the dance. But I met him from a different perspective.'

'You had no idea that he was a well–known singer?' Jessica sounded surprised.

'None at all. Then I found out he was the guy opening up the music recording studio. But I'd never seen him perform. I had to check out his concerts online. And look at his New York website to see what all the fuss was about.'

Nancy smiled. 'He's handsome as well as talented. I suppose you noticed that.'

'I did,' said Robyn. 'Brad is a heartbreaker. And that's part of the problem. I've worked hard to build my business, and I don't want to have my heart broken and my life turned inside out. Besides, I don't know if he's interested in me.'

'From what we saw of the two of you at the dance, and the gossip about you at the cove, he seems very taken with you,' Nancy told her.

Robyn felt a blush start to form across her cheeks. 'I don't think our lives fit easily together. I mean, I don't want a sort of summer romance and then have it fade when he has to go off on tour to promote his new album.'

'If you want my advice,' said Jessica, 'keep your options open and see where your friendship takes you.'

Robyn wasn't sure. There was the issue of writing the lyrics. That complicated everything.

Smiling, Robyn continued sewing and stopped when she came to the second corner.

Jessica showed her how to stitch the binding on so that the corner was neat. Robyn was glad that chatting about quilting techniques replaced the topic of romance.

Other members were talking about the market fair, and Robyn joined in, happy to find out more details about the event.

'Nate is delighted that Brad is going to sing at the fair,' said Nancy. 'Word is getting around, and people are looking forward to seeing him perform live.'

'Do you know what songs he's going to sing?' Jessica said to Robyn.

'I'm not sure,' Robyn lied. Brad wasn't revealing that he planned to perform two new songs to promote the album, so she couldn't tell them.

'Whatever he sings, everyone will enjoy hearing him,' said Nancy.

Robyn smiled tightly, and continued sewing.

Coffee, tea and cakes were served halfway through the evening, and members helped themselves. Members usually brought along home baked cakes and cookies to share at the quilting bee nights. Robyn contributed a box of chocolate chip cupcakes she'd bought from Greg's cafe. She helped herself to a strawberry cupcake that one of the ladies had baked.

Enjoying the bee night, Robyn managed to sew quite a bit of the binding on before someone else took a turn to finish it. Then she worked on her own quilt, making more progress and picking up tips from the other members.

As the evening finished, everyone packed up their things. Robyn folded her quilt, tucked it in her craft bag and walked outside while chatting to Nancy.

'If there is anything that Brad wants to know about the market fair, Nate will be happy to help him,' Nancy told Robyn.

'I'll tell Brad.'

'But Brad is used to performing on stage in front of an audience, so I'm sure he'll know what to do,' said Nancy.

Robyn agreed.

'A few of the quilting bee members are selling quilts, craft items, and things like that at the fair,' Nancy explained.

'I'm looking forward to buying items for my house, like quilted cushions and a throw for the sofa. And I know I won't be able to resist the home baking stalls.'

'It's a great day out,' Nancy assured her. 'Nate is always busy arranging things, and I try to help too. But I love wandering round the stalls and just having fun. We close the grocery store after lunchtime until late afternoon so that we can enjoy the day. A lot of the stores do the same or hire extra staff to cover for them while they're at the fair.'

'I'll be taking the day off to enjoy it,' said Robyn.

'Are you coming along to the wedding dance tomorrow night at the lodge?'

Robyn jolted. 'Yes.' She'd almost forgotten about it. But she did have a dress in mind. One from her party days in New York. Fashionable, pink, but nothing that looked like she was trying to outshine the bride or anyone else.

Nancy's expression showed a hint of mischief. 'You could invite Brad as your plus one.'

Robyn laughed and shook her head.

Waving goodnight to Nancy and the others, Robyn got into her car and drove along the main street. The lights were on in Brad's music studio, a soft glow, indicating that he was through the back still working.

She fought the urge to disturb him and continued to drive home.

Unpacking her craft bag, she tucked her quilt away in her fabric stash cupboard, then went upstairs and got ready for bed.

Sitting up in bed with her laptop, she checked out Snow Bells Haven's website. It listed all the town's events.

Snow Bells market fair was at the top of the list.

Pictures from previous years showed that the fair looked popular.

Robyn studied the photos from the last two years and noticed one or two faces she knew, including Nate and Nancy, Greg, Penny, and the people missing such as Mark and Kyle.

The stallholders had all put on a great display of their products, especially the craft stalls. There was a quilt stall from the previous year where Jessica had pinned up her quilts and piled up bundles of fabric too.

The knitting shop's stall offered a wonderful selection of yarn, plus knitted items.

And she saw various stalls serving everything from hot snacks to ice cream and refreshments.

The cake stalls were impressive with plenty of home baked cakes and cookies, and she knew she'd be tempted to buy cakes from them at the forthcoming fair.

The town's previous mayor was pictured up on the stage addressing the crowd, a duty that now fell to Mark.

The stage was larger than the one at the community hall, so Brad would have ample space to play for the audience.

Robyn sent a message to Brad.

Check out Snow Bells Haven's website. It has news about the market fair. Here's the link. Lots of pictures show previous years. The stage looks great. This could work well for you. I'd be happy to film your performance so you can add it to the New York website to help promote your new songs.

Closing her laptop, she settled down to sleep. Warm night air drifted in the open window along with the scent of flowers and greenery. Brad's house was in total darkness. No lights on whatsoever. She surmised he'd still be at the recording studio.

She was gradually learning how he worked, his process, playing his guitar to find the melodies, blending that with the lyrics, and then recording different layers of the track. He'd play the guitar version. Then he'd add the keyboards and drums. He played the sax too, and although she'd never heard him play, she imagined it would be incredibly soulful. The layers of recordings were then merged together into a single track that sounded as if it had been played simultaneously.

He'd explained that even when his session musicians backed him, he still added elements until the song sounded right to him. But apparently he really enjoyed playing with them because they inspired each other to raise their games. And he said there was an extra energy when they all played live together in the studio. She pictured that, with Brad playing lead guitar and singing.

Wondering what new songs he'd created using her lyrics, she fell asleep in the silent night thinking about music.

CHAPTER ELEVEN

Just because I loved someone else
Before I fell in love with you
It doesn't make you my second choice
It makes you the right choice
I love you deep and true

Brad breathed in the late night air, emerging after a long working day that blended into an equally long evening at the music studio.

He locked the door, securing another night of songs and lyrics to the past.

Lamplights cast a glow along the quietude of the main street. In the depths of the night the only light that shone was from Greg's cafe opposite the studio.

Putting the acoustic guitar, that tended to accompany him everywhere, in the back seat of the car, Brad took a moment to look over at Greg, lit up in the window of the cafe. The busy figure moved around baking cakes, even at this late hour, with an energy and urgency that Brad often noticed in himself whenever he had a melody in his mind that he wanted to capture before it faded.

If he'd been more skilled at baking, he'd have gone over there and helped the guy. But Greg looked like he didn't need anyone's help or well–intentioned hindrance.

He figured Greg was baking cakes ready for the following day. Customers turned up early, often making it their daily breakfast stop.

Maybe tomorrow he'd have pancakes with maple syrup there himself, like he kept meaning to do.

Steeped in his own busy bubble, Greg never noticed Brad watching him and then getting into his car and driving away.

Brad arrived home happily weary. This hit two right notes. He was happy with the song recording work he'd achieved that day. And he was so tired he'd fall asleep as soon as his head hit the pillow. Win, win.

Glancing over at Robyn's house, he felt a pang of longing. No lights were on. She'd be asleep. He'd received her message, about checking the market fair on the town's website, just before he locked up the studio, and replied. She'd see his response in the morning.

Taking his guitar with him inside the house, he didn't turn the lights on, and instead let the moonlight glow that poured through the windows illuminate the way upstairs to bed.

He didn't remember falling asleep. But he remembered dreaming about Robyn.

The next morning, he noticed Robyn's car was gone, indicating that she'd already left to get on with her working day. His started later, having slept in to catch up on some rest.

It was around eleven in the morning as he drove down the main street, listening to his latest demo recording. As he approached the studio, he wondered why there were pretty banners blowing in the warm breeze, draped across a few of the street lamps. They weren't there the previous night, so someone had been up early to hang them up.

Parking outside the studio, he squinted against the bright sunlight. Was that Kyle running full pelt down the street from the direction of the lodge towards Greg's cafe? Yep, that was Kyle alright. He wore his chef whites, and was running so fast that he had to hold his hat on to prevent it blowing off in his rush to reach the cafe.

Greg's station wagon was parked outside the cafe with the trunk open. Dwayne and Herb, wearing their usual cafe attire, were trying to strong–arm Greg away from the car. Greg wore a smart dark suit, white shirt and tie, looking dapper. A buttonhole, a rose, was pinned on his lapel, like he was dressed to attend a wedding.

Fascinated by the fiasco unfolding across the street, Brad watched as Kyle skidded to a halt and attempted to take charge of the situation.

Hustling Greg inside the cafe, Kyle disappeared after them and emerged moments later balancing a tray piled with white cake boxes. Brad held his breath, thinking that the whole pile was going to tumble like a stack of cards.

Greg appeared for a second at the open door of the cafe, and was then pulled back inside by Dwayne, while the distraught face of Herb peered out the window at Kyle's balancing act.

Leaving his guitar in the car, Brad walked over to the chaos, offering to help.

'Grab the large boxes of cupcakes and stack them in the back of the car first,' Kyle instructed Brad. No hesitation whatsoever in accepting the helping hand.

Without knowing the perimeters of the ring of trouble he'd stepped into, Brad went into the cafe, picked up as many boxes of cupcakes as he could handle safely without dropping any, and loaded them into the back of the car.

Passing each other going in and out of the cafe to the car, Kyle managed to explain the situation.

'It's Zack and Sylvie's wedding day. Greg offered to bake the cupcakes for the reception at the lodge. I'm catering for the entire event, but Greg's cupcakes were ordered specially, along with other sweet treats.'

Brad glanced at the banners fluttering. They made sense now. Wedding banners to celebrate Zack and Sylvie's special day.

'For a small wedding, there's been a ton of trouble,' Kyle said, now carrying the bottom tier of a beautiful white iced wedding cake on a silver tray.

'Let me help you with that,' Brad offered.

Together they carefully loaded the two tiers of wedding cake into the back of the car.

Kyle closed the trunk. 'Phew! Now all we need is to unload it at the lodge. Jump in the passenger seat. I'll drive.'

Having offered to help, Brad jumped in while Kyle drove the short distance to the lodge with the car loaded with cakes.

'Why were Greg's guys stopping him helping with the loading?' Brad said to Kyle.

'Greg is Zack's best man. They were worried he'd mess up his nice suit.'

Brad noticed he had sugar dust and sprinkles on his dark denim shirt and black jeans. 'Smart move.'

Kyle parked outside the front entrance of the lodge that was festooned with flowers, ribbons and wedding regalia. The lodge was dressed for the wedding, unlike the two men in a rush to get out of the car.

Jumping out, Kyle ran round to the rear of the car, opened the trunk and tugged his hat on tight.

'Okay, let's lift the wedding cake in first. Remember, we cannot drop it,' Kyle warned Brad.

'Do you want me to carry the bottom tier while you carry the top one?' Brad offered.

'Yes, that would work.' Kyle lifted the top tier. 'Steady as we go.' He led the way, hurrying up while trying to take his time.

Brad surmised there was chaos in the kitchen. The catering for the wedding had gone awry somehow. But this wasn't the time to ask for the details of what had gone wrong. Lifting the bottom tier of the cake, that felt like a solid ton of fruit cake decorated with white icing and fancy fondant flowers, he concentrated on not tripping and followed Kyle inside.

The wedding decorations inside the lodge made the exterior look underdressed in comparison. Bouquets of flowers and garlands trailing with white ribbons filled the air with their floral fragrance. A bridal banner emblazoned with Sylvie and Zack's names arched over the doorway of the restaurant and function room.

Kyle led the way through to the function room. A table at the side of the dance floor was ready for the wedding cake to be set on the white linen table cover.

'Put your tier down first,' Kyle instructed him. 'There are no pillars, so they just stack on top of each other.'

Brad carefully put the bottom tier of the cake down on the table and straightened it.

Kyle placed the top tier on, stepped back and took a deep breath.

'We did it,' Kyle announced, and then scattered silver heart confetti around the edges of the table cover.

'Very nice,' said Brad.

'Greg's wedding cakes are wonderful. Look at his fondant roses and ornate sugar craft. I wish I could bake half as well as him. I'm not as skilled in patisserie work. But I'm planning to be.'

'Will we bring the cupcakes in?' Brad started to head out.

'Yes, we'll take them through to the kitchen.'

Unloading the boxes of cupcakes, they carried them into the kitchen and placed them down out of the way of the main dishes being prepared by a handful of catering staff buzzing around.

'Thanks for mucking in, Brad.'

'Sure. I'm glad I could help.' Brad glanced around the kitchen. Everything looked clean, well–designed, and clearly Kyle was a capable chef. Baking specialist cakes, like a wedding cake, just wasn't his top skill yet.

Before taking charge of the cooking for the wedding meal again, Kyle handed Brad the car keys, expecting him to drive Greg's car back down to the cafe.

Brad accepted the keys, headed out of the kitchen, and waved to Penny at the reception desk on his way out.

Penny had been through in the office dealing with the wedding guests' bookings, and had missed the calamity.

'Hi, Brad. Are you coming to the wedding dance tonight?' she said lightly. She wore a pastel silk dress, suitable to attend the wedding, and a rose was pinned near her neckline and pearls.

He paused. 'No, I'm not on the guest list. Zack helped design my studio, but I'm not a close friend.'

'I thought you'd be Robyn's plus one. She's been invited to the dance later on. All the quilting bee members were invited,' Penny told Brad.

'Eh, no, Robyn didn't mention this. But I hope the wedding event goes as planned.' He smiled, waved and headed out to the car.

Grinning to himself at the quirky start to his day, he drove Greg's car back and parked it outside the cafe.

He went in and handed the keys to Dwayne.

'Thanks,' said Dwayne, and pocketed the keys. He planned to drive Greg up to the lodge soon. No way was Greg wrinkling his nice suit driving the car.

Herb was telling Greg not to be nervous about messing up his best man duties. And going over his best man's speech with him for the umpteenth time.

There was something about standing up in front of people to give a speech that sent Greg into a tizzy. He would've preferred to hide behind his cakes and let someone else take the verbal limelight. But Zack had wanted him to be his best man. He couldn't let him down.

'Don't fiddle with your tie when you're giving your speech,' Herb advised Greg. 'And try to smile, like you're calm and confident.'

'I'm not,' Greg confessed.

'Fake it, while we bake it, that's our motto,' Herb reminded him. On days when the cafe was busier than a bee hive in summer, the three of them kept their game faces on for the customers.

Greg took a deep breath and forced a fake grin. Then he noticed Brad leaving and called after him with a genuine smile. 'Thanks for your help, Brad.'

'No problem.' Brad waved and left them to it. Although customers were in the cafe having breakfast, and those pancakes smelled really tasty, he decided to leave and not add to their burden. He'd come back another day when things were less hectic.

Walking over to the studio, he gazed up at the wedding banners. Would he ever have a day like this in Snow Bells Haven? A day when his name and the name of the woman for him would be written in silver on the banners and hung up for the town to celebrate.

Grabbing his guitar from his car, he went into the quiet seclusion of the studio and locked the door, shuttering himself into his own world while a wedding was due to shine in the summer sunlight.

It was around lunchtime when Brad noticed he'd run out of milk for his coffee and went across to the grocery store.

Two of the quilting bee ladies were manning the store so Nate and Nancy could attend the wedding ceremony. He'd met them at the group photo taken at the community hall dance, and they smiled as they served him. They put his milk, a pack of salad sandwiches and a shiny red apple in a bag as he paid for his groceries.

Stepping out into the midday sun, he was aware of two tall figures approaching him.

'Hey, Brad,' the sheriff called to him as he walked closer, accompanied by a young man, lean and fit, with dark blond hair. 'This is my new deputy, Wyn.' The introduction was warm, as if the sheriff was pleased to introduce them.

Another acquaintance made for Brad. He stepped forward and shook hands. 'Pleased to meet you.'

'Likewise,' said Wyn. His cool, green eyes glanced across at the music studio. 'Those are two fine guitars you got there in your window.'

Brad noted the interest. 'You play guitar?'

'Used to, a while back, when I was young,' Wyn replied.

The sheriff guffawed. 'Listen to him, talking like he's an old man. I'm in my forties. I'm not old, and he's just turned thirty.'

The three of them smiled.

'I thought about having a career like yours,' Wyn explained to Brad.

'What happened?'

'I figured that you've got to have two main things to make it in your industry,' said Wyn. 'First, real talent. You need to be a ten or a ten plus. I was seven on a good day. Six most times. You, of course, are off the chart.'

Brad smiled at the compliment.

'I don't even figure on the lowest bar,' the sheriff added. 'Unless a minus three has merit.'

They laughed, and the cheery conversation circled round to romance.

'I never believed in love at first sight,' said the sheriff. 'But when I first set eyes on Jessica, that was it for me. I was smitten.'

'I've heard that Snow Bells Haven is a town where romance thrives,' said Brad.

'It sure does,' the sheriff agreed. 'But I first met Jessica when I worked as a security guy in New York.'

Brad looked surprised. 'You're from New York?'

'I am. Then Jessica walked into my life. She attended a quilt fair in New York where I was working security. We started dating, and I upped sticks and moved to Snow Bells. Never figured I'd become the town's sheriff, but I've found the place where I belong with the woman for me.'

'I'm from another town,' Wyn told Brad. 'I moved here for the deputy's job. I've got myself one of the cabins up at the cove.'

'It's nice up there, right by the sea, but near enough the main street,' said Brad.

Wyn nodded and then revealed the second reason he didn't aim for a music career. 'You have to want to travel around a lot and perform, be away for weeks on the road. You need to want that more than anything. And I don't. I want a steady life, to find a woman to love, settle down with and raise a family. If I achieve any of that, I'll consider myself a lucky man.'

'Well, you came to the right town to find romance,' the sheriff said to Wyn, glancing up at the wedding banners fluttering in the sunny breeze.

As the pleasant conversation came to an end, the sheriff and the deputy walked away, and Brad went to cross the street towards his studio.

'See you tonight at the wedding dance,' the sheriff called over his shoulder to Brad.

Brad's quizzical expression made the sheriff clarify the remark.

'Jessica said you're going as Robyn's plus one.' The sheriff waved and continued on his way with the deputy.

Brad walked over to his studio, wondering if the deck was stacked, and a dance date with Robyn was already on the cards.

The farmer's horse had taken a shine to Robyn, probably because he'd showed her how to feed it. The tour of the farm had taken twice as long as the meeting for marketing their produce. She'd started in the morning with a chat, sitting out on the porch with the farmer and his wife. It was a family–run homestead, and recently their homemade products, including their maple syrup, had seen an increase in sales since Robyn tweaked a few things around on their website remotely. Now, they wanted her to design a new logo for one of their product labels and had insisted she come out to the farm, on the outskirts of the town, to take a look around.

She'd never been near a horse, let alone fed one. Watching them in movies and seeing pictures was the closest she'd ever been. Standing beside the friendly, chestnut horse, one of three horses they owned, she felt tiny in comparison.

'Would you like to go for a ride around the farmland?' The farmer offered her.

'On the horse?' She needed to clarify the mode of transport. She'd never ridden a horse before.

He laughed. 'We can take the truck if you prefer.'

She did.

Patting the soft coat of the horse, she then walked away from the stables, and got into the truck for the extended tour.

The wheels trundled over the rough terrain, and she hoped it disguised the rumblings from her stomach. She should've eaten breakfast before dashing out early in the morning. And taken the farm folks up on having something to eat along with the coffee she'd accepted. Not imagining the meeting would stretch out into a full excursion, she was now functioning on the fumes of the coffee and nothing else.

A late lunch in town was on the horizon, she reminded herself, admiring the beauty of the farmland that took priority right now.

Robyn finally left with a basket of fresh farm produce, a notebook full of ideas for their logo design, and a feeling that she'd enjoyed another new experience.

Driving back into town, she rewound Brad's reply to her message.

I'll check out the link for the market fair. And I need to talk to you about something.

About what? Lyrics? The market fair? What was so secret?

With these thoughts running through her mind, she pulled the car over at his music studio instead of Greg's cafe where she'd intended treating herself to anything remotely delicious. And everything was delicious in his cafe.

The lights were on in Brad's studio. She knocked on the door and waited.

'I'm not in,' a deep voice piped up behind her. He'd been to the post office.

Jumping, she looked round at Brad standing there grinning at her.

'Don't do that!' she scolded him playfully.

He threw her one of those smiles that melted her heart.

'I got your message,' she said. 'What do you want to talk to me about?'

He dug out his keys and went to unlock the studio door. 'Let's talk inside.'

Robyn didn't budge. 'On one condition.'

'What's that?'

'Food. I need something to eat.'

'That type of day, huh?'

'Oh, yeah.'

'Okay, how about I treat you to something sweet in the ice cream parlor?' He reckoned the chaos in Greg's cafe was unlikely to have completely subsided.

Robyn's reaction wasn't what he expected. 'I was thinking more like a late lunch in the cafe.'

'That could be tricky today.'

She frowned.

'I'll explain later. So how about I buy groceries and make us something to eat? A tasty snack. Nothing too heavy. You don't want to feel too full when you've a night of dancing on the cards. With me.'

Robyn blinked. 'With you?'

'Apparently, people think I'm going as your plus one.'

'Do they now?'

'Yep. So we can't disappoint them.'

'Certainly not.' She tried not to giggle. 'Okay, let's do the grocery run together. Then you can tell me all your secrets.'

'Only if you help with the cooking.'

'You've got a deal.'

'I hope that's not the first time you say those words to me today,' he said, teasing her.

'You're up to something. Fair warning,' she said, teasing him back. 'I play to win when it comes to mind games.'

Brad grabbed her hand and ran with her across to the grocery store. 'Game on.'

Robyn indicated the farm produce in her basket. 'I've got eggs, pickles, sweet potatoes and...some surprise items that look tasty. But we need fresh bread.' She put a loaf on the counter.

'And butter and cheese.' Brad added those to their selection.

'Milk.' She selected that.

He'd bought milk, but planning to make them an omelette, and copious amounts of coffee, extra milk was handy.

'Herbs?' he said.

Robyn tapped her basket. 'Got those covered.'

'I think we're good to go.'

She nodded.

Brad paid for the groceries and then they went over to the studio and through to the makeshift kitchen where she was surprised to find it kitted out with more utensils than she'd expected.

'Are you moving in here? It's like a home from home,' she remarked.

'Sometimes it feels like I live here more than in the house. But I'm planning on changing that ratio.'

'To live here full–time?' she quipped.

'That's the type of remark that won't get you invited here again.'

Robyn pretended to zip her lips and throw the key away.

Whipping up the ingredients for their omelette, he then chopped the red and yellow peppers from her farm treasure, while she prepared a crisp, green salad.

It was a little kitchen without windows, but she enjoyed the comfort of feeling like the whole wide world couldn't get to them. No interruptions, unless they invited them in, which they'd no intention of doing until after they'd had lunch and discussed whatever topics needed aired.

Moving around each other, Robyn thought they'd look like a well–matched couple, used to each other, if an outsider was able to peer in. There was a comfort in being there with Brad, especially after what felt like a full day's work at the farm. And she had a wedding dance date with Brad. Another few ticks on her dance card, she thought to herself, wondering if she'd waltz more with Brad than anyone else. Or would she encourage him to mingle like before? Truth be told, she was inclined to keep him all to herself. That was a dangerous thought, even though it secretly thrilled her.

Brad thought they moved in–sync with each other as they cooked the food. Like a well–orchestrated piece of music, with him as the strong base and Robyn as the high notes. They complemented each other perfectly. He wanted to tell her how much he was looking forward to them going dancing. And he hoped that by bringing up the subject of her doing marketing work for the New York studio it wouldn't dispel the feeling that they were becoming more in tune with each other every time they were together.

'What was the highlight of your morning?' he said, breaking into both their wayward musings.

'Making friends with a horse.'

Brad laughed. 'You win. I can't top that one.'

She explained about her meeting at the farm and the marketing work she was doing for them.

'Well, I'm sure you'll help boost the farm's sales.'

'What was the highlight of your morning?' she wanted to know, even if he couldn't get any further than second place.

Brad looked thoughtful. 'It's a close run thing between the conversation I had with the sheriff and his new deputy. And helping Kyle deliver Zack and

Sylvie's wedding cake to the lodge, while Dwayne and Herb held Greg in check.'

'I'm not so sure my horse acquaintance is the winning hand now.'

While they finished preparing the food, made the coffee and settled down to their meal, he unrolled the details of the events, causing Robyn to laugh so much she couldn't tuck into her food as fast as her hunger pangs intended.

CHAPTER TWELVE

Celebrate a wedding on a summer's day
Hearts and smiles and flowers
I waltzed with you at the wedding dance
Wishing it was ours

'What did you want to talk to me about?' Robyn said to Brad, after they'd finished their meal in the studio kitchen. They sat there at the small table, relaxing and drinking their coffee.

Brad took a sip of coffee. 'About marketing the New York studio. My manager likes your marketing ideas for the studio here. We'd like you to help promote the New York studio too.'

Robyn frowned. 'I'm happy to do the marketing for the Snow Bells studio. But the New York studio?' She shook her head. 'That's a whole other game.'

'Think about it. Your ideas are fresh, they're a clear perspective on my music and the studio. You wouldn't need to be in New York, just able to offer promotional ideas.'

Robyn considered this. 'So I'd make suggestions on advertising and promotions from here in town?'

'Yes. Surely you've got ideas from looking at the New York website. You seem to have a talent for giving suggestions for news updates, how to present the studio.'

She had, but she'd kept most of her comments to herself. Their website was lacking solid information on Brad's forthcoming album. But that was none of her business, and she knew she had a habit of poking her nose into things and interfering.

'Tell me,' he said, reading her well.

'I don't get why you're not promoting your new album. There's nothing on the New York studio website to catch fans' attention. The only thing is the link to the new studio opening here. That mentions you're working on songs for the forthcoming album. But again, there's nothing to excite people's interest about the actual songs.'

'Is that why you suggested we put a recording of the live performance at the market fair on the New York website?'

'Yes.'

'We're going to take your advice and do that.'

'You should. And as I'm being allowed to meddle, you should arrange for your session musicians to be at that performance.'

Brad admired her forthright attitude. 'Okay, I'll check the date of the fair, call the guys, and then tell Penny to book their accommodation at the lodge.' He took another sip of his coffee, relaxed back in his chair and smiled at her.

Robyn gave him a steely–eyed look.

'What? Have I said something wrong?'

'No, but you should do it now.'

'Right now?'

'Yes. Check the website link I gave you.'

He checked it on his phone. 'Here we are. So if the guys were here two days before the event, and extended their stay for another day...' Brad continued to figure out the dates and then called them. All three were happy to accept the invitation to come to Snow Bells.

'Now phone Penny and make the booking at the lodge,' said Robyn.

'Won't she be busy with the wedding?'

'Maybe, but if she is, you can leave a message. The sooner you secure the accommodation the better.'

Brad agreed and phoned the lodge. Penny took the call.

'I hope I'm not interrupting you at the wedding,' said Brad.

'No, not at all, Brad. It was a lovely ceremony out in the garden under the floral arch, and now guests are sitting down to their meal in Kyle's restaurant. I'm not having the meal, but I'll be at the dancing later on.'

'I'll be there at the dance tonight too, with Robyn.'

Robyn shot him a smile.

'Oh, great. I'll see you both then,' said Penny.

'I'm phoning about making a booking for the musicians.' He told her the dates he needed.

Penny checked the availability. 'I have three lovely rooms in the lodge that I think your friends will find very comfortable.'

Having made the booking, Penny chatted to him some more, giving him details about the wedding and how the cake cutting was a success.

'I'm glad everything is going well,' Brad said to Penny. 'Robyn and I will see you tonight. And thanks again for making the booking.'

'See you later,' said Penny.

After the call, Brad smiled at Robyn. 'We've got the ball rolling now. Thanks for pushing me to do it.'

'Now we just have to get ready for the wedding dance.' She stood up and picked up her bag, along with the basket of what was left of the goods from the farm.

Brad walked her out. 'What time should I pick you up for the dance?'

'Seven.'

'Okay.'

As she walked to her car she cast a comment back to him. 'Remember to wear your dancing shoes.'

Brad laughed as he watched her drive off.

Heading back inside, there was a new urgency to push on with the song writing to have everything ready for the guys arriving.

Taking Robyn's forthright attitude to heart, he set up the studio to record a demo for them to hear the songs he'd been working on. They'd record complete versions in the studio after rehearsing the material. Years of working with him at the studio in New York, and on his tours, had given them plenty of experience of backing him.

He'd messaged his manager with the news of what was happening. His manager called him.

'I got your message, Brad. The guys are getting ready to head to Snow Bells. How are the new songs coming along?'

'I'm happy with the new material. Still working on it, but it feels exciting. I'll send you more rough demos later today. Oh, and...I spoke to Robyn about her doing the marketing for New York. She was hesitant at first, but I think she's going to take it on. She suggested some things she thinks need work — like promoting the new songs on the website. She thinks we're missing out on letting people know what we're up to.'

'I'm inclined to agree with her. So let's see what she comes up with and we'll talk about it.'

'I'm seeing her tonight. I'm her plus one for a wedding dance at the lodge. But it'll be a chance to talk to her. I'm betting that mind of hers will be full of ideas of what we could do to promote the new songs.'

'A wedding dance? Sounds romantic.' There was a teasing tone to his reply.

'It's nothing like that,' Brad said, feeling like he was lying somewhat to himself.

'You don't sound too sure about that.'

'We're keeping things on a friendly, business arrangement. For now,' Brad told him.

'The *for now* has potential. That's a good thing.'

'I'm complicating her working life already. First the Snow Bells studio marketing, then writing lyrics, now including the New York studio in with the marketing work. It's a lot.'

'Robyn sounds the whip–smart type who can handle it.'

'She is, but romance...that's something for further along the line, if at all.'

His manager laughed. 'Keep telling yourself that, Brad. Maybe you'll convince yourself, because you sure aren't selling it to me.'

Brad brushed off the comment. 'Okay, I'm going to keep working on the demos. I'll send them to you later.'

'Enjoy your dance night with Robyn.' He laughed as he hung up.

Taking a deep breath and trying not to smile, Brad settled down to play the keyboards and record a track to add to one of the songs. He'd played it with his guitar, and now he wanted to hear a richer version.

While he played, the words that Robyn wrote resonated in his heart. Were any of the lyrics about her feelings for him? Romance was the brief, the theme, but some of them felt personal. Or maybe her lyrics were supposed to cut deep, to make listeners feel part of them. Her words certainly made him think deeply about her.

As he played the keyboards, he went to shake off the feelings her words evoked and then decided to keep them and maybe transfer some of that extra emotion into the music.

After Robyn arrived home, there was time to spare before she had to get ready for the wedding dance.

Sitting in her office, she made a start on designing the new label for the farmers. She had a couple of ideas for their logo design and began creating these so that she could email the rough copies for them to have a look at.

Sitting alone in the studio, playing the melody and singing the songs, Brad became lost in the music, and almost lost for the time.

He flicked the lights off and dashed along the shadowed hallway that was lit by the fading sunlight streaming through the front window and street lamps blinking into life. The wedding banners barely fluttered in the calm, early evening air.

Locking the door, he put his trusty guitar in the car and glanced up the main street towards the lodge. Even from this distance, he could see the lights indicating that the wedding event was now in the party mood. And so was he.

Before getting into his car, he ran across to one of the shops to buy a little something special, then dashed back.

Jumping in the car, he drove home, showered and changed into a sharp suit, white shirt and tie.

Steeped in her ideas for the logo design, Robyn almost lost track of time. But she'd finished the roughs and emailed them to the farmers, before running upstairs to get dressed for the dance.

She put on the fashionable pink dress she'd had in mind to wear, refreshed her makeup, wore neutral tone heels, and went back downstairs.

Tonight definitely felt like a date, but she told herself it wasn't. If other people hadn't expected Brad to be her plus one, she would've been going to the dance on her own.

Seeing his car drive up, she stepped outside.

His hair was brushed back, but still damp from the shower. As he got out of the car and walked towards her, she noticed he had a corsage in his hands. A wrist corsage made from flowers and greenery. He'd bought it from the local florist shop.

Brad handed it to her. 'I thought you'd maybe like to wear this.'

Robyn put it on her wrist. 'It's lovely, thank you.'

He smiled, pleased that she was happy with his gesture. 'You look...' *Beautiful, you're breaking my heart.* 'Very nice, tonight.'

'Thank you.' She smiled casually, and hoped he didn't sense the effect he had on her. It was a warm night, but Brad ignited all sorts of emotions in her, and she felt herself blush. He looked heartbreakingly handsome.

They got into the car and drove to the lodge.

'I almost lost track of the time,' she confessed. 'I was working on the label design for the farmers.'

'So did I. The time flew in. I was laying down tracks in the studio.'

She glanced at the guitar on the back seat. 'Planning on being a wedding singer this evening?'

Brad laughed. 'No, not tonight. I forgot to leave my guitar in the house.'

Robyn tapped her stylish bag that matched her dress. 'I never go anywhere without a notepad and pen.'

'Force of habit?'

'Yes, but although I don't intend to work tonight, I can't promise not to meddle.'

'What's to meddle in at the wedding dance?' He was genuinely intrigued.

'It is first and foremost a wedding,' she said, making that clear. 'But Penny and Kyle are hoping to include pictures of Sylvie and Zack to help promote the lodge and the new restaurant. Everyone is happy to do this.'

'Where do you come in?'

'Experience. From my experience, none of them will have pictures that are suitable for promotional purposes. Yes, they'll have tons of pictures of the wedding. But to promote the lodge as a wedding venue, and Kyle's new restaurant... Well, they need to be specific. And people just don't always do that.'

Brad nodded. 'So you'll nudge them in the right direction.'

'I'll tactfully try. Plus, Sylvie and Virginia will want to promote the wedding dress on their websites. The fabric is one of Sylvie's designs. That's newsworthy for her website, and for the company she works for. Virginia made the dress. And as I'm helping Virginia to market her dress shop, this is a great opportunity to tie in the wedding dress. But I'm betting they won't have taken pictures of the dress being made, which would've been handy for both their websites. So I'll probably meddle to make sure they have close–up pictures of the wedding dress that will work for promoting their businesses.'

Brad laughed lightly. 'That sounds like a ton of meddling.'

'It sounds a lot more complicated trying to explain it. But it'll only take a few minutes to include the pictures they'll need for their promotions.'

They pulled up outside the lodge. It was busy, and there was a sense of excitement in the air as he escorted her inside.

Music and chatter from the function room pulled them into the hub of the dance night. Sylvie was wearing her beautiful wedding dress, and she was dancing with Zack. She wore her light, caramel brown hair up in a chignon, pinned with diamante clasps. Zack was tall, dark haired and handsome in his expensive suit. They were an attractive couple.

A few people paused and looked at Robyn and Brad arriving together.

Penny was the first to come over and welcome them.

'I'm glad you could make it,' said Penny. 'Everyone is having a wonderful time.'

'Sylvie's dress is beautiful,' Robyn said to her.

'It is,' Penny agreed. 'The wedding photographer they hired is still here to take pictures of the dancing, and video it too, so if you see him, that's what he's up to.'

'We're looking forward to the dancing,' Brad told Penny. 'The function room looks great tonight.'

'Thank you, Brad,' said Penny. 'And I emailed you confirmation of the bookings for your friends, along with information about the accommodation and meals. If they have any special requests, let me know.'

'I appreciate that, Penny.' He glanced around. 'I think they're going to be impressed with their stay at the lodge.'

'I'll make sure they're well–fed,' Kyle said approaching them. He'd changed out of his chef whites into a suit.

'My manager said it sounded more like a vacation than a working trip,' Brad mentioned lightly. 'He's talking about coming here too.'

'Your manager would be more than welcome,' said Penny.

While they chatted, Robyn noticed that the wedding photographer was taking pictures of the bride and groom while they were on the busy dance floor. For a moment, she thought about not interfering, but then that wasn't her style. She spoke up to Penny and Kyle.

'You mentioned that Sylvie and Zack were happy for their wedding photographs to be featured on your website, to help promote the lodge as an excellent wedding venue,' Robyn said to them.

'Yes, that's right,' Penny confirmed.

'And it'll help to promote the new restaurant too,' Kyle added.

'Is something on your mind?' Penny said to Robyn.

'It's just that...are you sure that you have the right type of photos for the lodge's website?' said Robyn. 'And I imagine that Sylvie will want to promote her fabric designs. She'll surely want to have pictures showing her wedding dress that's made from her own fabric.'

'Sylvie did mention this to me during rehearsals for the wedding,' Penny recalled. 'I would think that she'll have plenty of photos to choose from.'

Robyn wasn't convinced. 'I probably shouldn't interfere, but...'

Penny and Kyle exchanged a glance. They knew how smart Robyn was when it came to marketing. Penny beckoned Sylvie to come over. Zack came with her.

'Robyn was wondering if you've got the right type of pictures of your wedding dress to promote your fabric designs,' Penny said to Sylvie.

Although Sylvie didn't know Robyn too well, she'd heard how effective she was at promoting businesses. 'What did you have in mind?'

'Images of you standing over there, near the twinkle lights,' Robyn explained. 'A clean shot, showing the function room, the atmosphere of the wedding reception, but without clutter and others obscuring the view of your entire dress. And close–ups of the fabric. I see that it has a white on white floral print. That needs close–up shots with the atmospheric background.'

Brad smiled to himself. Here we go, he thought. But he trusted that Robyn was right.

'The wedding photographs, by the hired photographer, will be excellent,' said Robyn. 'But for publicity shots, you need more focus on your dress fabric. And pictures of you and Zack with Penny and Kyle so that they can use those on their website.'

By now, Virginia had overheard them talking, and came over to join them.

'I'd suggest that you have separate photos taken to promote your dress fabric, the lodge function room, and Virginia as the dressmaker,' Robyn added. 'You all need different pictures suitable for each of your promotional needs.'

All of them started to plan what they needed to promote each different aspect. Robyn advised them, while Brad enjoyed the excitement.

'And what about you, Zack, standing in the restaurant,' Robyn said to him. 'You're the restaurant's architect. You'll want to promote that on your website too.'

Zack blinked. 'Yes, I would. I hadn't thought about it. I've been too busy with the wedding.'

Zack beckoned the wedding photographer over and explained that they needed specific photographs taken.

With Robyn moving everyone around like pieces on a chess board, more photos were taken. Robyn used her phone to take extra pictures, knowing exactly what she wanted, just in case they needed back–up shots.

The dancing wasn't disturbed. Guests were interested to see what was going on, and eager to take part when needed.

A few guests came over to meet Brad, and he was happy to chat to them while Robyn was busy.

'Robyn's a whirlwind, isn't she,' Mark said to Brad, wandering over to talk to him.

'Oh, yes,' Brad agreed.

'But in a good way,' Mark added.

'Everyone involved is going to be happy with what she's advising them to do,' said Brad.

It didn't take long for the whirlwind to be over, and the dancing continued.

Robyn came back to Brad. 'I couldn't help it. I've seen so many times during events where publicity pictures are supposed to be taken, but people end up with lots of photos and nothing they really need.'

Brad grinned at her.

'Say it.'

'I'm saying nothing.'

'Just say it,' she insisted.

'Okay, you meddle in things, but it works.'

'I'm trying to meddle less.'

'Don't do that. It's part of what I love about you.'

A blush started to form across her cheeks.

'What I meant is—'

'I know,' she assured him.

He held out his hand. 'Let's dance.'

'Okay. I can't meddle when I'm waltzing.'

Brad led her on to the dance floor and took her in his arms. 'I wouldn't bet on that.'

Robyn laughed.

As they danced, Brad started to hum a new melody that came to mind.

The music they were dancing to was a slow waltz, and he leaned close to Robyn, murmuring as they waltzed around.

'I like that. What song is it?' she said. It was obviously not the one they were dancing to.

'I don't know yet. I can just start to hear the melody...'

'Will you remember it?'

'I hope so.'

Robyn stopped dancing and pulled him away, leading him outside the lodge.

'Where are we going?' Brad said, laughing.

'Don't talk, just sing.' She pulled out her phone. 'I'm recording. Go for it.'

Brad hummed the tune that was in his mind, and in the warm night air, another part of the melody came to him, and he sang that too.

Robyn didn't say a word. She recorded the tune, until Brad stopped singing.

'That is such a beautiful melody,' she said.

Brad nodded. 'I'll work on that tomorrow.'

Robyn sent him a copy of the recording. 'There you go. So you don't forget a note of it.'

'Thanks. But now...'

'What?'

'You'll have to come up with the lyrics.'

'Ha! It never ends, does it,' she said, smiling.

He shrugged. 'What?'

'My meddling and your music.'

She breathed in the night air and gazed up at the stars. 'Maybe I should include a starry night sky in the lyrics.'

'Sounds romantic,' he said, admiring how lovely she looked in her pink dress with her blonde hair falling around her shoulders. Her face was so beautiful in profile as she gazed up at the stars, not knowing how much he wanted to wrap her in his arms and kiss her right there and then. And forget the consequences.

'There are few things more romantic than a wedding,' she said wistfully, still admiring the night sky. 'I'm glad their wedding went well. Sylvie's dress was gorgeous. I'd love a dress like that when I get married.' Then she tried to retract her words. 'Not that I'm planning on getting married or being a bride—'

'Don't you want that one day?' Brad cut-in.

'Well, yes, I do, but...' She threw her hand out in a faraway gesture. 'That's so far in the future that I'm not even thinking about romance.' This was part truth, part lie. Heavier on the lie. Romance and Brad crossed her mind more often than she liked to admit.

Brad started to hum the melody again, adding to it.

'Go grab your guitar from the car,' she told him, getting her phone ready to record again.

He hurried back and began to play the opening riff, the chords that came to mind, while she captured the melody that filtered out into the air.

They were alone at the front of the lodge, lit by the twinkle lights and wedding decorations.

As Brad played the melody on his guitar, Robyn murmured lyrics that came to mind.

You waltzed into my life one starry night
Promising romance, then you were gone
Leaving behind a feeling that warmed my heart
And warned my heart...

Robyn shrugged. 'I don't know where the lyrics would go from there.'

'Write them down on your notepad,' he urged her.

She dug it out of her bag and scribbled the words down.

'Hold the lyrics up so I can read them while I play,' he said. And then sang them as he played the melody.

'Oh, I think we've got an audience,' she said, noticing the faces peering out at them from the entrance of the lodge.

Brad stopped playing and put the guitar in his car, while she tucked her notepad in her bag.

They walked back inside, grinning, like they'd been caught.

Penny and Kyle were there, along with Nate and Nancy and a few others.

'We didn't mean to interrupt you,' said Nancy. 'But someone mentioned that Brad was singing outside.'

'It was lovely to hear you serenading Robyn,' Penny said to Brad, smiling at them.

'Brad wasn't serenading me,' Robyn clarified. 'He was working on a new song. The romantic atmosphere of the wedding inspired him.'

'But we're here to enjoy the dancing,' said Brad. Escorting Robyn through to the function room, they started waltzing around. Nate and Nancy, Greg and Lucie, Jessica and the sheriff, and others joined in.

For the remainder of the evening, Robyn refrained from further meddling and they enjoyed the wedding party, dancing late into the night.

At the end of the evening, Robyn and Brad went over to wish Sylvie and Zack well and thank them for inviting them to the dance.

'Are you going away on honeymoon?' Robyn said to them.

'No, we're taking time off work, but staying here in town,' said Sylvie.

'We thought about heading somewhere else, then we decided that there's nowhere we love more than being here, at home, in Snow Bells Haven,' Zack added.

'We're planning to relax at Zack's cabin up at the cove,' Sylvie explained. 'And have our dog, Cookie, with us.'

'That sounds perfect,' said Brad.

As others came over to say their goodnights to the newlyweds, Brad escorted Robyn out to the car and drove her home.

He walked her up to her front door.

'Be prepared for a secret delivery, a parcel, being left outside your house tomorrow morning,' Robyn told him.

'A secret delivery? What is it?'

She gave him a mischievous smile. 'It's a secret.' Smiling at him, she went inside.

Brad walked away, wondering what was in the secret parcel.

When he got home, he phoned her. 'Give me a hint.'

'I can't.'

'Come on, Robyn.'

'Okay. It's something to keep you warm at night in bed.'

The first thing he thought of was — her. But he kept that thought to himself.

'Is it the something that I'm not supposed to have and know nothing about?' he said.

'Remember to be surprised,' she insisted.

'I will,' he assured her. Before hanging up, he said, 'I had a great time tonight.'

'So did I.'

'Sleep tight.'

'You too, Brad.'

CHAPTER THIRTEEN

I've never been the starry–eyed type
Except when it comes to you
I feel you mesmerize me
And there's nothing I'd rather do

Robyn's working day started at Virginia's dress shop. Sunlight tried to stream through the front window where three dresses were displayed on mannequins, but was calmly shaded by the floral canopy.

Virginia had called to say that Sylvie had sent her copies of the promotional pictures taken the previous night at the wedding dance. Robyn arrived to help her select the pictures for her dress shop's website and write the captions to go with them.

Rails of dresses, from pretty and practical day dresses to cool summer shifts and party frocks, tempted Robyn to rummage through the rails and buy what she hadn't come in for.

Robyn resisted, and kept her focus on Virginia sitting at her sewing machine behind the shop counter working on her latest creation — a chiffon number in shades of sea blue that Robyn imagined would be wonderful for wafting around in on a hot summer night. That one still might be going home with her once it was finished.

The dresses were real bargains in comparison to the ones she used to buy in New York. Except for the thrifty vintage pieces she bought. Pre–loved dresses were a stylish way to spruce up and extend her wardrobe. And there was something special about wearing classics from the past, like the sky blue chambray dress she was wearing. Chic, cool, comfortable. It hit all the right notes.

Seeing Robyn arrive, Virginia stopped sewing.

Virginia wore a pretty dress, one of her own designs. Her silky chestnut hair framed her pale features, and her deep blue eyes matched the flowers in her dress.

'Sylvie was thoughtful enough to send me the pictures so that I can promote my dressmaking,' Virginia explained, showing Robyn the images on her laptop.

Virginia's shop sold a selection of dresses, a large percentage designed by Virginia and sewn herself. But she had a small team of local seamstresses and those skilled in embroidery and beadwork to help her. The online demand for her dresses had increased recently since Robyn had suggested a few alterations to the dress shop's website. And local sales had picked up too, especially the summer designs for daywear and evenings. She sold accessories too, including beaded purses to match the dresses. Rolls of fabric were kept in the stockroom through the back, and a changing room allowed customers to try the dresses on.

Virginia was around the same age as Robyn, and trying to make a real go of her business. Currently, she wasn't dating any of the local guys though she lived in hope. She had experience of making wedding dresses, but had only created a few since opening her shop, including Ana's wedding dress in the spring. Ana and her husband, Caleb, were a local couple, and now Ana worked as one of the shop's seamstresses.

But Virginia hadn't promoted Ana's gorgeous wedding dress. Designing Sylvie's dress was now the ideal opportunity to advertise the bridal fashion side of her business.

'This would be my lead photo,' Robyn advised, pointing to one that showed Sylvie's beautiful wedding dress. 'The classic design of the dress looks gorgeous. Then I'd add this close–up shot of the fabric showing the white on white floral print.'

Virginia nodded. 'The fabric was wonderful to work with.'

'Did you take any pictures of the pattern cutting, sewing the dress, how you made it?'

Virginia sighed heavily. 'No, I should've, but I was too busy making it.'

'Do you still have a copy of the paper pattern?'

'Yes, I keep all my patterns in these folders. Some of them are my grandmother's original patterns that I alter and update.' Virginia lifted one of the folders, flipped through it and stopped at the pattern she'd designed for Sylvie's wedding dress. 'This is it here.'

Robyn studied it. 'What about the fabric, do you have any pieces of it left over?'

'I do. I kept samples from the off–cuts.' Virginia opened one of the deep drawers where a neat stash of dress fabrics were kept. The white wedding dress fabric was near the top.

Robyn lifted a piece that was about the size of a pillowcase. Other smaller off–cuts were stashed too. 'We could set this up on your cutting table, along with the pattern. I could take a close–up photo of those, and then one with you in the picture.'

'Yes, I'll clear my cutting table and we'll do that.' Virginia sounded eager to do this.

Robyn helped to set it up and then took several pictures to highlight what they'd discussed. She showed Virginia the images.

'These are wonderful, Robyn. They'll look great on the website. From now on I'll make sure to take photos of the dressmaking in progress.'

'Your customers will love to see how you created the dress, from the initial sketches, to the paper pattern, making a toile from plain cotton before cutting the precious fabric, and then sewing it expertly.'

'You make it sound so enticing,' said Virginia.

'It is. I enjoy seeing the whole process of a beautiful dress being created. You should include the different types of dresses you make, from the pretty day dresses you sell to the evening gowns.'

'Is that vintage you're wearing?' Virginia admired the blue chambray dress.

'It is. I used to buy vintage dresses like this in New York. They're timeless pieces. I love the blue tones and the softness of the chambray.'

'I often admire the dresses you wear,' Virginia told her. 'You've got a great eye for style and what suits you.'

'I appreciate the compliment coming from a dressmaker like you.'

They continued to chat about business, and Robyn wrote the brief descriptions for the website photos, adding one of the pictures she'd taken the previous night.

'You and Brad seem to be getting along really well,' Virginia remarked.

'We work well together.'

'He was serenading you last night at the lodge.'

'No, I understand that's how it looked, but he was just playing a new song, working on the melody,' Robyn explained.

Virginia grinned.

'Really, Brad wasn't serenading me.'

'He seems very into you.'

Robyn tried not to blush. 'Brad is into his music.'

'Okay,' Virginia said, sounding like she didn't believe this.

'I'm putting romance on the back burner so that I can concentrate on building my marketing business.'

'I understand, but...' Virginia sighed. 'I love Brad's music. I read in the newspaper that he's working on a new album. I'll definitely buy that when it's released. Though I've no idea when his new songs will be available. I checked his website, but there were no details about this. Do you know anything?'

'Brad is working on new songs in the Snow Bells studio, and he's already recorded a few tracks for his next album.'

Virginia looked excited. 'I hear that he's going to be playing live on stage at the market fair.'

'He is.'

'I've hired a stall for the fair. I'll show a selection of my dresses. But I'll be there to hear Brad singing.'

A customer came in, interrupting their conversation, and Robyn left the shop to let Virginia get on with her work.

Robyn walked down the main street to her car when Brad phoned.

'I got the secret parcel.' He sounded pleased. 'It's a beautiful quilt, and there was a card signed by the members of the quilting bee. I want to thank them. If I write a card, should I give it to Nancy or Jessica? Or one of the other members?'

'Nancy. She'll make sure everyone sees it.'

'I'll send a little extra thank you when they have their next quilting bee night at the community hall. Cake, chocolates.'

'That will go down well at the quilting bee,' said Robyn.

'Where are you?'

'Main street. I was at Virginia's dress shop helping her update her website with pictures of Sylvie's wedding dress. Virginia is a fan of yours by the way. She's pleased that you're performing at the market fair. But she mentioned that she'd checked out your New York website for information about your new album, and came up empty.' She explained the details.

'Well, you said the website needed updated to promote the new songs, so I guess we'll have to do something about that soon. Are you busy today?'

'Mega busy. I'm heading to the lodge to chat to Penny and Kyle about promoting the lodge as a wedding venue now that they have photos of Sylvie and Zack's special day. Then I have to discuss the new label for the farmers, and a couple of other things.'

'A packed day. But what about tonight? Could we discuss ideas for the website this evening?'

'Okay. I'll call you when I've finished work for the day.'

'To then start work with me,' he said jokingly.

'No rest for the wicked. Or marketing consultants.'

'Or lyricists.'

Robyn laughed. 'Just pile on the pressure, Brad.'

'See you tonight.'

After the call, Sylvie walked along in the sunshine to the lodge to get on with her working day. She mulled over having to write lyrics, and as she thought about this, more lyrics came to mind. Taking her notepad out, she jotted them down, and then tucked it away as she headed into the lodge.

Penny stood behind the reception desk dealing with booking in guests, but nodded acknowledgement to Robyn.

Kyle darted by to the kitchen. 'Hi, Robyn. I'll be with you in a few minutes. Take a seat in the function room. It's quieter in there and we can talk.'

Noticing that the restaurant was busy, she headed through to the empty function room and sat down at one of the tables at the side of the dance floor where the bridal buffet had been set up.

Lyrics continued to spring to mind, so out came the notepad again. She was so intent on writing them down that she didn't notice Penny walking in.

'Sorry to have kept you waiting, but I see you're busy writing...' Penny tried to fathom what Robyn had been so steeped in.

Robyn closed the notepad and put it in her bag. 'Marketing notes.' Not a total lie. Just a slanted variation of the truth.

After spending time to advise Penny and Kyle on promoting the lodge as the ideal venue for weddings, and phoning the farmers to confirm they liked their label, Robyn walked back along the main street and picked up groceries, fresh vegetables and fruit, from Nate and Nancy's store.

Nancy was pleased to show her the card she'd received from Brad thanking the quilting bee members for the quilt they'd made for him.

'Brad handed this in,' said Nancy.

Robyn admired the card and the message he'd written thanking them for the beautiful quilt.

'He's really pleased with the gift,' Robyn remarked.

Nancy was beaming. 'I've told Jessica and a few others and I'll make sure to take the card along to the next quilting bee night so that everyone sees it.'

Taking her fresh groceries out to her car, Robyn went to head home, but then decided to drive up to the cove first. The sun was shining bright in the long afternoon, and she parked the car and walked along the coast, breathing in the sea air.

She sat down on the grass and looked out at the sea sparkling as the sunlight reflected off the surface. People were in swimming, enjoying picnics and making the most of the gorgeous day.

Taking her notepad out, she sat there writing lyrics, adding to the lines she'd written earlier, feeling the warmth of the sun and fresh sea air remind her of summers she'd never had, but imagined how wonderful they'd be, when she was in the hot, midsummer city. New York was lovely in the summer months, but sometimes she thought about driving off into the countryside and stopping in a small town for lunch.

Now, she didn't have to imagine it. She was right there. Days like this were meant to be lingered over rather than swept aside by work that could wait until sundown. But she was working on her lyrics.

As the afternoon mellowed into an amber glow, Robyn tucked her lyrics away, and drove home.

She noticed Brad's car was parked in his driveway. He was home from the studio.

Unpacking her groceries in the kitchen, she then walked over to Brad's house and knocked on the front door. When he didn't respond, she went to phone him, but then heard him singing. His voice carried through from the back yard, and so she headed round the side of the house, following the tune, listening to the words she'd written leading her to him.

And there he was, singing while tending to his garden, stripped to the waist, wearing only his low-slung jeans that clung to his lean hips and long legs. He was barefoot too, walking on the grass while pottering around the flowers.

'Oh! Sorry, I didn't expect you to be—' She cut short her comment about him being half naked. This was the second time she'd seen his toned physique, but the effect was far more potent now. He looked so...sexy handsome standing there with a grin on his face, unperturbed that she'd encroached on his privacy.

She started to walk away quickly.

'Robyn, wait! It's okay. I was just planting a few flowers for that moon garden effect you mentioned.'

She paused, still not knowing where to look as she glanced round at him.

'Where do you think I should plant these white gardenia?' he said, showing her the plants he'd bought.

'You're more experienced at gardening than me, but I would think over there, near the iris would be ideal.' She heard the nervous excitement in her tone, and scolded herself. Calm down. Brad is cool about this. Don't let him see the effect his fit physique has on you. She smoothed her hands down her chambray dress.

Brad took her advice and lifted the gardenia over to the iris and started to plant them with expert ease.

'There's a jug of cold lemonade in the kitchen,' he said. 'Help yourself. It's a hot day. You look a little flushed. Maybe you've caught the sun today.'

Eager to run away, she hurried into the kitchen. And breathed.

Opening the refrigerator, she poured herself a tall glass of lemonade, and gulped down a mouthful before adding extra ice and meandering outside again.

'I was at the cove. I'd been indoors for most of the day with the marketing meetings, and then I gave in to temptation, to drive to the cove in the late afternoon.'

Wiping the soil from his hands, he strode towards her. 'You should always give in to temptation.'

Oh, if only he knew... She took another gulp of the ice cold lemonade, but it didn't help to cool the blush forming across her cheeks as he moved closer.

He gestured to her rosy cheeks. 'You've definitely caught a glow from the sunshine. It suits you.'

Grabbing his empty glass from the table in the garden, he smiled. 'I think I'll join you. I could do with a cold drink. It's been a hot day.'

And getting hotter as the sunshine started to fade into an amber twilight, she thought, watching him walk past her into the kitchen. She didn't know where to look as he came back out with his glass refilled. Or rather, she did. And the view was tempting. All lean muscles and raw masculinity. But she certainly wasn't giving into temptation. No way.

Despite telling herself this, the ice rattled in her glass for a second before she steadied and silenced it.

'Something wrong?' He frowned as he studied her. He seemed comfortable around her, and now that they knew each other quite well, he didn't feel the need to rush away and put a shirt on.

Arguably, she'd seen men stripped to their swimming trunks at the cove, but none of them had rattled her calm like Brad.

'No,' she said. 'I was just thinking that...your blond hair looks highlighted from being in the sun at the cove and now spending the afternoon outdoors.' Part truth. Mainly bluff to cover feeling flustered. She usually didn't do flustered. Not like this anyway. But Brad had a potent effect on her.

He ran a hand through his thick hair, a sexy gesture that didn't help the thundering of her heart. 'Yeah, it always goes real light blond in the summertime.' Then he reached over and brushed a strand of her hair back in a casual gesture. 'Like your hair. Something else we have in common.'

Wow! She felt herself melting and the fluttering of her heart seemed wild enough for him to sense it.

'Take a seat.' He sat down on the swing chair and gestured for her to join him.

She did, wishing she'd phoned him and not placed herself into this tinder box of hot temptation.

But he seemed at ease, and so, taking a steadying breath, she calmed her wayward thoughts and enjoyed just being there with him, unwinding after their busy days.

And there they were, she thought, like a couple again, or the couple they could be. Comfortable with each other, sipping cold lemonade in the warm amber glow.

Putting her empty glass down, she took out her notebook. 'I was working on those lyrics you wanted for the new song. I wrote most of these while I was at the cove. Though Penny almost caught me scribbling them before our meeting at the lodge.'

'Don't you feel like telling them you're my lyricist?' He seemed to think there was no issue with this.

'No, not yet. I think it'll change how they perceive me. They know I'm into my marketing. And a hobby quilter and knitter. But writing lyrics for you? That's another league as far as they're concerned.'

He nodded. 'I won't tell until you've told them.'

She smiled at him.

He leaned close and read her lyrics. 'I like that opening line.'

She felt his masculine strength so close, mixed with his genuine warmth and interest in her lyrics.

Handing the notepad to him, she thought he'd lean away again, but instead he remained close, pointing to the phrases as he read them.

'I love the atmosphere your lyrics evoke,' he said.

She watched his gorgeous profile and those blue eyes of his, and felt her heart break a little. Break a lot. An ache like she'd never experienced took her aback, but she hid it well. He never noticed as she kept her response light and bright.

'I wrote more lyrics than you'll need for the song. I wanted to have something new for our meeting tonight.'

He looked right at her. 'Have you had dinner?'

'No I drove here, from the cove. Just dropped off my groceries in the house.'

'No ice cream? Gingerbread cupcakes? Or cookie dough ones?'

She shook her head. 'Nope. Barely anything except coffee and a snack that Kyle made for me at the lodge while I was discussing their marketing.'

'You must be hungry.'

'I could eat something.'

Brad stood up. 'Let's have dinner, and then we'll talk about the lyrics, and your ideas for the New York website.'

'Okay.' She wondered if he planned to take her out for dinner, or...

'I have pizza and plenty of salad stuff.' He headed into the kitchen. 'I know you like pizza.'

Dinner at home, she thought, following him inside. 'Want me to help?'

He looked at her as if this was a given.

'I'll prepare the salad and the coffee,' she said, while Brad washed his hands, dug out a pizza from the freezer and put it in the oven.

Wondering if he was going to put a shirt on, she rearranged her thoughts instead to...having a gorgeous, half–naked chef cook dinner wasn't a bad thing after all.

He sang some of her new lyrics as he set up the dinner plates on the kitchen table.

'*I've never been the starry–eyed type*'
'*Except when it comes to you...*'

'I love those opening lyrics.' He looked over at her. 'What was the next line?'

'*I feel you mesmerize me*,' she prompted him.

He walked across to where she was preparing the salad to pick up another plate and napkins.

Those fabulous blue eyes of his gazed down at her as he sang the line.

'*I feel you mesmerize me...*'

Robyn spoke the final line.

'*And there's nothing I'd rather do...*'

For a second, she felt the connection between them, as if he was going to give in and kiss her.

Then he stepped back, and shook the temptation aside, not wishing to compromise her. She needed to trust him. She could trust him.

He evaluated the kitchen table, glanced outside the kitchen, and then grabbed the table, lifted it up and carried it outside to the patio. The plates and cutlery barely budged as he sat it down.

His broad shoulders and strong, lean arms lifted it as if it was lightweight, but she knew she would've had to drag it out. Brad was even stronger than he looked. And he looked pretty strong. All that guitar playing, she assessed, had built a deep, core strength.

Stop it! She scolded herself as her thoughts drifted to wild meanderings that would only lead to trouble.

He came back in. 'It's too beautiful an evening to eat inside.'

Robyn agreed. 'Dinner in the garden suits me.'

She couldn't remember the last time she'd dined outdoors. Certainly not like this, on a hot summer evening, and never with a man like Brad.

His clean, white shirt was hanging over the back of a kitchen chair. He put it on, buttoned it, but folded the sleeves up.

While the pizza cooked and she prepared a bowl of salad, he talked about her lyric writing process again.

'Did you hear the music that I'd played last night when you wrote these lyrics?'

'No, it's like a write in a bubble of silence, or more accurately, I hear the words in my mind. I can remember the melody of the song, but I didn't write with that in the background. Writing at the cove was relaxing. But I think I write well in the depths of the night. There's something about the evenings that I've always loved.'

Brad gazed out at the darkening sky. Stars were starting to blink in the wide arc of blue. 'Looks like another starry night for us.'

It was the way he said, *for us*, that jolted her heart, like a shooting star of excitement charging through it.

The timer pinged on the stove. He grabbed the oven mitts and pulled the tray of pizza out. The rich topping of cheese and peppers smelled tasty.

Brad put it on a serving plate and carried it outside while Robyn brought the coffee.

They sat down and he cut them generous slices and put them on their plates.

Robyn dished out the salad, and they helped themselves to dressing and seasoning.

Robyn gazed up at the sky as it became darker by the minute. Hundreds of stars blinked into life, as if timing their glow to shine down on them while they had dinner in the garden.

'This is nice,' she said. 'Dining outdoors.'

Brad nodded. 'I could get used to this. Maybe I should buy heaters for the colder months so we can still sit outside. Snow Bells Haven's name is a hint of what the winter is like here.'

He was planning that far ahead? she thought.

'Apparently, Greg grows pumpkins in the fall,' she told him. 'He has a house with a fair bit of land. And the town has a market fair in the autumn.'

'The town probably looks amazing with the trees all copper and gold.' He looked at the trees now silhouetted against the night sky, picturing them in their autumn finery.

'I like that the town has beautiful seasons,' she said.

He nodded thoughtfully. 'I really did strike gold when I moved here.' He cast a smile her way. 'Especially meeting you.'

CHAPTER FOURTEEN

Queen, king, rook
Her opening love gambit
Doesn't play by the book
I'm just a pawn in her romance
Playing against her, I don't stand a chance
Making all the wrong moves
She's got me in checkmate
I'm too late
I sacrificed too many pieces of my heart
To play the game of love
Queen, king, knight
She won the fight
I resign my heart to her

Brad cleared the dinner plates away and came back out to the garden with his laptop.

'Show me any ideas you have in mind to update the New York website.' He sounded eager to hear her thoughts.

'For a start, you need to highlight the forthcoming album.'

'Like a news update?'

'More than that. I don't pretend to know how you launch a new album, but could you show the cover, like the one you showed me?'

'We could do that. The cover's finished. We usually keep that under wraps until nearer the launch, but we're willing to adjust things around.'

'Use a clear headline.' She gestured across the top of the website's banner. 'New album coming soon.'

'Okay.'

'Are you able to release any excerpts from the album? To create a buzz for what's on the tracks?'

'I was talking to my manager about releasing a lead single. We usually release the first single before launching the album. He thinks the new material has two or three hit singles. And he loves the one from last night. I let him hear the melody. Now that you've written the lyrics, I'll work on finishing it.'

'I did love that melody,' she said.

'The guys are arriving in town tomorrow to stay for a few days. The three of them are driving in the van from New York, leaving early, and should be here before lunchtime. That'll give us almost a whole day to start rehearsing in the studio.'

A ripple of excitement charged through her. 'It's all coming together.'

'It is. Music needs that spark, a sense of energy that transfers to the songs. They've played backing instrumentals on my songs for years, so we all know our faults and foibles. And assets and strengths.'

'Do they play guitar or other instruments?'

'They're multi–instrumentalists — guitar, keyboards and drums. We all mix and match well. But I'm the only one to play sax.'

'Saxophones always sound so moody and sexy.' She immediately wished she'd stopped at moody.

He saw her reaction. 'They are. When I need that sort of vibe for a song, I play sax and overlay that on the track.'

'I'm sure you've got it all figured out, what you need for the new songs.'

'You should come down to the studio and meet the guys,' he suggested.

She nodded in a non–committal way. She didn't feel like she belonged in that musical mix.

He picked up on her reluctance. 'You're part of the music now. The lyrics are the verbal heart of the songs.'

'Okay, I'll drop by, but I'll give you guys a chance to rehearse before I poke my nose in.'

'Speaking of that...what else does the website need?'

She started listing off several suggestions.

'Whoa there! Let me keep up.'

She laughed. 'Sorry, I'm used to moving ideas around like pieces on a chess board. It's like a promotional game. Often there are standard opening moves that work well whatever type of business it is.'

'What moves are those?'

'Tell people what they need to know. Nothing fancy. Don't be too clever for your own good. Say you've got a new album coming out. Explain that you're working on new songs in the Snow Bells studio, but that several tracks are in the bag and were recorded in the studio in New York. Be clear. Use visuals to add interest and help explain what you're saying.'

'Including the album cover?'

'Yes. If they see the cover, they'll immediately know that it's forthcoming. It'll create a sense of the theme. The romance of it.' She took a deep breath.

'These suggestions sound simple, but you'd be surprised how many companies miss out on doing that.'

'Would you be able to list these ideas? Could you write the headlines, the captions for the website and select photos from the ones you took at the studio?'

'Yes, I'll do that.'

He smiled. No hesitation from Robyn. He loved her quicksilver methods.

Taking charge of his laptop, she wrote the notes he needed. Then she started to scroll through the photos on her phone. 'I'll earmark the pictures you need.'

He watched her fingers type at speed across the keys, imagining sparks were flying.

'You've obviously given this some thought,' he said.

'I have. Now it's up to you to decide whether you'll follow through with these ideas. Everything will work better if it's all done at the same time. Create an overnight buzz. Advise your manager to have the website updated. Light the touch paper. Then watch the sparks fly as the news ignites interest with fans.'

They chatted about the marketing, the music, and he made them more coffee.

After discussing the ideas for the marketing, Brad phoned his manager and told him what needed updated on the website. He forwarded the list Robyn had written and links to the photos.

'I'll start coordinating this tonight,' his manager confirmed. 'These are solid ideas from Robyn.'

'You should have all the information you need, but call me if you want anything else,' said Brad.

Finishing the call, Brad picked up his guitar and started playing the latest melody.

'Do you think this will be one of the songs you'll play at the market fair?'

'Yes, and with the guys on stage with me, I think it'll be a surprising performance.'

'I'll film it, as promised. Then you can add that to the website. That'll really cause a sensation.'

He heard the confidence in her voice and felt that the excitement was building, along with his feelings for Robyn herself.

'What's that serious look for?' she said to him.

About her, about him, and whether he could risk upturning her lifestyle by bringing her full force into his world. 'Nothing,' he lied, and continued playing his guitar, adding the lyrics she'd written, while she wandered around the lounge.

The way she moved, her face, her beautiful nature and her ability to spark things into action, set his heart thundering so loud he was sure she could hear it above the guitar playing.

And there he was, singing from the heart, while he was falling for her.

But he liked her too. Really liked her company, and admired her talent. And because he liked her, this was the main reason he wasn't willing to ask her out on a date...and take things from there. He knew where that would lead him. He was concerned where it would lead her.

Breaking her heart was the last thing he ever wanted to do. Though the strength of his feelings for

Robyn indicated he was the one in jeopardy of having his heart broken by her.

The lyrics from another song highlighted this sentiment.

You're worth a broken heart
I'll take my chances with you
They say it won't last
Maybe that's true
I know I should play it smart
But you're worth a broken heart...

Robyn sat down and studied the website again, and came up with other ideas on how to market the music.

Her marketing experience, working with a wide range of businesses, enabled her to evaluate the things that would help boost the music company. Often it took an outsider with a clear perspective to see what was missing. Or what was unnecessary.

'These lyrics work so well,' Brad remarked, now playing another tune.

'Will you release your new songs online or as CDs?' she said.

'The singles and the album are released as digital downloads first. We've had huge success with those. And we take pre–orders for the album's CD. We've done this for a while, and work with the same people, so the whole process is usually smooth.'

Brad's phone rang. He smiled when he saw the caller's name.

'Hi.' Brad paused and listened. 'You're where?' Another pause. 'No, head to the lodge. I'll meet you there. And I'll call Penny right now to see if your rooms are vacant. If not, you can stay overnight at my house. Yes, no problem. See you shortly.'

'Something happening?' said Robyn.

'The guys are heading into town right now. I have to call the lodge.'

'I thought they weren't arriving until tomorrow.'

'They packed the van ready for the trip, then decided to jump in and drive here tonight.' There was laughter in his voice. 'They can't wait to see the studio.'

He called the lodge and Penny picked up.

'Penny, it's Brad. Listen, my guys are going to be in town tonight. I was wondering—'

'Their rooms are ready,' Penny cut–in. She'd deliberately kept the rooms vacant and all set for Brad's special guests. 'They're welcome to book in early.'

'Thank you so much. I didn't know they were going to do this,' Brad explained.

'It's fine,' Penny assured him.

'I'm heading to the lodge now.'

Brad started to grab a few things. 'Want to come along and meet the guys tonight?'

'No, I'll leave you all to catch up. It's been a busy day and I should get home.' She was happy to let Brad deal with them, and relax a little.

He picked up her notepad. 'Can I take your lyrics with me? I'll give them back to you tomorrow. But if I know the guys, they'll want a tour of the studio tonight after they book into the lodge. I'd love to let them hear the latest lyrics.'

'Yes, take them with you.'

He smiled at her. 'I hope I won't be taking your grocery list this time.'

'Unfortunately, I didn't write it on the notepad.' She shook her head and sighed. 'I guess I've missed out on more free groceries delivered to my door.'

'Too bad,' he said, smiling.

They headed out together. He got into his car and she started to walk over to her house.

'Thanks again for all the marketing advice,' he called to her before driving off.

She waved in acknowledgment and watched him drive away.

It was later than she thought. The night had flown in, but she pictured that Brad's evening was about to begin.

Easing the tension from the effects of a busy day and an evening with Brad, she went into her office and checked and answered her messages.

One message was from Mark asking her if she'd read over the speech he planned to give at the market fair.

She read the speech, made a couple of adjustments to it, and then sent it off to him, not expecting a quick reply.

Can I call you, or is it too late at night?
It's okay to call, Mark.

Mark phoned her. 'I'm reading the changes you made to the speech. They're ideal. As it's the first time I'll be making the opening announcement as mayor, I wanted to run it by you.'

'It's good to keep the speech relatively short, concise but welcoming. I just added a few words here and there.'

'Bill me for your time. I don't take your advice for granted.'

'This one is on me, Mark. You're always welcome to run your speeches by me.'

'You're very kind, Robyn.' He paused. 'I hope Brad appreciates that.'

'Brad's been okay to work with. We get along fine. His session musicians have arrived in town. They're staying at the lodge.'

'Will they be playing with him at the market fair?'

'I think so, but they're mainly here to work on his new songs at the studio.'

Mark sighed heavily. 'I feel responsible for getting you involved with Brad and his studio. If I hadn't told him to contact you to help with his marketing...'

'I would probably have become involved somehow,' she said. 'You know how I meddle in everything.'

Mark laughed. 'What have you been meddling in today?'

'Things I never thought I'd be involved in.'

'That sounds interesting.'

'I'm keeping it a secret for the moment.'

'So, I'm guessing it involves Brad. You'll know what you're doing. But be careful, Robyn.'

'I will, Mark.'

'Has Nate contacted you?' he said, changing the subject to a lighter note.

'No, why?'

'He said he wants to ask you to help with the market fair, advise on promoting it. Including the news about Brad playing. He'll likely talk to you soon.'

'Okay, thanks for letting me know.'

After the call, she closed her laptop, and got ready for bed.

She didn't remember falling asleep. But she did recall waking up in the early hours of the morning with lyrics in her mind. Instinctively, she reached for the notepad that wasn't there.

Getting up, she wandered downstairs to her office, picked up another notepad and pen, and went back to bed after scribbling the lyrics.

Before falling asleep again, she noticed that Brad's car wasn't in the driveway of his house, and she pictured he'd be playing an all–night session with the musicians at the studio.

Somewhere in the depths of the night, she woke up again and saw that Brad's car was parked in his driveway. He was home, and his house was in darkness.

Closing her eyes, she tumbled into a deep sleep and didn't wake until the dawn.

Penny waylaid Kyle in the morning as he prepared the breakfasts for the guests.

'Brad's musicians arrived late last night,' Penny whispered urgently.

'I thought they weren't—'

'They decided to come to Snow Bells early,' Penny cut–in. 'Their rooms were ready so I booked them in. They dropped their luggage off and then went along to the music studio with Brad. It was late when they came back. They told our night porter they wanted a wake–up call for breakfast, so they should be coming through soon.'

'I'll handle them,' said Kyle, and hurried away.

A call came through for Penny from Nancy. 'Hi, Nancy.'

'Is it true that Brad's musicians are at the lodge?' said Nancy.

'Yes, Kyle is about to cook breakfast for them. They arrived last night. Three of them.'

'Oh, how exciting. What are they like?'

'They're around the same age as Brad and Kyle. But they're all happily married.'

'So there won't be any gossip about romance with them.'

'No, but I still think there's a romance brewing between Brad and Robyn,' said Penny. 'Despite her saying he wasn't serenading her the other night.'

Nancy giggled. In the background, she heard Nate hectically dealing with customers. 'Sorry, the store's getting busy. I have to help Nate. Speak to you later.'

Kyle whispered quickly to Penny as he hurried by, busy with the breakfast orders. 'The music guys have just asked me if Brad and Robyn are a thing.'

'Really?'

'Yes, apparently when they were at his studio playing last night, he kept talking about Robyn. They said he sounded smitten. What will I tell them?'

'Tell them the truth,' said Penny.

'That Brad was serenading Robyn outside the lodge during the wedding dance?'

'Nooo! Say you don't know for sure.'

'Know what for sure?' Brad said, walking into the lodge and hearing the tail–end of their conversation.

'If we'll be serving pancakes with maple syrup and raspberries for breakfast every morning,' Kyle rambled.

Penny pressed her lips together to stifle a giggle.

'Are you joining your friends for breakfast?' Kyle said to Brad.

'Eh, I wasn't planning to. But I've been meaning to have pancakes lately, so yes, count me in for breakfast too.'

Kyle showed him through to their table in the guests' dining room.

Robyn ate her breakfast in the kitchen, and then took her coffee and laptop out to the garden where she sat enjoying the warm, sunny morning. The rose trees had settled into the garden where Brad had planted them, and the floral fragrance of the flowers set her up for the busy day ahead.

Checking her laptop, she saw there was a flurry of messages from local businesses all interested in the same thing. They wanted her help to promote them at the market fair. It was short notice as the fair was fast approaching, but she contacted all four businesses, agreeing to assist them. She'd dealt with them before, so there was a familiarity with them.

The messages dealt with, she went to sip her coffee and relax for a moment, but Nate phoned her.

'Mark was in the store for groceries,' Nate began. 'He said he'd mentioned to you that I'd like your advice to promote the market fair.'

'He did. How can I help you?'

'The summer fair is set to be one of the busiest we've had. Brad performing has created even more interest, but things were looking good anyway. But as one of the town's main event planners, I have to write the news articles on the Snow Bells website. It's not my strong point, so I wondered if you'd write the articles about the fair. You'll be there. Could you take notes and then write about the event?'

'I'll do that, and I'll take photos too. I'm familiar with the Snow Bells website, so I'll write what you need.'

She could hear the sigh of relief from Nate.

'Things have been extra hectic this year. In a good way,' he said. 'But I could sure use your help. You'll be paid of course from the town's fund.'

Robyn knew that Nate volunteered his time, as did others, to set up local events for the benefit of the community. She wasn't about to take their money.

'Consider it my contribution to the town's fund,' she told Nate.

'Oh, that's very kind of you, Robyn.'

'Do you have any details for the next market fair? The one being held in the fall,' she prompted him.

'Yes, but that's not for a few months yet,' he explained.

'I know, but I could tie in the summer fair's success with the news of the forthcoming fair in the fall. Get the interest going.'

Nate perked up even more. 'I'll send you the details today. Thank you again, Robyn.'

In the background, she could hear Nancy speaking. 'I'll call you back later, Penny. Nate has Robyn on the phone. I think she needs to know what you've just told me.' There was a pause. 'Don't hang up, Nate. I want to speak to Robyn.'

Nate's phone was handed to Nancy. 'Robyn, there's gossip brewing about you and Brad.'

'What sort of gossip?' Robyn sounded concerned.

'Penny says that Brad is at the lodge having pancakes for breakfast with his three music friends. Before Brad arrived to join them, the guys cornered Kyle to ask him if you and Brad were dating.'

'They what?'

'You know how people take to Kyle. He's so approachable. Anyway, they said they were in the music studio last night and Brad couldn't stop talking about you. They said he sounded *smitten*.'

'Smitten? With me?'

'Uh–huh!'

'What did Kyle tell them?'

'Nothing. He threw them some waffle about pancakes, but Brad almost overheard the conversation,' said Nancy. 'Penny and I thought you should know. Don't say anything about this to Brad or he'll know we snitched.'

'I won't say anything.' But she was thinking plenty.

'Sorry, I have to go. We've got a bakery delivery.' And Nancy was gone, leaving Robyn in a bubble of trouble.

Before Robyn could unravel her thoughts, her phone rang. It was Brad's manager.

'Hi, Robyn. Have you got a few minutes to chat?'

'Yes.' Just pile on the trouble folks.

'And call me, Tony,' he said.

But Tony wasn't bringing trouble. He was bringing great news.

'I worked last night and this morning with the guy who updates the website, and we've got the pieces in place to press the button to show the updates.'

Tony was in his late thirties, single, and had been involved in the music industry since he was in his teens. His experience was invaluable, as was his trusted friendship with Brad and the session musicians.

'Wonderful,' she said.

'The only pieces missing are the single releases. I wanted to let you look over the updates before we make them public. I'll call Brad and see if we can agree on the first single release. Then we can light the fuse all at the one time, like you suggested.'

Tony had forwarded a private link to the website updates. Robyn read them and noticed everything from her list of ideas had been instigated.

'This looks ideal, Tony.'

'Right, I'm going to call Brad now. And are you totally sure you don't want a proper credit as the lyric writer on the songs?'

'I'm sure. The little robin logo will suffice for now.'

'Okay. Speak soon.'

Robyn sat back in her chair and felt her world shift further into the music industry. Part of her was reticent. Part of her felt excited. Come on, she bolstered herself. Let this fly.

She was glad when a message came through from Nate with the information she needed about the fall market fair.

Diving right into the editorial, she wrote until the time flew in and she emerged having written an outline highlighting the features she wanted for the town's website news.

Filling in the gaps would be straightforward enough. Once she'd attended the summer market fair and written about that, she'd tie in the one due in the autumn.

In the back of her mind, she sensed Brad...and trouble brewing. Not with the website, because if the single was added to the updates, she'd seen in the past how fast something like this could soar. Were Brad and his associates ready to handle the sparks when they started flying?

She didn't think so, but maybe Brad would surprise her. He'd certainly surprised her with his talk about her to the music guys so much they reckoned he was smitten.

Then again, this was all gossip and whispers, and she'd learned not to rely on sources like that.

Next up on her trouble radar was Mark.

Can I call you? Or are you too busy? It was his usual thoughtful message approach.

Robyn phoned Mark.

'I'm in the main street,' he told her. 'There's gossip circulating that you and Brad are an item. I thought you should know. Unless of course you are, so...'

'We're not. It's just gossip. But thanks for the heads up, Mark.'

'Okay, I'll let you get on with your work.'

Robyn dared to take a deep breath, trying to find a moment to digest the morning's melee of events.

She watched butterflies fluttering around the flowers in her garden, feeling like she'd taken a similar route. Flitting from one thing to another.

Brad was probably in the studio now rehearsing with the guys, polishing the new songs, and maybe he'd selected one for the lead single release. Was Tony coordinating this for the website? Whenever anything notable happened in her world, she always sensed it. Right now, she sensed the whole marketing mix brewing.

Taking a calming breath, she took charge of the work in hand, writing, planning tactics and strategies for clients' marketing. Writing the piece for Nate about Brad performing at the market fair. No lies. Just skirting around the truth. Brad was performing two songs. People would assume it was two former popular songs. She didn't say it was, and leaned on their presumptions to keep his intentions a surprise.

Skipping lunch and sailing on through to the afternoon on coffee and bursts of enthusiasm mixed with anticipation, she jolted when Tony phoned her.

'We're about to launch the lead single as a digital release on the website, along with the updated information and pictures,' Tony told her. 'We've rearranged the running order on the album.'

Butterflies fluttered in her heart, making her feel she could've out–flown the ones in the garden.

'What's the single?' she dared to ask.

Tony told her. 'One of the first songs with your lyrics. It's a modern number with a touch of country. Brad recorded it and played all the instruments himself.'

'I know the one. Great choice.' She remembered it as a musical masterpiece.

'I'll be in touch again soon, Robyn,' Tony promised. 'Payment for your marketing work has been put into your account.'

He was gone before she could discuss this with him. Of course, she expected to be paid for marketing the New York studio. But seeing it deposited in her account, was something else. At this rate, she could get by with one main client. But that had never been her intention. Besides, goldmine clients rarely lasted and burned out fast. She liked the security of having numerous clients.

But still...that was quite a lucrative assignment she'd just completed for them. And she was due to be paid for the lyrics too.

Heading into the kitchen out of the heat of the afternoon, she poured herself a cold glass of orange juice. Then she wandered back out and relaxed for a bit in the garden, enjoying the sunshine, before refreshing the New York website on her laptop.

The updates had come through. There was the headline announcing Brad's new album with the front cover picture. The back of the album hadn't been revealed as the list of tracks wasn't final yet.

But there was the robin logo on the credits for the single's lyrics, and the cover art photo. The spark had been ignited.

CHAPTER FIFTEEN

I don't think about you these days
Even on stormy nights
When I used to hold you tight
I don't think about how you left that morning
Leaving me without any warning
But I don't think about you these days
I don't think about you...

Robyn closed her laptop. Throughout the day she'd worked between her office and outdoors in her garden. The garden won the last round of the day, and she sat in the amber light of the early evening relaxing for a few moments before deciding what to have for dinner. She'd tackled a load of work the whole day from home.

Brad had crossed her mind, along with the false gossip that they were dating. But she'd tried to concentrate on the tasks in hand, and figured he'd be busy in his studio.

Sitting in the garden, she didn't hear Brad knock on the front door, so she was taken aback when he came walking around the side of the house to the back garden carrying two bags of groceries. He wore jeans, an open neck shirt and a mischievous smile.

'Brad!' She stood up and smoothed her hands down her light floral print dress.

He held up the two heavy bags of groceries, one in each arm as if they were lightweight. 'Will I put these in the kitchen?'

She smiled. 'Free groceries delivered to my door.'

'I didn't want you to miss out even though they weren't listed on the notepad,' he said playfully.

He carried the bags inside. She followed him, eager to see what he'd picked.

'These are my tastes entirely.' She sounded impressed.

'The credit goes to Nancy. I went in to pick up your groceries. She knew what you usually buy.'

He helped her unpack the bags and put the groceries away.

She put the milk, butter, cheese and fresh salad items in the refrigerator. 'Tony called me.' And others, telling her about the gossip, but she'd promised not to snitch.

Brad unloaded the tinned items and stacked them in a cupboard. 'He told me. We're both grateful for your help with everything.'

'How did things go with you and the guys at the studio today?'

'Great, they love the studio and the new songs. We nailed a few tracks. They're having dinner at the lodge. Kyle is spoiling them with his cuisine.'

'Are you not joining them for dinner?'

'No, I had a grocery run to do,' he joked with her. And he'd wanted to see her all day. The delivery was an excuse to drop by. 'We're meeting up later tonight to work on the songs. I'm re–recording two songs I wrote in Snow Bells. I'm happy with the melodies, but I'm exchanging my words for your lyrics.'

'Really?'

He nodded. 'That's what we're working on tonight. And planning the two songs we'll play at the market fair.'

'Will you perform the lead single from the album that's been released?'

'No. Tony and I think we should let that song stand on its own. Then we'll add another two of the new Snow Bells tracks via the performance at the fair.'

'Giving fans three new songs to enjoy,' she said.

'Exactly. The lead single can be downloaded. But hopefully the video of the market fair's live performance will help us gauge other singles to release.'

'It's all so exciting.' She smiled up at him.

And so was she. His heart ached to take her in his arms and tell her how he felt about her. But common sense kicked in. It wasn't appropriate. Not yet.

'Tony's talking about coming to the market fair performance,' said Brad. 'On the condition he gets to stay at the lodge. The guys are teasing him that the food is top class and it's like a vacation.'

'I guess I'll be meeting Tony soon,' she said chirpily.

'And you have to meet the guys. I've been telling them all about you and your lyrics.'

Robyn smiled tightly. Oh yes, she could understand why the gossip was sparking about her and Brad being an item.

'You okay?' he said.

'Yes, it's been a hectic day. I've worked from home, which you'd think would be a breeze, but it's been a pressure–cooker of a day. Happily so.'

Brad nodded. 'I know what you mean. When I'm in the studio with a deadline to aim for, it gets pretty intense. But I love the music, and sometimes the pressure helps to spur me on.'

'I sat outside in the garden to work today. The rose trees you planted and the flowers have come along nicely.'

He smiled, sending a wave of excitement through her. Just seeing him standing there in her kitchen, so tall and sexy–handsome...

'You've got that pretty rose glow to your cheeks again. All the sunshine and fresh air I suppose.'

'Yes,' she lied, wishing her blushes didn't give away the effect he had on her. 'I was about to make dinner, now I'm spoiled for choice with all these groceries.' He was lingering, so she made the offer. 'You're welcome to join me. Again, nothing fancy.'

'I wish I could but...I only came to drop off the groceries.'

She smiled to hide her disappointment.

He smiled back at her. 'And to invite you to have dinner with me at my house.'

'You've cooked dinner?'

'No, I asked Kyle to give me items from his menu to take away with me, so we could have dinner and catch up on things.'

She nodded. 'Okay.'

Without hesitation, he led the way over to his house.

'I've set dinner up in the kitchen, but we can dine outside in the garden if you prefer. It's a lovely evening.'

She laughed. The table was set with dinner plates, cutlery and napkins. Whatever Kyle had cooked for them was put aside near the stove in four ceramic terrines.

'What's so funny?' he said.

'I'm just picturing you lifting the table, as is, outside to the garden again. Only this time you've got your shirt on.' She wished she could retract the latter comment, but it was out and she started to blush.

Brad leaned down and studied her. 'I'm thinking that rosy glow isn't always attributable to the sun after all.'

This made her blush even more. 'Stop it!'

He stepped up the teasing. 'I could take my shirt off if that helps.'

She held up her hands. 'No, don't.' She could barely stifle her giggles.

He laughed as he lifted the table and put it outside in the garden, while keeping his shirt on.

She didn't wait for him to offer her a cold drink and opened the refrigerator and poured a glass of lemonade with ice.

Coming back into the kitchen, Brad lifted the dishes Kyle had cooked and carried them outside.

Robyn sat down at the table, sipping her drink.

Brad gestured to the food. 'Help yourself.'

He hurried back into the kitchen and returned with a lit candle in a glass. He put it on the table and sat down to dine with her.

Robyn lifted the lid on one of the terrines. It was a pasta dish, with a rich, creamy sauce, sprinkled with herbs and chives.

'This looks tasty.' she said, scooping up a portion on to her plate. 'Would you like me to serve yours?'

'Yes, thanks.' He peeked at the other terrines. One had a mixed salad with roast vegetables. He added that to their plates.

'What's in the other dishes?'

'Two different desserts.' He lifted the lids to show a summer berry dessert with layers of fruit, jelly and cream in one, and two slices of rich chocolate cake with cream.

'Your friends aren't the only ones being spoiled by Kyle's cuisine,' she remarked.

They tucked into their pasta and chatted about the forthcoming market fair.

'It's two days from now,' she said. 'I'm going to be so busy tomorrow. Nate sent me lots of information. The stalls are being erected tomorrow, so I'm going to be there to help some of the businesses to set up for the fair.'

'I'll be there too, around lunchtime, with the guys. Nate phoned to ask if I'd like to come along to see that the stage set up is suitable for our performance. You could meet the guys then.'

'Yes, I'd like to meet them.' Even though she felt slightly embarrassed that they'd figured out a relationship was building between her and Brad. Whether it would lead to anything or fizzle out before it even began, time would tell.

'Great, I'll see you there.'

'Will you be rehearsing the songs on the stage?'

'No, I want the performance to be a complete surprise. We'll rehearse in the studio. Mainly, we'll ensure the stage is set for the numbers. The acoustics are suitable. Lighting if necessary. Nate says the fair continues into the evening, with a dance. So I hope you'll save a dance for me.'

'I will.'

He smiled over at her, causing her heart to squeeze.

'Any plans to make time for romance yet?'

Robyn blinked. 'I, eh...'

'Sorry, that wasn't what I meant to say,' he said, sounding like he was blustering.

She waited. What had he meant to say? She put him on the spot.

It was his turn to feel a glow across his cheeks. He feigned interest in his food as he waffled. 'I thought maybe you'd find a way to schedule romance into your busy life.' It was all he could come up with while pinned to the spot.

'I'm busier than ever at the moment. But maybe things will settle down soon.'

'Settling down would be nice.' He bit his lip. 'I mean...settling into a schedule that works for you.'

He heard himself talking himself into corners he couldn't get out of.

Was this what a man, supposedly smitten, looked like? She wanted to reach out and clasp his hand, smile at him and make light of everything. But that cautious streak in her nature, and experience of being burned when it came to romance, made her keep her gesture in check.

'I'd like to see how things are once the market fair is over. And the songs on the album are released,' she told him. This was true. Everything felt hectic and that wasn't the time to trust her heart to make the right decisions. Decisions she could easily wish she hadn't made.

He kept his gaze downwards and nodded. 'Smart decision.' Then he made a confession. 'I'm edgy about the songs being released.'

'I think people will love your new music.'

'It's always a gamble. But this time...I feel like I did when I had my first success. Like there's something in the air. I don't know...'

'A wave of success coming to hit you,' she suggested. Throughout the day, she couldn't shake off the feeling that something exciting was coming.

He shrugged and then those blue eyes looked right at her. 'Whatever the reaction, promise me you'll hold tight. Hold the line with me.'

'I promise.'

He gazed up at the early evening sky. For a moment, he wished that the world could be sidelined for a little while, to give him and Robyn a chance at romance. If he fell any deeper for her, he wouldn't be able to contain his feelings. And maybe that would be the wrong timing, and would push her away. He knew that feeling only too well.

She'd finished her main course and decided on the dessert. 'What one would you prefer?'

'How about we share both. There are two slices of chocolate cake. One each, with a side order of whatever that berry dessert is.'

'Kyle would never approve of us mixing his top class desserts.'

Brad leaned close, his eyes highlighted by the glow of the candle. 'I won't tell if you won't.'

Robyn served up two mixed portions. 'You are a bad influence on me,' she scolded him playfully.

He scooped up the chocolate cake and cream. 'I do hope so.'

Robyn laughed and then they tucked into their desserts, while knowing that after they'd finished, Brad was heading to the studio and she was going back home.

Time, circumstances and work were conspiring to keep them apart, she thought. But maybe the new song released into the wild would shake up everything.

Brad finally blew the candle out and they got ready to go their separate ways. She could've accompanied him to the studio, but this would surely have interrupted their recording session. So she decided to go home and relax. Maybe even do some quilting or knitting. Though probably she'd prepare marketing ideas for the fair. Another busy day was due to dawn.

Brad put the dishes in the picnic–style basket Kyle had given him, planning to drop them off at the lodge when he went to get the guys. They'd have finished their dinner by now too.

Getting into his car, his heart felt heavy as he watched Robyn walk over to her house. How he longed to go with her. One day maybe.

Robyn spent the remainder of her evening listing the things she needed to do for her marketing work at the fair. The stallholders she was helping included Jessica with her quilt stall, Virginia's dressmaking and the knitting shop. Plus a couple of the farmers.

The fair was being held in one of the farmer's fields. The stalls were being erected in the morning, so she aimed to go there early to help some of the businesses to set up for the fair the following day.

The excitement was building. She could sense it. But there was something else too. Something she felt was gathering pace.

Shaking off the feelings that interrupted her concentration, she checked that she had everything scheduled on her list for the morning. Then she went through to the lounge to relax for a little while and work on her quilt. The window was open, and warm air drifted in, along with a sense that something exciting was brewing.

The lights were on in Brad's studio until well after midnight, as he rehearsed and recorded the new songs with the session musicians.

None of them were watching the clock. They were just making sure they'd nailed the numbers.

Finally, they called it a night, and the guys headed along to the lodge, while Brad drove home.

Rolling down the car windows to let in the night air, Brad felt a rush of excitement hit him like a tidal wave.

As he pulled up in his driveway, he glanced across at Robyn's house. It was in darkness. If even a flicker of light had shone from the windows, he would've meandered over. He felt an ache to see her, even for a few minutes, as if this would settle his world and provide a solid night's sleep.

He surmised she'd be sound asleep, tucked up in bed. Something he should be doing, and was about to.

He got as far as trudging upstairs to his bedroom when a sense of anticipation went through him.

Getting ready for bed, he kept the lights off, letting the moonlight's glow illuminate the room.

He eased his weary muscles from all the intense guitar playing that often took its toll on him, but kept him whipcord lean and strong. For everything he'd achieved of value in his life, there was always a flip side that cost him on a personal level. He had a successful career, but an unfulfilled romantic life. He intended changing that balance now that he was here in Snow Bells Haven. But perhaps whatever was rolling in on a stormy sea of adventure was bringing a tidal wave of trouble with it.

Gazing out the window at the thousands of stars in the dark sky, the waves of excitement rippled through him.

He didn't make a wish upon any of the stars. He'd done that recently and was now waiting to see if they came true.

Lying down in bed on the silk sheet, he pulled the new quilt he now owned up to his waist.

Robyn and lyrics filtered through his thoughts as he closed his eyes to go to sleep...

We had our time together
In the sunny days
We were fine together
In so many ways
Then we drifted apart
You said I broke your heart

I said the same about you...

CHAPTER SIXTEEN

Make time for romance
Make time for you and me
Love doesn't work to anyone's timing
Fall in love, it was meant to be

The market fair was starting to take shape. Stalls were being erected around the hub of the field where the event was due to take place the following day. From bake stalls to crafts of all sorts, farmers and businesses alike were busy building the structures, helping each other, everyone mucking in.

Robyn raised her hand to shield her eyes from the dazzling sunshine. Even at this early hour of the morning it was shining through the clear, cobalt sky. Wearing a skirt, smart blouse and practical pumps to navigate the field's terrain, she looked around for familiar faces — and saw plenty.

The sheriff was hammering a stall together for Jessica, making sure there were rods where she could hang up her quilts.

Next to Jessica, was Virginia's dress shop stall. Volunteers lending a hand with erecting the stalls had finished assembling it. Beside Virginia stood the knitting shop's stall, creating a trio of quilting, dressmaking and knitting, with a clear view of the stage. Virginia had no intention of missing Brad's performance, and she wouldn't even have to leave her stall to have a great view of him singing.

The stage was built solid, put up the previous night, the first thing to anchor the event, with the stalls like satellites around the whole area.

Food and beverage stalls were dotted around, though there was a main hub where power was provided to cook snacks and hot drinks. If the weather continued to be warm, which was forecast, cool drinks would be equally popular.

Canopies shielded many of the stalls from the sunlight, while others welcomed displaying their products without being shaded.

Farmers' stalls looked like they were ready to hold a variety of fresh produce, such as fruit and vegetables.

Greg and Dwayne unloaded folding chairs and tables from the back of Greg's station wagon, and stacked them up beside the makeshift cafe stall.

Across the crowd, Robyn saw Mark deep in conversation with people delighted to chat to the mayor.

Everyone moved at a fast clip, and it felt like she was watching one of those videos where an event was filmed at speed as it was built by a lot of busy people.

The fair was due to open the following morning, so everything needed to be ready for the first arrivals. According to the news reports Robyn had read on the Snow Bells website, people turned up early, eager to snap up bargains and enjoy a full day out, often like a family outing.

Robyn took a deep breath. If she hadn't been involved in helping a handful of the stallholders, and filming Brad's performance, she'd have happily turned up to wander around and make a day of it herself. Still, she'd have ample time to buy items she didn't essentially need, like another bundle of quilting fabric, or yarn for knitting. Cake was definitely on her list. Apart from stalls like Greg had, she'd seen the schedule of participants and home baking stalls were included.

Holding a binder so she could take notes as required for the different clients, for Nate's news report, and ideas for Brad, Robyn glanced over at the stage. It looked even bigger than in the pictures on the town's website. It was fit for a performer like Brad, she thought, and his musicians.

Three men were standing on the stage talking to Nate. They seemed like they were agreeing where their equipment would be connected. The power was supplied at the back and side of the stage. She didn't want to interrupt them, and glanced around to see where Brad was. He'd maybe been waylaid by local fans, or was at the side of the stage out of view. The platform was quite high, providing a great view for the audience. She pictured the crowd gathered there tomorrow and felt the anticipation rising.

The voices of the musicians filtered over to where she was standing. Nate had gone to check the power situation, leaving the three musicians to talk amongst themselves.

'We'll put the drums at the back of the stage,' said the guy wielding an electric guitar. He was the only one of the three to have an instrument, which made sense she reckoned. The drum kit and keyboards would be brought with them the following day. 'The keyboards can go on the right,' the guitarist continued, seemingly used to taking charge of the stage set–up. 'I'll stand here, left of stage, while Brad stands up front.'

The other two guys nodded.

She still couldn't see where Brad was, and stepped closer. 'Excuse me,' she called up to them. 'Where's Brad?'

'He's not here,' the guitarist told her, plugging in his guitar for a sound check.

The guys made no indication that they knew who she was. It dawned on her that holding the binder and pen she probably looked like one of the event planners. She guessed Brad hadn't shown them the photos of her in the studio, so they'd no idea who she was.

Not inclined to make a cold introduction without Brad being there, she spoke up again to the guitarist. 'I thought Brad was going to be here this morning to see the stage. Where is he?'

'New York,' the guitarist told her. No details. Clearly, Brad's business was none of her business.

She took the hint and walked away, toying with the idea of phoning him, and yet, something didn't feel right and she hesitated.

'Hurry up and listen to this,' Virginia called to Robyn, waving her over urgently to her stall where she was listening to the radio while setting up the dress rails.

Robyn hurried over.

A few familiar faces were gathered round Virginia's stall, listening, including Jessica and Mark.

Everyone kept quiet, not wanting to miss a word of the interview on a New York radio station.

'*Your new song has taken off like a rocket trailing sparks.*' The radio interviewer sounded thrilled.

Robyn felt her world tilt when she heard Brad's voice reply.

'*Yes, Tony, my manager, phoned me in the middle of the night to tell me that digital downloads of the new single were through the roof, and we're getting mountains of pre-orders for the CD.*'

'*It was a surprise release for your fans. No one knew when your new album or lead singles were due. And then, bam! There it was on the website.*'

Brad agreed with the interviewer. '*I know. We decided to release it and ignite the spark.*'

Robyn's heart thundered in her chest. She'd encouraged Brad and Tony to do this.

'*You've recently moved to a small town up north called Snow Bells Haven and opened a second studio there.*' The interviewer prompted Brad to explain about this.

'*I wanted a fresh start. I still have the main studio in New York. But I've made Snow Bells Haven my home. It's a great town with great people.*'

Virginia, Jessica, Mark and the others couldn't contain their delight at the town being mentioned and praised on the radio.

'*Does that fresh start include a new, secretive lyric writer? No name is credited for the song's lyrics. Only a little robin logo.*'

'*Yes, I have a new lyricist.*' Brad didn't elaborate.

The interviewer persisted. '*Don't they want credit for their wonderful words?*'

Tired from working until after midnight in the studio, then being woken up by Tony around two in the morning, getting up, throwing his clothes on and driving to New York to arrive before the dawn, Brad made a mistake...

'*She doesn't want any credit for the lyrics. Not yet.*' He didn't notice his faux pas until the interviewer picked up on it.

'*She? Your new lyric writer is a woman?*'

Brad mentally kicked himself and fumbled to cover this up. '*That's not what I meant to say—*'

Virginia and the others didn't suss that it was Robyn. But Mark did. He gave Robyn a knowing glance, but said nothing as the interview continued.

'*Is she someone you've played with before? A singer? A musician?*'

'*No, she's not involved in the music industry.*'

'*Really? And she can write heartfelt lyrics like this? Wow! She sounds incredible.*'

'*She is.*' Brad's tone indicated he wasn't prepared to elaborate.

The interviewer knew him, had welcomed him on the show before, and moved on. '*I spoke to Snow Bells Haven's newspaper editor, and they said that you're due to perform at the local market fair tomorrow.*'

Brad couldn't deny it. '*I'm singing two new songs from the album.*'

'*I assume one of the songs is your latest release.*'

'*No, two other new songs. All three of them were written in Snow Bells. A video of the live performance will be put up on the website.*' He hoped this would help prevent the town being inundated with fans.

'*I hear too that the town is known for sparking new romances. Any truth in that regarding you?*'

'*No romance for me. I'm concentrating on my music.*' The denial gnawed at him.

It caused a dagger of disappointment to shoot through Robyn's heart.

'*Thank you for coming on the show this morning, Brad. Good luck with the new album, though considering the meteoric success of the single, you won't need it. We're finishing today's show with Brad's new single...*'

The song started to play, and the chattering began while people listened to the music. More stallholders had joined Virginia and the others.

Nate came bustling over from the stage area. 'We were mentioned on the New York radio show!'

'Brad acknowledged that this is a great town,' said the sheriff, sounding pleased.

Robyn stepped aside to talk to Mark.

He shook his head and looked worried.

'Don't say anything to anyone,' she whispered to him.

'I won't. But...' he shook his head again. 'Do you know what you're getting yourself into?'

'Yes...no.' She sighed in exasperation. 'It's complicated.'

'I bet it is.'

They went over to a couple of bales of hay and sat down to chat for a few minutes out of earshot of the others.

She gave him the short course of how she'd become embroiled in the lyric writing...

...'and then Brad and Tony asked me to do the marketing for the New York studio. I encouraged them to promote the new songs on the website.'

'You meddled.'

'I showed them how to spark interest in Brad's new songs.'

'The ones you wrote the lyrics for.'

Robyn sighed.

'What are you going to do?' said Mark.

'Brad dropped off a load of groceries at my house last night. I could hide there until the dust settles.' She was being facetious.

'Stardust doesn't settle. You've become involved in a life where music stars like Brad shine for all the world to see.'

'I like the small town life I have here. I'm not prepared to give that up.'

'It could give you up. It's obvious there's a spark of romance between you and Brad.'

She didn't deny it. 'We're not dating. We're not anything yet.'

'*Yet.*'

She sighed again.

Mark spoke in a concerned whisper. 'What are you going to do when Brad has to go away on tour to promote his album? Or perform at live gigs? Radio interviews? Press coverage? His world isn't private. I think you like your privacy even though you're a force to be reckoned with.'

'Who gave you the keys to my personality?'

Mark smiled. 'I know you better than you imagine. And I know I'm not the man for you. But I'm here if you need me, even just to talk. I won't tell anyone you're the lyric writer.'

'It'll come out in the wash sooner or later. Preferably later when I know how this will all work.'

Mark gave her hand a reassuring squeeze, stood up and then went over to join the others, agreeing with them that this had been great publicity for the town.

'We can cope with extra folk turning up to the fair,' said Nate.

Mark frowned. 'Are you sure?'

'Oh, yes. The more the merrier. Besides, it's such short notice. Folk won't be able to just drive here to Snow Bells tomorrow. Brad said the performance is going to be filmed and put on the website, so that should keep fans happy.'

Robyn gave the impression she was studying the lists in her binder, taking a few moments to gather herself. Hearing Brad's voice when he said... *No romance for me. I'm concentrating on my music.* The denial gnawed at her.

Electric guitar playing sounded from the stage.

She looked over and watched the guitar player test out the sound system. He played one of Brad's older numbers.

Nate hurried over to help them. 'Is the sound system suitable for you?'

'It's excellent, Nate. We'll be here tomorrow for the show with Brad.'

Robyn's heart lurched at the mention of his name. She checked her messages. None missed. He hadn't tried to contact her. He wasn't obliged to. But she'd been the instigator of the current fireworks on his website.

Standing up, she brushed stray bits of hay from her skirt and shrugged off the heaviness weighing down on her shoulders.

Walking away, she began getting on with her marketing work, and chatted to the stallholders about setting up for the fair.

An area for dancing was being cleared in the heart of the field, and edged with lanterns that she pictured would look magical lit up at night.

The dance was apparently a highlight of the fair, and she thought about what to wear. She aimed to wear her confidence–boosting red dress during the day. It would be fine for the evening too. But fine wasn't dynamic. If her heart was due to go down in a blaze of glory, she wasn't going to fade quietly into the night.

She had a couple of party numbers with a bit of pizzazz. Then she remembered she had a vintage cocktail dress, midnight blue fabric shot through with sparkle and dazzling with sequins. It reminded her of a starry night sky. She'd never had a firecracker reason to wear it...until now.

Around lunchtime, Robyn was chatting to people as more craft stalls were erected when a message came through on her phone.

Your marketing worked. It was the most understated message Brad had ever sent.

Robyn replied. *I heard you on the radio this morning.*

A sting of elation clashed with disappointment. Brad felt happy that she'd heard the interview so she would understand what was going on. But sad that some of his comments could have upset her. Or his disappearance without telling her he'd gone to New York. But as he'd driven off in the middle of the night he didn't want to wake her, or leave a message before he knew what was happening himself. He'd needed to go and talk to Tony and find out if the interest in the single release had truly skyrocketed. So, he'd kept quiet, and then was pulled into the fast–moving interview circuit. To say it had been a crazy busy day was the second biggest understatement.

Tony accepted every offer for radio and TV interviews. I'm running around New York from one studio to the next.

Run strong. That was the whole reason for doing it.

Two words. No one else he'd ever met would sum it up like Robyn.

I will. I'll be back in time to sing at the fair.

See you tomorrow.

And that was it. Everything understood with little explanation.

Brad wasn't sure this was a good thing. He wasn't sure of anything. Thrown back into the musical limelight was familiar territory. He'd always been able to handle that. An asset he valued. But now...there was an even more precious element in the mix to consider — Robyn. Where did she fit in without pulling her out of the life she had that she was happy with? The small town life he was happy with too.

Tony had news for Brad. 'Someone has spoken to the press. Media news sites have reported, from a so-called *source*, that Robyn is your lyric writer. They've even grabbed a picture of her from her website.'

They were sitting in the lounge of one of the radio stations drinking coffee before Brad was due to be interviewed.

Brad muttered under his breath and swallowed his anger. 'A source!'

'It wasn't me. I'm pretty sure it wasn't any of the guys,' Tony insisted.

Brad nodded. 'I trust all of you. So it was an outsider.'

'I'll find out,' Tony assured him. The decisiveness in his tone was clear. He had a wide circle of friends in the media and planned to call them.

'You're on air in five,' a radio assistant said to Brad, beckoning him through to the studio.

Brad downed the remainder of his coffee, and followed the assistant, leaving the detective work in Tony's capable hands.

During the interview, Brad side-stepped questions about Robyn being his lyric writer. Thankfully, the DJ was a friend and a fan, so he went easy on the questions, making the new single the focus of the interview. The music was of more interest to listeners. The Robyn issue was a personal deal.

Brad emerged virtually unscathed from the interview and joined Tony in the lounge. They had more interviews lined up for later in the day, and headed out of the studio to their next one.

Tony spoke as they were on the move. 'I found out the snitch. Aria.'

'That figures.' The bitterness in Brad's voice was evident. 'I guess she's still trying to step into my spotlight.'

'While throwing Robyn under the bus,' Tony added.

Brad checked his messages. 'Nothing from Robyn. She probably doesn't know yet.'

They got into the car. Brad drove off, heading to their next location across the city.

'Aria put two and two together,' Tony explained as Brad navigated the traffic. 'The robin logo, Robyn your marketing consultant, the *she* you let slip on the radio, and came up with an equation that serves her own interests. Forcing herself into the glow of your limelight.'

'This complicates things,' Brad said wearily.

'Even more,' Tony clarified.

Brad didn't argue. A whole web of trouble was being spun around him. Wanting a quiet life in a small town with Robyn was proving to be headline news.

Kyle served up lunch to the musicians in the lodge restaurant. 'I've added extra sweet potato mash with my secret sauce.'

The guys had gone there to relax after checking the stage at the market fair location. Tony had just called to tell them that Aria had ratted on Robyn writing Brad's lyrics. The atmosphere at their table felt heavy.

The guitarist held up his phone to his friends and pointed to Robyn's picture on one of the media links where the story was published. 'This is Robyn. I didn't know when I spoke to her this morning. I thought she was one of the event assistants.'

None of them had known. But now her interest in Brad made sense. They'd assumed she was another eager fan too. They were used to people trying to talk to Brad.

'Everything to your liking?' Kyle assumed from their frowns that there was an issue with their meal.

Assuring him the food was excellent, they told him about the latest predicament.

Kyle almost knocked his chef's hat off slapping his brow in surprise. 'Robyn is writing the lyrics for Brad's new hit songs! And Aria told the press.'

The guys nodded.

It took a moment for Kyle to process the news. He spooned the remainder of his special sauce on their plates, smiled, and then hurried away to tell Penny.

Penny was as surprised as Kyle. 'Does Robyn know about this?'

'I don't think so. The guys only just found out,' Kyle explained.

'I'll phone Nancy. We have to figure out what to do.' Penny called Nancy. The gossip started to snowball in Snow Bells.

Jessica linked her arm through the sheriff's and gave him a loving squeeze. 'Thanks for helping to put up my stall. I can't wait to hang up the quilts tomorrow at the fair.'

Volunteers were on hand to help anyone needing assistance with their stalls, but most folk tried to do it themselves to take the burden off the volunteers as they had a ton of work to do. Nate was buzzing about like a bee.

Virginia watched the sheriff walk away, after saying he'd see Jessica at home for dinner that evening.

She saw Sylvie was nearby with Zack, still in the throws of their honeymoon, but Sylvie was planning to show her fabric collections at the fair. Zack helped her put the stall together the way she wanted it. Another happy couple.

Then there was Lucie with Greg, sorting out their tables and chairs.

Looking around her, Virginia wished she had that type of happiness. As she viewed the numerous stalls shaping up, she saw Luke setting up his art stall. He didn't look over at her. She wished too that her heart would take heed of her head. Luke wasn't interested in her romantically. That didn't make him a bad guy. Just not the guy for her. So why did she keep pining when it was in vain? Maybe having a crush on Luke was a habit she needed to break.

Brushing these thoughts aside, Virginia went over to chat to Jessica about quilts and dressmaking.

Nancy phoned Jessica a few minutes later. 'Is Robyn there?' The call sounded urgent.

'Yes, she's over at the dance area talking to a couple of the farmers.' Jessica wondered what was wrong.

Nancy explained the situation.

'We should've figured out it was Robyn when Brad was interviewed on the radio,' said Jessica. 'But we were so pleased Snow Bells was mentioned that it didn't dawn on us.'

'Someone has to tell Robyn,' Nancy explained. 'I don't want to tell her over the phone, and I can't leave the grocery store. Nate has enough burdens on his plate so...'

'I'll tell Robyn,' said Jessica.

'Assure her that the quilting bee members will rally round her, shielding her from whatever is coming her way.'

'I will. Virginia is here too. We'll go talk to Robyn right now and call you back.'

As they walked over to where Robyn was talking to the farmers, Jessica told Virginia what had happened.

Their surprise that Robyn was Brad's lyricist played second fiddle to their need to protect her from getting hurt from the gossip.

'Robyn, can I talk to you?' Jessica beckoned to her.

Glancing round and seeing Jessica and Virginia, she smiled. 'Yes.' She thought it was something to do with displaying the quilts. She had notes in her binder for suggestions to highlight Virginia's evening dresses as well as an idea to put pictures up showing Sylvie and Ana's wedding dresses. Notes for Jessica included making a big deal of the fat quarter bundles of fabric, while tying in some of Sylvie's fabrics from her new collections.

But as Jessica and Virginia led Robyn away from eavesdroppers, and neither of them were smiling, Robyn knew something was wrong.

'Aria has told the media that you're Brad's secret lyric writer.' Jessica felt terrible seeing the impact this revelation had on Robyn. But there was no way to sugar the pill.

Jessica and Virginia instinctively moved closer and kept their voices soft and assuring. 'The quilting bee members won't let the media sharks get you,' said Jessica.

'They won't get past us,' Virginia added.

'I was going to tell everyone,' Robyn began to explain.

'It's okay, we understand you needed to keep this a secret until Brad's album was out,' Jessica assured her.

The relief of everyone knowing helped alleviate the thundering of Robyn's heart. A storm was brewing. She'd sensed it as soon as the website had been updated. It had built up last night, like warning waves coming to wash away her happy life in Snow Bells. Her senses about things like this had never been wrong. Now, what were her senses telling her? Run? Hide? Challenge them all? Despite the odds, her own self–defiance kicked into overdrive. Option three. No doubts.

For the remainder of the day, Robyn continued helping with the preparations for the market fair. Jessica and Virginia had gone back to tend to their shops, as had others, now that the stalls were ready. Lots more lanterns and twinkle lights had been hung around the dance area, and there was a feeling of anticipation in the air about the forthcoming event.

Later, Robyn drove home and closed the door, intending to make a dinner and relax in the evening.

There were no more messages from Brad, and she figured they'd talk when he got back from New York.

CHAPTER SEVENTEEN

Playing music with you feels so right
Singing songs way past midnight
Sitting with you under the starlight
Playing music with you tonight

Brad drove home at night with Tony in the car. Tony planned to spend a couple of days in Snow Bells Haven and then hitch a ride back to New York in the guys' van. No point driving there in two cars.

On the way, Brad phoned the lodge. 'Penny, it's Brad.'

'How many rooms do you need?' she said lightly.

'One. For my manager, Tony. We're on our way back to Snow Bells. We should be there within the hour.'

'I have a nice room available for Tony,' Penny was happy to tell him.

'Thanks, I appreciate you accommodating him,' said Brad.

Tony had packed a couple of cases for his impromptu working vacation. This included carefully folded shirts and a spare suit. Tony didn't do casual. He wore bespoke suits, shirts, ties, waistcoats. Expensive. He looked more like a lawyer than Mark. He handled the business side of Brad's affairs with aplomb.

Born and raised in New York, Tony was street smart. An asset that money couldn't buy. His loyalty to Brad and the other musicians couldn't be bought either. Brad considered this to be priceless.

Virginia had finished altering the hem of Penny's new dress, and dropped it off to her at the lodge that evening.

They stood at the reception area chatting about the dress Penny had bought from Virginia's shop to wear at the market fair. It was classy, but fashionable.

'Thanks for bringing this over,' Penny said to Virginia.

'No problem. I'll see you tomorrow at the fair.' Virginia went to leave when Brad walked in with Tony.

Tony's first impression of the lodge was excellent. He liked the decor, the welcoming atmosphere.

Brad introduced him to Penny and Virginia.

'Tony, this is Penny.'

'Pleased to finally meet you, Penny,' said Tony. 'The guys are full of praise for your lodge.'

Penny smiled and looked delighted at the compliment. 'Welcome to the lodge, Tony.'

'And this is Virginia,' Brad added. 'Virginia is a dressmaker and owns the dress shop in the main street.'

Virginia's heart reacted seeing Tony standing there in a bespoke suit. He was marginally shorter than Brad, with well–cut dark hair, blue eyes and a fit build, disguised by his elegant suit.

'Tony's my manager,' Brad elaborated, wondering why Virginia was staring at him.

Virginia snapped out of her wayward thoughts and smiled. 'Pleased to meet you.'

Tony stepped forward and smiled at her. 'Nice to meet you too, Virginia.'

The introduction was barely a moment or two, but there was an instant spark between Virginia and Tony.

Brad glanced at Penny. She'd clearly sensed it too.

'I'm looking forward to hearing you perform at the fair tomorrow,' Virginia said to Brad, and then headed out of the lodge.

'I'll go bring in my luggage,' Tony told Brad.

'Let me give you a hand,' Brad offered.

'No, I can manage.' Tony hurried after Virginia.

'Are you thinking, what I'm thinking?' Penny said, smirking at Brad.

Brad laughed. 'It's been quite a topsy–turvy day. Nothing would surprise me.'

Moments later, Tony came back into reception carrying the two, large, heavy suitcases as if they were lightweight.

Brad muttered under his breath to Penny. 'I withdraw that last comment.'

Penny stifled a giggle.

Tony glanced back to see that Virginia had gone, and dumped the cases down.

'I hope it was worth wrenching your arms out of your shoulder sockets to impress Virginia,' Brad said to him.

Tony straightened his tie and cuffs. 'I'm stronger than I look. This suit hides a multitude.'

'Of sins or stupidity?' Brad stated.

'There's nothing dumb about romance,' Tony told him.

Brad blinked. 'Romance? Smitten in Snow Bells already?'

'Virginia seems like a lovely young lady, that's all. I'm not likely to see her again.'

Penny cut–in. 'Virginia has a dress stall at the market fair.'

Tony reacted well to that news. 'I guess I'll see her tomorrow.'

Brad made a throwaway comment to Penny. 'What's in Snow Bells *secret sauce* when it comes to stirring up romance?'

Kyle came scurrying out of the kitchen, overhearing a snatch of the conversation. 'My secret sauce is an old–fashioned recipe that I've brought bang up to date with my own sprinkling of herbs and spices.'

'Sounds delicious,' said Tony.

Brad introduced them. 'Kyle is Penny's nephew, a top chef. He's opened a new restaurant in the lodge.'

'Brad's manager, Tony, is staying with us for a couple of nights,' Penny said to Kyle.

They shook hands.

Kyle gestured through to the restaurant. 'Are you joining the guys for dinner? I have plenty of my secret sauce left. And my special chocolate chilli dip if you're up for it.'

'I'm the adventurous type when it comes to dining out,' said Tony. 'So lay it on me, Kyle.'

Kyle beamed and then glanced at Brad.

'Count me in too,' Brad confirmed.

'I'll show them through to the restaurant,' Penny said to Kyle, helpfully shooing him through to the kitchen, while a member of staff took Tony's cases to his room.

They were all seated at the one table. Nearby, Penny noticed Luke sitting dining with a couple of artist friends here for the fair. She leaned down and confided to Tony. 'That's Luke over there. Virginia is single, but she's had an unrequited crush on Luke for a while now.'

Tony was interested to glean more details. 'Which one is Luke?'

'The tall, good looking, dark haired one,' Penny told him. 'He owns the art shop in town. He created the fancy music symbol for Brad's studio wall.'

'Oh, I heard about that guy. The artist.' Tony nodded to himself, and then said to Penny, 'What's so special about Luke that Virginia thinks he's a hot potato?'

Kyle walked into Tony's comment and served up two main courses to Brad and Tony. 'It's sweet potato mash,' Kyle explained to Tony. 'With my secret sauce.'

Tony smiled and nodded his thanks, and then resumed his chat with Penny.

'Luke is a real fast runner,' Penny told Tony. 'Some of the local ladies are impressed with his speed.'

'I used to outrun the cops when I was a kid,' Tony revealed, forgetting to keep his voice down. 'It didn't make me no heartthrob.'

Luke glanced over and met a steely gaze from Tony.

Brad nudged Tony, and the equilibrium settled to a calm watermark as they ate dinner. No ripples of contention from Tony. On the surface anyway. He hid the riptide bubbling under the surface well.

'Luke seems like a bit of a cold fish,' Tony remarked to Brad.

Kyle walked in with extra chocolate chilli dip. 'I have chilled salmon,' Kyle offered him.

'Thanks, Kyle, I'm good,' Tony told him.

Kyle continued serving the busy restaurant.

'Let it go,' Brad hissed to Tony.

Holding up his hands, Tony nodded. 'Okay. But it just grates on me that a guy like Luke causes heartache for a sweet woman like Virginia.' He shrugged. 'But, that's the way the cookie crumbles.'

'Two chocolate cookies coming up,' Kyle said, sweeping by their table.

Tony shook his head and grinned at Brad. 'You think if I mention gold bullion, Kyle will have a recipe to match?'

Brad smiled, and the conversation at the table, as they enjoyed dinner, circled around the preparation for the performance at the fair. And the forthcoming whirlwind when the video was released.

'Do you think Aria will turn up for the performance tomorrow?' Brad said to Tony.

'No, she's too busy cashing in on the glam–shot interviews she exchanged for snitching on you and Robyn,' Tony assured him. 'When she can't share your limelight, she's happy to nudge the spotlight in her own ambitious direction.'

Brad nodded. Tony was always right about people's moves and motives. Another plus in their long–standing friendship.

'The woman in the red dress is the one to speak to.' One of the farmer's pointed across the stalls to where Robyn stood near the stage.

The morning of the market fair dawned bright and sunny. It was going to be a scorcher, in more ways than one.

The media reporter made a beeline for Robyn, mistakenly thinking she was due to encounter an easy target.

Robyn didn't see her coming and was unprepared for a microphone to be shoved in her face.

'Robyn,' the reporter said with an inappropriate fake familiarity. 'Did you write the lyrics for the two new songs Brad is due to perform later today?'

Robyn iced her with a look that even a hot day like this couldn't melt. 'Excuse me, I'm busy with my marketing work.' This was true. She'd been there since the first stallholder arrived, taking photos as the fair sprang to life. She planned to create a montage of the images leading up to the official opening of the fair when Mark made his speech within the next hour. A video for the town's website.

'But can I just ask...' the reporter's words trailed off as Robyn walked away, leaving behind her an impression that jarred the news hound's plans.

After breakfast, Tony and the guys were in Brad's studio. Tony was given the tour of the studio, loving the layout of it. While the guys rehearsed the songs for the performance, Tony left them to get on with their playing.

'I'm heading out for a look around the town before we go to the fair,' said Tony.

Brad walked him out, so that he could lock the door after Tony left.

Tony stepped outside into the sunshine, wearing a sharp suit, as always.

Brad thumbed along the street. 'Virginia's dress shop is that way.'

Tony opened his arms wide. 'I'm just having a look around the town.'

'Sure you are,' Brad said, with an unconvinced smile.

Tony waved and headed up the street while Brad locked the studio door.

The sheriff and his deputy were walking down the street. Tony smiled and introduced himself.

'Hi, I'm Tony, Brad's manager.'

The mention of Brad's name sparked interest from them, and they were pleased to meet him.

'Are you going to the market fair for Brad's performance?' said the sheriff.

Tony nodded. 'Wouldn't miss it.' He looked around the main street. 'I keep hearing all these great things about Snow Bells Haven from Brad. Tell me, what's the real estate like around here?'

The sheriff was glad to extol the benefits of the town's property market.

Brad and the guys had just finished playing one of the new songs when a message came through for him from Robyn.

Remember to take pictures of you and the guys outside the studio. It'll be handy to add context to the video of your performance.

This was something she'd mentioned to him recently, and he'd clean forgot about.

'We should get some photos of us all outside the studio in the sunlight. Grab a guitar or whatever else you want, and let's do this now.'

Following Brad outside, they gathered in a group in front of the studio and asked a passer–by to take a couple of photos of them all together.

Then Brad snapped a few of the guys themselves, making sure to show the studio.

Meanwhile...Wyn told Tony about the cove.

'I recently moved to Snow Bells to work as the sheriff's deputy. I got myself a real nice cabin up at the cove,' said Wyn.

Tony looked interested, and surprised. 'The town's got a cove? Like a coastal residence area?'

'Yes,' Wyn was keen to tell him. 'It's only a stone's throw from here.' He gestured to the narrow road leading to it.

'I think I'll take a quick look at that before heading back to the studio,' said Tony. 'Is it far to walk? I came from New York in Brad's car. I left mine in the city.'

'Hop in the back with us.' The sheriff offered him a lift. 'We'll give you a quick tour.'

Tony took them up on their kind offer and got into the back of the sheriff's car, with Wyn in the front passenger seat.

The traffic was fairly busy in the main street due to everyone turning up for the market fair, causing them to drive slowly by the studio.

Brad blinked, thinking he was seeing things. But no, there was Tony sitting in the back of the sheriff's car with the deputy riding up front.

The guys noticed too, and laughed rather than looked concerned.

Brad jokingly checked his watch. 'Usually it takes a few days before Tony gets on the wrong side of the law.'

None of them thought that Tony had been arrested. But it looked like it. So they weren't totally convinced that everything was okay.

Brad sent a message to Tony. *Should I have your mail redirected to the sheriff's office?*

Tony replied. *The sheriff and Wyn are giving me a tour of property at the cove. See you shortly.*

'Everything's fine,' Brad told the guys. 'Just Tony being Tony.'

Bunting was draped across the stalls at the market fair, and the stallholders were starting to become busy with people buying their products as the fair was officially opened. Mark's speech up on the stage went down well, and from the number of people arriving to enjoy the fun of the day, it looked to be one of the town's most successful market fairs.

But gossip had filtered through to some of the quilting bee members. Penny had been coming out of Nancy's grocery store and had seen Tony in the back of the sheriff's car. Word soon reached Virginia at her dress stall, and her heart sank when she heard that Tony was obviously a troublemaker.

Robyn had clapped and cheered Mark at the end of his speech, and had avoided a couple of city journalists trying to waylay her about her lyric writing. She approached Virginia's stall to take photos of it.

But Virginia wasn't in the mood for smiling. 'Why do I always like the wrong guys?'

Robyn glanced over at Luke tending to his art stall.

'No, not Luke,' Virginia said with a sigh.

'You like someone else?'

Virginia fussed with her dress rails and shrugged. 'Maybe, or I was starting to, then he goes and gets arrested by the sheriff.'

'Do I know him?' said Robyn.

Virginia couldn't look up as she revealed his name. 'Tony.'

'Brad's manager!' Robyn was totally surprised. 'I didn't know you knew him.'

'I met him last night at the lodge.' Virginia explained about their brief encounter, and Tony's attempt to impress her with his luggage lifting. 'He's the first guy I've felt something special for in a long time. Apart from Luke.'

'Wait a minute. You're saying that the sheriff has arrested Tony?' Robyn sounded aghast.

Virginia nodded, and tried to shrug off her disappointment. 'Penny saw Tony in the main street being driven off in the back of the sheriff's car. Deputy Wyn was there too.'

'I have to phone Brad,' Robyn said urgently.

Brad was in the studio rehearsing with the guys, but his heart soared when he saw the caller's name.

'We took the photos outside the studio,' Brad told her, before she could tell him why'd she'd called. 'Thanks for reminding me.'

She could hear from his chirpy tone that he didn't know about Tony's predicament.

'Brad, Tony's been arrested by the sheriff.' She spoke blunt and clear.

'No, it's fine,' he assured her, explaining what had happened.

Robyn felt the relief wash over her. 'Thank goodness. The gossip is circulating at the fair. I'll set things straight with Virginia and any others.'

Brad kept his voice down. 'Is Virginia there?'

'Yes, why?'

'Tony's sweet on her,' he whispered.

'The feeling is mutual.'

'It's nice that they like each other, but Tony's only here for the fair. I don't see how things could work for them.'

'Neither do I, but I'm going to tell her about the gossip being wrong,' said Robyn.

'Okay, I'll see you later. We're coming to the fair just before it's time for the performance in the afternoon. I don't want any fans or fuss to disrupt the event.'

'That's thoughtful.'

'And Robyn, we need to talk about things. Just you and me.'

'Yes,' she agreed. 'We'll do that later.'

He ached to tell her that he missed her, but this was something he wanted to tell her personally. When he'd been in New York, all he could think of was that he wanted the interviews to be finished so that he could get home to her.

After the call, Robyn was pleased to reveal the misunderstanding about Tony to Virginia.

'I'm so glad.' Virginia beamed and Robyn felt the need to remind her that Tony's visit to town was temporary.

'Tony's only here for a short stay.'

'I understand that. It was just nice to feel...you know...a sense of romance.'

A customer came up to Virginia's stall, eager to buy one of the evening dresses. 'This is so lovely. I'd like to wear it to the dance tonight.'

While Virginia dealt with the customer, Robyn phoned Penny to explain about Tony. Then she wandered around the stalls, buying a few items, like yarn, fabric from Jessica, fashion bracelets from one of the craft stalls, and a home baked vanilla and buttercream cake. She carried them over to her car and put them in the back.

From the edge of the parking area she took photos of the market fair, showing how busy it was with people and activity. A lead photo for sure for the news feature she was due to write for the town's website.

Wearing a smile along with his sharp suit, Tony arrived at the fair ahead of Brad and the guys, eager to look around. There were so many stalls, and the aroma of fresh pancakes being cooked by Greg and Lucie, along with other food stalls serving refreshments and snacks, wafted in the air. He looked around for Virginia's stall, but bumped into the sheriff and Wyn.

'Hey, Tony.' The sheriff said, pleased to see him. 'Enjoying the fair?'

'Yes, it's an impressive event,' Tony told him.

'Nate says it's the busiest in a while,' Wyn added.

'But there's always something fun going on in our town,' the sheriff said to Tony. 'Another element to consider if you decide to move here. We're a big small town, with lots happening.'

Tony nodded. 'It would be a huge wrench to uproot from New York, but it's something that's been on my mind this past year or so. Brad moving here, talking about how great the town is, it's made me want to rethink things.'

'If it's any help, I moved here from New York,' the sheriff confided.

Tony looked surprised. 'You're from the city?'

'Sure am. I worked in security. One day at a quilting event I was working at in New York, I met Jessica. The day I met her, that was it. I fell for her there and then. She'd never been to a quilting event in New York before, and I'd rarely been outside of the city.'

'What happened?' Tony was keen to know.

'We started dating. She had her house and quilt shop in Snow Bells, and I'd drive there, even just to see her for an hour or so. People thought it wouldn't work between us. Two different worlds.' The sheriff sighed. 'But driving back to New York kept feeling heavier. One day, I knew that my home was with her in Snow Bells, and New York was in my past.'

Tony revealed his situation. 'I have an apartment with a great view of the city. I have a nice office with another wonderful view of New York. I have a successful career there, but no one to share my life with. Something always feels like it's missing these days.'

The sheriff nodded. 'I felt like that. There comes a time when I think a man feels the need to settle down. Before I met Jessica, I'd thought about living in a small town, but meeting her was the spark I needed to leave the city. I think if I hadn't met her, I could still be working security in New York, throwing tough guys like you, Tony, out of city clubs.'

Tony laughed. 'My tough past is long gone, if it was ever really there.'

Wyn smiled. 'You probably need a strong character to succeed in your business.'

Tony agreed.

'When I moved to Snow Bells, I moved in with Jessica,' the sheriff explained to Tony. 'I didn't have a house of my own. I applied for a job at the sheriff's office, and now, here I am. But if you move here, you can afford to buy a house at the cove. And you won't need to change your job. You'll still work as Brad's manager, work in the music industry. The only thing that will change for you is the view from your window.' The sheriff smiled at Tony, and got ready to walk away. 'Think about that.'

'I will, thanks,' said Tony.

The sheriff and Wyn headed away into the crowd, leaving Tony with lots to consider.

Brad and the guys drove in the van to the market fair and unloaded the guitars, keyboards and drums.

Entering the stage from the side, they started to set up their equipment behind the curtain shielding them from view.

Their years of experience playing live concerts enabled them to make short work of setting up, and they indicated to Nate that they were ready to play at the scheduled time.

The curtains were pulled back.

A crowd had gathered at the front of the stage, eager to hear the performance.

Robyn was ready to film the performance, and another volunteer was there with a back–up camera. News reporters were there too.

Tony stood with Nate at the side of the stage out of view of the audience, but was on hand if Brad needed him.

A ripple of excitement charged through the crowd that included fans who'd arrived specially to hear Brad.

Wearing jeans and a pale blue shirt, Brad walked to the front of the stage with his electric guitar slung around his neck and spoke to the audience. A cheer erupted before he'd even spoken.

'Thank you for welcoming us,' Brad began. 'I've just released a new single. But these are two other new songs from the forthcoming album. I hope you like them. All of these new songs were written, right here, in Snow Bells Haven.'

Brad nodded to the musicians and started playing his guitar, building up the introduction to the song. The anticipation rose up from the crowd. Then with another nod to the guys, he played the opening riff, causing the audience to burst into applause as the exciting melody filled the stage and resonated out to the audience.

The summer air carried the song across the whole of the market fair.

Robyn felt tingles at the energy of the riff, and then Brad started singing, causing another cheer from the crowd. She wanted to cheer too, getting swept up in the excitement of the live performance, but had to keep herself steady to film it.

Hearing the song, with her lyrics, being performed on stage was an experience she knew she'd always remember. The atmosphere, Brad's talent, backed by the other musicians, the warm summer day and a cobalt blue sky. It was perfect.

Her heart felt such a strong longing to be with Brad, so happy that she was part of his world.

The melody built to a rapturous finale, with the sound of Brad's guitar playing taken to a level that displayed his talent as a singer, guitarist and performer.

Whatever she'd been expecting, and it was a lot, Brad's performance outshone all her dreams.

The second song, drifted in slowly, deeply, a moody number with an underlying beat and memorable riff. The audience was captivated.

And so was Robyn. Her heart felt fit to burst. There was Brad up there on the stage creating a piece of musical magic. But she kept getting flickers of the moments they'd shared together, lying in his garden under the stars, cooking meals together, the laughter and teasing, how he made her smile, how he made her feel...

As the song ended on a high note, the crowd went wild.

Robyn brought her focus back to the task in hand. Capturing the footage, the happy faces of the crowd, and Brad and the musicians standing up there on the stage.

'Robyn.' Brad's voice called out above everything. He held out his hand and beckoned her to come up on stage. There were steps at the side, and she walked over, taking his hand as he pulled her up on to the stage beside him.

Brad spoke to the crowd. 'This is Robyn, my new lyric writer.' No hiding now.

The cheer from the audience filled her heart with a sense that she was welcome in Brad's world, while still welcome in Snow Bells. She could see the faces of strangers alongside others she knew, like Nancy, Penny, Virginia, Jessica and Greg. They were all happy for her and cheering her on.

Brad waved goodbye to the audience.

A roar of appreciation for the live performance, and the chance to be the first to hear the new songs, charged the air with a feeling of friendship and fun.

Robyn then took photos of Brad on stage standing beside Nate, Mark and others, including the sheriff and Wyn. Precious images of those involved in the market fair, alongside Brad, the guys and Tony. These pictures were going up on the town's website for sure.

Jessica, Virginia, Nancy, Penny and other members of the quilting bee joined them for a group photo. Tony stood next to Virginia.

With all the photos taken, everyone filtered into the fun of the market fair.

Brad and the guys drove back to the studio in the van.

Robyn gave Tony a ride with her.

'So...you and Virginia, huh?' She couldn't resist teasing him.

He didn't deny it. 'I like her. I think maybe she'd like me, if she could see past the shadow of Luke.'

'Oh, the times they are a changing.' Robyn gave him a knowing glance.

Tony perked up. 'Seriously?'

'Oh, yeah,' Robyn confirmed. 'But I said nothing.'

'Nothing about what?' Tony joked with her.

They laughed.

'I heard gossip that you were up at the cove checking out the cabins.'

'Wyn's got a cabin up there. He let me have a peek inside. Homely luxury. Just my vibe. Apparently, there's a cabin due to be up for sale soon. I'm thinking of buying it.'

'Does Brad know?'

'Nope. Only Wyn, the sheriff and now you. Though probably half the town knows considering the way gossip spreads in Snow Bells.'

'That's a good thing. It's better to have things like that out in the open.'

'Like you writing lyrics for the songs.'

She couldn't argue with that. 'It's a relief not to keep it a secret. But now with the other two new songs about to be released on the video, I'm concerned that I'll be thrown back into the media spotlight again as the lyric writer.'

'You should know the best way to handle a news situation like that,' Tony prompted her.

Her response was instant. 'Release the news first.'

Tony nodded firmly. 'Put your name on the video as the lyricist. Shout it loud.'

She hesitated. 'I kind of like the little robin logo.'

'Have both. Your name and the logo. Let them all know you're not hiding now.'

'I love that idea.'

'Run it by Brad, so we all agree,' Tony advised.

'I will.'

'And maybe tell him that you're rescheduling some of your other plans.'

Robyn frowned. 'Like what?'

'Like waiting to make time for romance.'

'Someone's been telling tales.'

'Brad mentioned that he doesn't want to disrupt your plans, especially the bit about you putting love on ice until you can *make time for romance*.'

She threw him a side eye.

'You're a smart cookie, Robyn, but that seems like a dumb idea to me.'

They arrived outside the studio. She parked behind the van and they headed inside to join Brad and the others.

The plan was for Robyn to prepare the video so that they could get it up on the website as promised.

Inside the studio, everyone bustled around while Robyn set up her laptop to check the video and edit it.

Brad smiled, seeing her work like lightning, concentrating on the task in hand. She was experienced in making short clips for websites. This was a bit longer, but she kept going, working through the footage of the two songs, the whole performance. Then she quickly top and tailed it with a couple of photos showing Brad and the guys standing outside his new studio, and one of the group shots from the fair that included them with everyone from the mayor to the sheriff.

She glanced at Brad and Tony for their approval to include a picture showing them with everyone.

Brad and Tony gave her a thumbs up.

The whole editing process took about an hour, but the time went by in a blink, with the guys talking about the new songs, having coffee, and buzzing around the studio. The excited vibe hadn't calmed down.

Robyn sent the finished video to Tony and waited...

Tony uploaded the video to the website. 'Here we go!' He pressed update.

Robyn checked the website on her laptop, as the guys gathered around to look too. And there was the video, playing for all to see and hear.

Closing the laptop, Robyn let out a sigh of relief. 'Job done.'

'If the work's done, how about we all go and enjoy the fair,' Brad suggested. 'I hear there's dancing.' He checked the time. 'It should be starting soon.'

Robyn stood up. 'My dress is in the car.'

'You look terrific in your red dress,' said Brad. He'd been admiring her.

'I'm upping the starry sparkle for the evening.' She headed out to her car, glancing over her shoulder at Brad smiling.

Grabbing her dress, she came back in and went upstairs to change. Even under the dim lighting, the fabric sparkled like stars. Hooking one of Brad's denim jackets on to her finger, she threw it over her shoulder, intending to wear it to the fair. The light pouring in the top window indicated that the daylight had mellowed, but she didn't want to arrive there looking like she was overdressed.

Walking downstairs to the studio, she gasped and laughed. The guys had played a joke on her. They were all standing there wearing sunglasses, pretending to shield their eyes from her dazzling dress.

She couldn't stop laughing.

Brad pushed his shades up on to his forehead and squinted. 'Nice dress, I think.' He pretended to cover his eyes from the glare.

Tony kept his sunglasses on, as did the musicians.

'Where's Robyn?' said Tony. 'I'm seeing nothing but stars.'

Swiping at them, Robyn giggled. 'This is muted compared to my silver sequin dress. But I'll save that for the next time.'

'Warning noted,' Brad said, playing along. 'Nice jacket by the way. I have one just like that.'

'I'm stealing it.' Robyn draped it around her shoulders. It was large enough to cover most of her dress. 'I don't want to turn up to the fair overdressed. It's not quite time for the dancing.'

Tony checked the time. 'Not far away. Shall we?' He gestured for them all to leave.

They piled into Robyn's car and Brad's car, leaving the van parked outside the studio.

Tony went with Robyn again, along with one of the guys in the back.

They pulled up at the field and walked over to where the dance area was lit with lanterns and lights.

Robyn gazed up at the sky's amber glow overtaking the daylight. 'It's a beautiful evening.'

Brad walked beside her and murmured, gazing at her, not the sky. 'So beautiful.'

She smiled up at him.

'I'll catch up with you at the dancing.' Tony took a detour over to Virginia's stall to invite her to dance with him.

The guys headed to the stalls to buy gifts to take back to New York, and grab something to eat at the snack stalls.

Brad and Robyn continued over to the edge of the dance area, lit by the decorative lights. She shrugged the denim jacket off to reveal her sparkling dress. The sequins scintillated under the lanterns and twinkle lights.

Before the dancing began, Robyn told Brad about her discussion with Tony to add her name to the lyric credits.

Brad was delighted. 'I love that you're keeping the robin logo too.'

'It's cute.'

So was she, a heartbreaker in that dress.

'Oh look.' Robyn pointed up at the evening sky. 'Two shooting stars. Did you see them?'

'Yes,' he confirmed. 'Maybe it's a sign.'

As he said this, a message came through from Tony. *I just checked the video on the website. The views for the new songs are skyrocketing.*

Brad smiled and showed Robyn the message.

'Wow! Maybe wishing on stars comes true after all,' she said.

'Is that what you wished for? Success for the songs?'

That telltale blush she'd tried to keep under control gave the game away.

Brad moved closer and gazed down at her. 'Or did you wish for something closer to home, closer to your heart?'

His tempting lips were a breath away, and she thought for a moment he was going to kiss her.

An announcement that the dance was about to start, inviting couples to take to the floor, interrupted the moment.

He held his hand out. 'Shall we?'

Robyn took his hand and he led her on to the dance floor.

The opening number got the dancing off to a lively start, and Brad twirled her around, causing her to gasp and giggle.

Other couples, including Tony and Virginia, Nate and Nancy and Jessica and the sheriff had joined in the dancing, filling the floor, as everyone enjoyed themselves.

Under the strings of twinkle lights entwined across the dance floor, Robyn's dress sparkled like the starlight above them.

After a few songs to get the dancing going, the music changed to a romantic melody.

Brad took Robyn in his arms and held her close as they slow danced around the floor.

'I missed you when I was in New York,' Brad murmured to her.

'I missed you too,' she said, feeling him wrap her closer in his strong arms. 'You were incredible on stage today.'

He gazed at her. 'You're incredible every day.'

She blushed again, but didn't care to hide it. Brad had this effect on her. He'd affected her like this since the first time they'd met. They hadn't known each other long, but she felt they knew each other well. Sometimes, that was just how it was meant to be.

'We can make this work, Robyn.' His voice was deep, loving. 'I think we were meant to be. I know I'll have to tour for a few weeks when the album is released, but you can come with me, if you'd like. The guys make it work. We wouldn't be apart too long.

And then you'd have months on end putting up with me working at the studio and seeing you every day and night.'

Her heart ached, hoping this was true.

Brad needed Robyn to be that incredible woman he'd fallen in love with. The one who said yes to challenges. The woman to challenge him. Deep in his heart he urged her to give him the reply he longed for. Say yes, Robyn, he thought, wishing again for what he'd wished for before. To get together with her.

Robyn smiled up at him as they danced. 'Yes,' she murmured.

Brad lifted her up and swung her around, then kissed the breath from her.

His firm lips claimed hers, and everything she'd felt for him ignited.

'I love you, Robyn,' he said, holding her close.

'And I love you too.'

'We can make this work,' he assured her.

'Yes,' she said.

A few couples cheered, including Tony and Virginia, seeing the start of a whole new happy future for Robyn and Brad.

Tony whispered to Virginia as they waltzed together. 'That could be us soon. I'm aiming to buy a house here in Snow Bells. Change my view of the world from my window. Maybe have a view of the sea.'

'I hear that one of the cabins up at the cove will be for sale,' said Virginia.

Tony smiled, and they continued to dance.

During a break in the dancing, Brad went to get Robyn a refreshing, cold drink. Tony joined him, getting one for Virginia.

'Did you ever meet a woman and liked her from the get–go?' said Tony, out of earshot of the ladies.

Brad thought of Robyn.

'Dumb question,' Tony muttered. Brad had told him he'd liked Robyn from the start.

Brad grinned and paid for the four drinks.

'Penny tells me that the lodge caters for weddings,' Tony remarked to Brad, accepting two of the drinks.

'I haven't even had an official date with Robyn yet,' said Brad.

Tony smiled knowingly. 'For once, I wasn't thinking about you, buddy.'

Brad laughed lightly, and they joined Robyn and Virginia again to dance the night away.

A couple of weeks later, after the first rush of excitement had settled down from the release of the singles, Brad and Robyn sat outside in his garden. It was approaching midnight. Another warm, summer evening. He was back from a day in New York, giving interviews about the singles, and talking about the forthcoming album.

Robyn had worked locally, dealing with her clients' marketing. And writing lyrics. Her notepad was filled with gold dust. That's what Brad called it. Her lyrics made him write great songs. It worked. They worked.

They'd had a late dinner together, sitting outside in the garden.

Robyn relaxed on the two–seater garden swing chair and sipped her coffee, while Brad sat beside her and played one of his latest songs. His melody. Her lyrics.

Under the stars shining bright in the dark sky arching above them, Brad sang to her and played his guitar.

Love and lyrics
It was meant to be
I'm in tune with you
You're in tune with me

Music and romance
I know it's true
You're in love with me
I'm in love with you...

End

About the Author:

De-ann Black is a bestselling author, scriptwriter and former newspaper journalist. She has over 100 books published. Romance, thrillers, espionage novels, action adventure. And children's books (non-fiction rocket science books and children's fiction). She became an Amazon All-Star author in 2014 and 2015.

She previously worked as a full-time newspaper journalist for several years. She had her own weekly columns in the press. This included being a motoring correspondent where she got to test drive cars every week for the press for three years.

Before being asked to work for the press, De-ann worked in magazine editorial writing everything from fashion features to social news. She was the marketing editor of a glossy magazine.

She is also a professional artist and illustrator. Embroidery design, fabric design, dressmaking, sewing, knitting and fashion are part of her work.

Additionally, De-ann has always been interested in fitness, and was a fitness and bodybuilding champion, 100 metre runner and mountaineer. As a former N.A.B.B.A. Miss Scotland, she had a weekly fitness show on the radio that ran for over three years.

De-ann trained in Shukokai karate, boxing, kickboxing, Dayan Qigong and Jiu Jitsu. She is currently based in Scotland.

Her 16 colouring books are available in paperback, including her latest Summer Nature Colouring Book and Flower Nature Colouring Book.

Her latest embroidery pattern books include: Floral Garden Embroidery Patterns, Christmas & Winter Embroidery Patterns, Floral Spring Embroidery Patterns and Sea Theme Embroidery Patterns.

Website: Find out more at: www.de-annblack.com

Fabric, Wallpaper & Home Decor Collections:
De-ann's fabric designs and wallpaper collections, and home decor items, including her popular Scottish Garden Thistles patterns, are available from Spoonflower.
www.de-annblack.com/spoonflower

Also by De-ann Black (Romance, Action/Thrillers & Children's books). See her Amazon Author page or website for further details about her books, screenplays, illustrations, art, fabric designs and embroidery patterns.

Amazon Author page:
www.De-annBlack.com/Amazon

Romance books:

The Cure for Love Romance series:
1. The Cure for Love
2. The Cure for Love at Christmas

Scottish Highlands & Island Romance series:
1. Scottish Island Knitting Bee
2. Scottish Island Fairytale Castle
3. Vintage Dress Shop on the Island
4. Fairytale Christmas on the Island

Scottish Loch Romance series:
1. Sewing & Mending Cottage
2. Scottish Loch Summer Romance

Quilting Bee & Tea Shop series:
1. The Quilting Bee
2. The Tea Shop by the Sea
3. Embroidery Cottage
4. Knitting Shop by the Sea
5. Christmas Weddings

Sewing, Crafts & Quilting series:
1. The Sewing Bee
2. The Sewing Shop
3. Knitting Cottage (Scottish Highland romance)
4. Scottish Highlands Christmas Wedding
(Embroidery, Knitting, Dressmaking & Textile Art)

Cottages, Cakes & Crafts series:
1. The Flower Hunter's Cottage
2. The Sewing Bee by the Sea
3. The Beemaster's Cottage
4. The Chocolatier's Cottage
5. The Bookshop by the Seaside
6. The Dressmaker's Cottage

Scottish Chateau, Colouring & Crafts series:
1. Christmas Cake Chateau
2. Colouring Book Cottage

Snow Bells Haven series:
1. Snow Bells Christmas
2. Snow Bells Wedding
3. Love & Lyrics

Summer Sewing Bee

Sewing, Knitting & Baking series:
1. The Tea Shop
2. The Sewing Bee & Afternoon Tea
3. The Christmas Knitting Bee
4. Champagne Chic Lemonade Money
5. The Vintage Sewing & Knitting Bee

Tea Dress Shop series:
1. The Tea Dress Shop At Christmas
2. The Fairytale Tea Dress Shop In Edinburgh
3. The Vintage Tea Dress Shop In Summer

The Tea Shop & Tearoom series:
1. The Christmas Tea Shop & Bakery
2. The Christmas Chocolatier
3. The Chocolate Cake Shop in New York at Christmas
4. The Bakery by the Seaside
5. Shed in the City

Christmas Romance series:
1. Christmas Romance in Paris
2. Christmas Romance in Scotland

Oops! I'm the Paparazzi series:
1. Oops! I'm the Paparazzi
2. Oops! I'm Up To Mischief
3. Oops! I'm the Paparazzi, Again

The Bitch-Proof Suit series:
1. The Bitch-Proof Suit
2. The Bitch-Proof Romance
3. The Bitch-Proof Bride
4. The Bitch-Proof Wedding

Heather Park: Regency Romance
Dublin Girl
Why Are All The Good Guys Total Monsters?
I'm Holding Out For A Vampire Boyfriend

Action/Thriller books:

Knight in Miami
Agency Agenda
Love Him Forever
Someone Worse
Electric Shadows
The Strife Of Riley
Shadows Of Murder
Cast a Dark Shadow

Children's books:

Faeriefied
Secondhand Spooks
Poison-Wynd
Wormhole Wynd
Science Fashion
School For Aliens

Colouring books:

Summer Nature
Flower Nature
Summer Garden
Spring Garden
Autumn Garden
Sea Dream
Festive Christmas
Christmas Garden
Christmas Theme
Flower Bee
Wild Garden
Faerie Garden Spring
Flower Hunter
Stargazer Space
Bee Garden
Scottish Garden
Seasons

Embroidery Design books:

Sea Theme Embroidery Patterns
Floral Garden Embroidery Patterns
Christmas & Winter Embroidery Patterns
Floral Spring Embroidery Patterns
Floral Nature Embroidery Designs
Scottish Garden Embroidery Designs

Printed in Great Britain
by Amazon